Stilettos
in the
Sun

NADEL HARVEY

Cover design by Carrie Spencer
Interior design by Jennifer Zaczek

This is a work of fiction. Names, characters, places, and incidents are a product of the author's imagination. Any resemblance to actual persons, living or dead, or to events or locales is completely coincidental.

STILETTOS IN THE SUN
ISBN-13 (pbk.): 978-0-9911840-0-2
ISBN-13 (ebk.): 978-0-9911840-1-9

To my father, George Harvey, a tireless reader and great letter-writer.

*The soul that can speak through the eyes
can also kiss with a gaze.*
—GUSTAVO ADOLFO BECQUER

*If you but knew the flames that burn in
me which I attempt to beat down with
my reason.*
—ALEXANDER PUSHKIN

Acknowledgments

I would like to thank the following people whose reading of my work in various stages of completion contributed to its fruition: Sheryl David, Glen Miller, Carmen Piner, Ernest Waugh, Rafiq Howard, and finally, my editor, Lourdes Venard.

Part 1

I left behind everything, save the memories locked in the
cedar of my guitar.

1

Colón, Panamá—1980

It had rained all day and the cobblestones of *Callejón de la Lechera* (Milkmaid Alley) were slippery and uneven from centuries of wear. In spite of the rain, there still lingered a smell of urine that the pockmarked walls absorbed, clinging to it with the tenacity of the blood and bullets of wronged lovers and double-crossed thieves that also lodged themselves there. Still, the magnetism drew me threefold: sound, scent, and sin.

I went there on Saturdays for guitar lessons with Jorge Ortega. El negrote, the big black one, was the term of endearment by which he was known. He played in the brothel midway up the alley. It took me a while to summon enough courage to ask him, though I knew from the time I first heard him that I would. He was an imposing figure with a head the size and color of a bull; his hair, wavy and white. His lulling voice was as clear as the bells announcing mass early Sunday morning. He introduced me to Tarrega, Sor and Villa-Lobos. No one seemed as enthralled as I. What did a drunkard care about sixteenth notes or *molto piano non troppo*? But Jorge cared and so did I. He told stories of the vihuela and the oud, and how the wedding of those two instruments gave birth to the guitar we both loved so much.

"No, Roberto, así. Como si fuera una mujer." That's how Jorge would explain playing some delicate passage: Approach it *as if it were a woman*. Caress the string as if they were the hairs on a woman's head. Except that I had never held a woman in my arms. I wanted to, though.

My job was to scrub the floors and clear the latrines. I was only eleven and couldn't ask for much. I suppose that is why I got the job: I had underbid the competition. Jorge took a liking to me and began giving me lessons for a dollar. I must have shown some talent because, after a month, he stopped charging me.

Working in a brothel exposed me to life in the rawest way. If I had been a painter I am sure I could have produced some beautiful renderings. At the time I was not aware of Toulouse-Lautrec, Elizabeth Catlett, or Diego Rivera, but in time I came to see how they took full advantage of their immediate surroundings. It was there at *Hotel Saltamonte* that I first discovered women. There was Bella, a woman twice my age, the most beautiful woman who graced that place. And while there was no official vote to my knowledge, she was one woman that every man wanted. Walking past two sailors in the hallway, I heard their conversation.

"¿A tí te gusta el café?"

"Claro, con poca crema."

"¡Igual que yo!"

I was no less selective than those two liking my coffee with just a little cream, too. But coffee was good even without cream!

I would leave the brothel smelling of a peculiar blend of sweat, cheap rum, and rose petals, and the hopes of Bella's thighs pulling at my loins. What would it be like to have her like the men who held her full hips; hips that jiggled under her cotton dress with all those smiling flowers? I would eventually know and I would never forget the mole I kissed on her rib cage: The cage that held me captive.

After coming home one day, my Mother had *good news* for me: I was going to the United States to stay with Tío Carlos. I was devastated! Why? My Mother's eyes told the story: I wasn't going to end up like my beloved Jorge Ortega. She had dreams for me and I would have to leave Panamá to realize them.

"Si, por supuesto, puedes llevar la guitarra contigo." Yes, of course. I could take my guitar—but not Bella. And given the choice, I wondered if I could fashion a contrabass case with airholes so Bella wouldn't suffocate, God forbid.

* * *

PanAm flight 1642 to *Nueva York* found me weeping as the plane circled around a mountain range and the lady seated in front of me remarked *"¡Qué montaña más bella!"* And all I could think of was how Bella was not there to view it. The letter my Mother gave me to read "after the plane takes off" told some of what was on my Mother's mind: *Aquí no hay futuro para tí, mi único hijo. Siguiendo con esa jeba vieja, ibas seguramente a una pérdida infinita. No me odias, mi amor. Te quiero más que puedo poner en palabras. Con tiempo me entenderás, si Dios quiere.* So, my Mother was getting me away from that woman. How had she found out about her anyway? I would need time to appreciate her wisdom; time and maturity. There was more that she wrote. I would return to that note through the years, away from all I knew, whenever I needed to smell the salty air and feel the thunder in my heart, the rain on my body.

That was so long ago. Why was I still lost in the past that never materialized, nor would it ever? A labyrinth as confusing as Soberanía National Park. Where was Bella today? Somewhere raising grandchildren, or with a pillow

3

propped under her black mane, giving someone her bittersweet brand of pleasure?

2

This Louisiana heat had me delirious, like crawfish in a boiling pot! On the way home I kept replaying the words Professor Andrews told me, after I completed my last assignment in Electronics Circuits Lab 303: "You have to find some way to relax. Make some friends. Enjoy your life." At least there would be no assignments for a time.

Gee, was my depression so visible? My mask so transparent? I did wear a veil of seriousness. Nothing was funny anymore. Concerns revolved around the essentials of life: food, clothing, and shelter. My only outlets were work at the nearby 7-Eleven, the loaves of bread I baked for strangers, and playing my guitar. To hear people tell it, I had become quite the baker. Loaves of challah, whole wheat, and *pan dulce* were favorites I had become good at baking. My Mother had taught me to make *mallorcas*: twisted dough, baked then sprinkled with white sugar. That was one I especially enjoyed. The neighbors might have wondered about all the people who trafficked through our front door. Yes, I would have to find a way to relax.

I left Dr. Andrews' office glad to have found out I had earned a "B" in his class. The hours we spent troubleshooting those broken frequency-generators had paid off. I was even ready to take a look at my black-and-white thirteen-inch television set and take it apart, completely. It was already broken, so what harm could I do? And the electric piano I had started to build? I had a full summer ahead of me.

I walked over to the bookstore. I had three books I hoped to sell: *Intro to Differential Equations, Linear Algebra*, and one from my favorite course, *Electromagnetic Field Theory*. I might walk away with seventy-five dollars. Less than a third of their total cost. While it was unusual for engineering students to sell books in their major, I was the exception. I needed the cash for groceries.

On the way I ran into two fellow students, Ghani, a Nigerian, and Steve, an African-American.

"Hey Newton, want to come with us?" asked Steve.

"Where to?"

"The Black Forest," said Ghani.

"I'll catch up with you," I said.

"Have a great summer, if you don't," said Steve.

"And keep from under those apple trees, Newton!" joked Ghani.

We shook hands in the fashion of black students and continued in our separate directions. I laughed at how the nickname, *Newton*, had stuck since the early days of Calculus. I held the peculiar distinction of having worked all of the problems—save for the proofs—in the first-year text. Without a question, I became popular with the lazy students. I remember one young woman *earned* the name *Xerox* for her penchant of blindly coping other people's homework. In retrospect, I wonder how many circuits have blown on her account. And the blackout that claimed fifty million households in North America in the late summer of 2003? Was she a factor in that catastrophe?

No, I didn't think I'd end up at the Black Forest. It *was* a popular German restaurant in downtown Baton Rouge, though. That day they would surely sell out of *Dinkelacker,* bratwurst, and *stollen.*

I arrived at the bookstore and ran into Alejo and Sixto, both Venezuelans.

"*¡Hola!*" I said.

"*¿Qué tal 'mano?*" asked Alejo.

"*Bueno, voy a vender éstos.*" I motioned to the books. The electromagnetic field theory one was in excellent condition.

I walked away with eighty-five dollars. My alternative would have been to take them to LSU, but they used different texts for those same courses.

The car lot which surrounded the assembly hall was still full of steaming cars, which from the distance resembled a kaleidoscopic checkerboard. I approached my car and opened the door, then windows, while standing outside. The Digital Logic textbook (left open on the backseat) displayed pages curled, heart-shaped.

"Hey Roberto, going home this summer?" It was Sidney from New Orleans.

"No way. Maybe this winter."

He waved and drove off.

No, I wouldn't be going home. Where was home anyway? Philadelphia? No. That was my respite here in North America. Tío Carlos, my Uncle Carlos, opened his door to me several years earlier. It was a great favor to both my family and me. My Mother, who championed my industry, presented a persuasive argument in my favor: How I was very diligent at everything I did; that I was brilliant *"Él puede hacer de todo!"*; how good I was at figures; that I would be a great help to my uncle at his hardware store. Tío saw the benefits immediately, as did my cousin, his son Carlito. To call him a sloth would not be completely fair. Why work when you have an ever-so-willing galley slave leaping up at every opportunity to do the dishes; teaching my

African-American aunt how to make meals my Uncle had forgotten how to pronounce, and washing and waxing the car weekly?

Upon arriving in the States I was cheered by the thought that I might see the Pittsburgh Pirates, the team of Manny Sanguillén, Roberto Clemente, and Willie Stargell, players my father and country revered so much. I showed my gratitude to my extended family, but (in the end) I ached in equal silence for my Mother's touch and Father's firm *abrazo*. I was *their* son, blood and bone. No Fourth of July "rockets' red glare" could change that.

A letter to my sister, Isa, contained a poem I wrote of my longing:

> *O, Panamá*
> Broken, divided like the night and morning
> I find my heart bleeding
> In bed I cry silent drops of hope
> down the slope of my shoulder
> I want nothing more
> than to see and touch
> my Verdant Ribbon so full of life
> toucan and red moth
> eagle and gray sloth
> ocelot in lush fauna
> I want to play guitar to you
> *O, Panamá*
> To sing the memories of my isthmus
> the corn silk of my Mother's hair
> the laughter of my Father's voice
> cracking through the air like thunder
> *O, Panamá*
> wife of two oceans
> who bathe you night and day
> At dawn as at crepuscule you don an auburn satin
>   gown

At midnight, the magenta moon shimmers on
　　your swollen breasts
O, Panamá
to see the pelicans soar high then dive
into the rippling blueness
Waves sweeping, frothing against the shore
send sand crabs scurrying
Rocks are their refuge
as is the salt-filled breeze
O, Panamá
Where are the bridges I used to cross?
Arms of every color:
oblique steel handshakes
embracing the copper sunrise
To stand on sand white and yellow
and have you swallow my feet
so I can be your son once more
O, Panamá

But Carlito made me pay for all the good I did. With him I was on permanent probation from the very beginning. First came the boxing matches. He loved to don the gloves. I wasn't keen on getting my nose bloodied. That was something *he* enjoyed. Nor did I like his insinuation that I fought like a girl. He wasn't a bad boxer. That is something I have to admit.

"*¿Qué te pasa, primita?*" he was fond of saying. He never missed an opportunity to belittle me.

But I wasn't going to be his little *girl* cousin. *Le iba a meter una patá en el culo!* Yeah, that's right! They were going to have to cut my foot off at the ankle, after burying it in his ass! I had to build myself up, though. Push-ups and jumping-jacks! I went to the Police Athletic League and worked out on the big bag. That bag became Carlito. I called him every name that I felt fit him: *vagabundo*, *zopenco*, and *zoquete*. I called him those same things when boxing him, too, though between his limited knowledge of Spanish and my mouthguard their meaning was lost to him. Even when I learned to say the words in English, they lost their sting because he either laughed at my accent or the meaning of vagabond, drone, and zygote elicited only a shrug. I soon realized if I wanted to communicate, I would have to learn to mumble in fragments of street-level English, where words come out like shards. No, he didn't make it easy. He fought with a ferocity he never put in his other endeavors. Endeavors? No, what did he ever really put an effort into—besides being rude to *me*? Oh, he mopped my body across the canvas plenty, before I overcame my fear of being hurt. I started fighting to win instead of fighting not to lose. He had backed the timid mouse into a corner for the last time! Funny, after I discovered that boxing was 80 percent footwork, Carlito learned some lessons from me! I learned to take a punch and to counterpunch off of his momentum as naturally as $m1v1 + m2v2 = m1v1' + m2v2'$. Thanks to Carlito, I came away with my first lessons in the conservation of momentum. I felt the internal forces of his punches, both physically and mentally. I had to find a way to survive them. Oh, math was so beautiful when it was adding up the body punches and head shots to the cowering Carlito. The tiger wasn't so menacing anymore. As we say in Spanish *tigre no come tigre!* The tiger won't eat another tiger! Carlito wasn't so tough after all. What was once a growl was now only a throat-clearing. A tough mutt, barking behind the protection of a fence, but after perceiving the stick in your hand, he became a cowering bitch. After a time, he didn't want to put on the gloves anymore. He liked it even less when I started calling myself Roberto *Durán* Dávila, now with a tight uppercut. And he hated math, but learned to respect geometry: that the shortest distance between two points was a straight horizontal line—to his jaw! The pattern of right-crosses and uppercuts in varied succession gave him something to think about, too. It gave me a chuckle to ask him, *"¿Qué te pasa, primito?"* At least I didn't call him *girl* cousin. Finally, it gave me particular joy to answer my Uncle, when he asked where Carlito had ended up after our last match.

"¡Pa' el piso!" I said, for Carlito was stretched out on the canvas.

From that day on Carlito took up basketball, hiding away the gloves—forever!

Not only did I have to endure the pain of my cousin's cool welcome, there were still the neighborhood thugs who wanted to know who this new kid *thought* he was. I had no reason to dislike anyone. I just wanted to make friends and fit in. My interest in electrical engineering got me into Carver High for Engineering and Science. Carlito took up printing at Dobbins Vocational High.

One spring Carlito and I attended the Penn Relays, and were stopped by a small group of black teens that wanted something from us.

"Where you from?" one of them said to me.

"*Panamá*," I answered, and felt proud pronouncing it.

"You trying to be funny?" he said.

"Do you know them?" I asked Carlito. He shook his head that he didn't.

"Yeah, you know me. I *go* with Joann Ritter. The girl I saw you talkin' to in school."

"¡Vámonos, Roberto!" said Carlito, discovering his Spanish.

"No you ain't!" said the short one in the back. There were four of them. "I'll knock the fuckin' curls outta your head!" said the short one again.

"And I'll knock the kinky rocks out of yours!" I said.

Well, I don't know if it was what I said, or whether he didn't like the way I bent my vowels; or if I had offended his family. I never slept with his mother, though somebody in that bunch did call me a motherfucker. All I know is that it *did* feel good cracking some jaws with those uppercuts. I heard the short one yell for help, and saw the one who didn't want Carlito talking to Joann doubled over like the Pillsbury Doughboy—but he wasn't laughing. Suddenly it was two against two. At that point, they had enough. I looked over at Carlito. His right eye was swollen closed. Rubbing his sore jaw he mouthed, " 'Knock the kinky rocks.' You some kind of poet?"

"They got the message," I said.

I had taken shots to my back and ribs, but I felt the exhilaration of having beaten four guys with Carlito. It had all ended too quickly for me. I wanted more and looked around for that wise-mouthed shorty. He had gotten away into the myriad. It was the first activity into which we had put a mutually, concerted effort. Carlito and I had seen enough of the Relays and Franklin Field. We would have to hear the outcome of which schools had taken away the most medals on the news that evening. I don't know if Carlito ever talked to Joann again, but he never mentioned her. It made me happy to hear him say, "I'm sticking to Latinas."

"Then we can speak Spanish from now on," I said, smiling. It seemed that from that day forward, I had graduated to a new level of probation with Carlito. There would be no more tests of toughness; just the acknowledgment that he was older (by a mere margin of four months). It is amazing how a closed eye can make you humble.

* * *

All of that was a lifetime ago. My present life revolved around Jennifer Jean Drive. My housemates: Euridice, Ginebra, Gerardo and I shared a townhouse. Euridice and I had private rooms. Ginebra and Gerardo shared the largest bedroom with a private bathroom. The two of them lived as if married. If life was ever comfortable between them, it was before I moved in. Gerardo enjoyed staying out on weekends, going to parties. I noticed some evenings I only heard one pair of footsteps passing my closed door: Ginebra's. Studying late on the weekends was usual for me. When I retired at four a.m. one time I remember the fireworks down the hall.

"*¡No te burles de mí!*" said Ginebra. Her voice trembled as she spoke. I was not comfortable hearing them argue. I wished the sheetrock that separated our rooms were soundproof. The chaos like an earthquake was unsettling. I liked them both but noticed respect lacking on his part. Why should he *make fun of her*? Why should she put up with his infidelity? Could he be rightfully considered unfaithful if he did not take a vow? Did the birthday cards to "My Husband" have any more meaning than toilet paper? Why did she love him to the point of humiliation?

I wondered what Ginebra's mother thought of the entanglement her daughter had woven around Gerardo. During one of her visits Senora Nuñez invited me to Caracas. While she might have just been feeling happy from the rum she was drinking as it coursed its way through her body, I was not interested in being a replacement for Gerardo. She did like a party. We twirled to the two-step of one *merengue* after another. Was she really married? And if so to what? Her own definition of fun? I felt the heat between us and took full advantage of the dim blue lights, swirling on the living room floor. She found her groove and was at one with the bass line and congas. And as my passion rose between her—enough to make the flower on her silk dress wilt—I felt the familiar warmth of the rainforest. Yes, I could see she liked me, but I did not want to be in anyone else's place.

3

I chose a new route home through an area of Baton Rouge called The Bottom. The August humidity blackened my mood as I perspired in my blue cotton shirt. A fly bounced erratically against the inside windshield, until the airflow carried it back out into the dizzying ochre sun. As I turned the corner at Delpit Drive and Terrace Avenue, my heavy eyelids were lifted by the sight of a woman standing some twenty yards ahead of me.

What was this Panamanian woman doing so far away from Colón? Was I seeing Bella?

"I ain't no pick-up or nothing. I'm just looking for a ride to the bar." She leaned languidly forward into the window, forming a triangle against my passenger door. My response to her request was instinctual. I opened the door and she climbed in.

"So do you live around here?" I asked.

"Not too far," she said, looking out the passenger window. Sitting next to her I picked up the scent of roses mixed with sweat. It pricked my nostrils. Her fingernails were polished pink. She wore a gold ring on her left hand. It was set with an opal. No, not a wedding band, I thought.

"And what about you?" she asked, this time looking forward.

"Not too far," I said. *Now, don't we sound like a pair of parrots?* I looked away from the road to catch her profile and registered the gentle slope of her nose, the fullness of her lower lip.

"So, we're neighbors," she said. She smiled at me and took a deep breath. The air-conditioner needed Freon.

"Wind the window all the way down," I said. I drove without a plan. I looked down at her hands again. She moved her left hand up and down her thigh as if massaging it. "You've got nice hands," I said. She smiled again, without a word. Where was I taking this woman? I looked at her and this time caught a glance at her black brassiere. "So where am I taking my neighbor?" I asked.

"Keep straight," she said, rubbing her leg once again.

"Are you sore?" I asked.

"I just need a rubdown," she said.

"A massage?" I asked, gripping the steering wheel tightly.

"Just a little one," she laughed. "You know anybody who gives them?"

"My specialty."

We continued down the road. I smiled at the thought that occurred to me: There was a building that once housed a Turkish bath, now in ruins. I wondered if in its day women ever ventured into it. Probably not. Before long I caught sight of a faded sign that read *Falstaff*. This was the place she was after, since she raised her arm, motioning to the bar. It would not have been such a long distance for her to walk, had it not been for the infernal heat and swirling dust.

"You coming in?" she asked.

"Sure," I replied, not at all sure, but not wanting to go home right away either. I surprised myself at how spontaneous I was. *Now what kind of walking was she going to be able to do in those black stilettos?* With legs like that she wouldn't have to walk far: from the lamppost to the car of her choice. (Heels were a fashion black college women were fond of sporting. It was something seldom seen at

15

northern schools; certainly not a popular fashion among whites.) I watched as she moved with confidence up to the wooden steps that led to the screen door. She glanced over her shoulder just before opening the door. This was actually more a gate than a door; a gate in need of painting and screen repair. By dusk a squadron of mosquitoes would find its way through to needle some new flesh.

She walked ahead of me to a table situated under a ceiling fan. Dust stuck to the fan like Spanish moss. The four oak blades rotated in a lazy circle. The clicking sound of her heels would have been enough to call attention to her arrival, had the place not been empty. The bartender, whose back was turned to us, spun his head, then full torso around. He held a sudsy glass and a head full of perspiration.

"My name is Cathy," she said after taking a seat in the basket-weave chair opposite mine. The square pine wood table squeaked as she leaned against it. This caused her to stop short, raise her eyebrows, and make the sound Oo! We both laughed.

"Roberto Dávila."

"Cathy Moore," she said, giving her last name. She looked to have been walking a long time. Her bare arms glistened dark brown.

"Roberto. You don't hear that name much, around here anyway."

"I'm not from around here."

"No, I didn't think so. Your English is too clear."

"Thank you, I took some trouble to learn it." I was smiling.

"And what beautiful teeth you have!" she said.

"The better to bite you with, my dear."

"It's 'the better to eat you with, my dear'," she corrected me.

"Actually, I'm more thirsty than hungry," I said, motioning to the bartender, and then, with the same gesture, to the Budweiser sign behind him. Moments later he moved toward us, in all his sweaty corpulence, with two frosty longnecks.

"To our appetites!" I raised a toast. She clicked her bottle against mine. The cold liquid felt good going down.

Cold river water passing over hot, sooty rocks
Rocks now washed clear and clean

Her gray blouse was sun-blanched; probably old as well. She said she was from Baton Rouge, though I doubted that. Her language showed none of the familiar lilt my four years here had come to recognize. She mentioned Chicago, and I was more inclined to believe that *that* was her home, or somewhere—anywhere—north of Louisiana. For the moment, I allowed myself to pretend she was from Colón. She showed off a single dimple in her right cheek when she smiled.

"And what is Roberto doing here?"

"I'm studying electrical engineering at Southern. I have another year to do. Then I'm going back to Panamá."

"And just like that you'll up and go?"

"Just like that." I saw no reason to lead her into thinking that I would be around longer than I had to be. There was new resolution in my voice. A Bud can do that. "Do you like it here?"

"I like it where I am right *now*."

I felt a chill of nervousness. I didn't know if I could keep this pretense up. No, she wasn't from Colón, though I felt I was in the wild. She was far too accommodating, or did she smell fear in the air, and was closing in for an effortless kill? *The panther crouched low in the jungle; the unsuspecting marmoset savored berries for perhaps the last time.* She tilted the bottle up vertically.

"So are you single?" I asked.

"I've been married six long years."

"You make it sound like a sentence."

"Didn't mean to."

"So what does your husband do?"

"Time."

"I think I need a translation."

"He's in Angola."

"An African freedom fighter?"

"No, Angola Prison right here in Louisiana."

"Oh! Sorry to hear that. I see what you meant by *long*."

"Robbery with a knife got him eight years."

"He'll be out soon?"

"Not soon enough. I wasn't cut out for this waiting game."

She played with the neck of the bottle and then with her fingernail eased away the corner of the label. Being wet it came off easily. I felt myself less compelled by what had initially drawn me to her: those stunning legs and slender ankles. I felt I was going to run out of topics of conversation. I didn't really want to spend the afternoon talking about incarceration, the times he tried to escape, or how often she wrote him. There was no reason to rush things, though.

I wished that I could fill her with a knowledge of science and numbers: the world of Faraday and Kirchhoff; of Euler and LaPlace. That would at least begin to justify the lust in my loins. The algebraic sum of things wasn't adding up to zero. But who was I kidding? Who did I expect to find on that parched road to inferno: Madame Marie Curie?

And what about this new information? How did this woman get involved with that unfortunate man? Of course, if Cathy's husband were out, *I* might be the unfortunate one. He didn't sound like a man given to reason before taking action.

¡Cuida'o camarada en la acera!
¡Cuida'o camarada que el que no corre vuela!

I wanted to go to heaven, but not so soon. Life was very precious to me.

"And children?"

"I have a daughter. She's eight. And you?"

"No, I'm single. No kids." Somehow my life seemed much less complicated than hers: a life of strikeouts and no runs scored. I had to ask myself if the route home I had chosen that day was all I had hoped to find.

"Does she stay with you?"

"We live together with my mother-in-law."

A photograph of her daughter, her arms resting on her desk with an apple to her left, showed her smiling. A blue and white plaid outfit gave the impression of a Catholic School, something she said was not the case.

"She looks like you."

"She *does*."

Cathy put away the photograph as quickly as she pulled it out. It was a chapter of her life she seemed less interested in sharing. That was fine with me.

"How about something to eat?" I suggested. She smiled. Perhaps she welcomed the diversion from the pain of discussing her husband, her daughter. They were vague figures, hardly traceable. Charcoal images on black paper are hard to discern. Even while wanting to remain detached from what didn't involve me, I was still the inquisitive one, panning for gold in every silt-filled creek.

We ordered the staples of the state: fried chicken with red beans and rice. The bartender returned with our food and two more Budweisers. I started thinking about what Dr. Andrews had said earlier. I was actually enjoying myself like no other time I could immediately remember. I had not gone out with a woman in well over a year, apart from reviewing notes over coffee with my Venezuelan housemate, Euridice Betancourt.

"That's a nice blouse."

"This?" she said, looking down, touching her left shoulder. "It's silk, but I ruined it." *There!* I was sure she wasn't from Baton Rouge. The way she pronounced *ruined* told me so.

"Still, you can tell quality," I said. I could see that she was at ease in the company of strangers, *foreigners*? She had the smoothness of a politician; the coyness of a cat. A woman who shared the proximity of a complete stranger from an afternoon ride to sitting in a bar . . . One had to wonder.

"Do you dance?" I asked, motioning to the jukebox.

"Yes."

I selected three slow songs. The voices of Smokey Robinson, Stevie Wonder, and Al Green were familiar to us down in our isthmus, even if their faces were not. The singing touched a time long ago, even if the language was different. West Africa resonated on all the shores of the Americas. We could identify with it, no matter how straight the hair, aquiline the nose, or green the eye. It painted our hearts with its dark crimson hue. Its subterranean blue bathed us.

I stood and held out my hand. Then Cathy stood, too. We walked onto the floor, hand in hand as if we had done this so many times, her heels tapping out the paces. We were as old partners: Bella was with me again. My Mother could not keep us apart. No, this was Cathy. We found ourselves in our own private fantasies. She with her partners; I with mine. With my eyes closed, we began our slow spin into oblivion. The light weight of her head on my shoulder, the trace of perfume in the air. My lips rested against her neck of pure satin. Her left hand laced in my right like clay in a mold, my right hand against the small of her back.

I held her firm body for fifteen minutes, the duration of the records. We must have sanded an impression in the circle below us, judging by the dust on our shoes. Cathy's breast still beat against my chest after she had clicked her way back to our table. For these fifteen minutes the importance of my studies and subsequent jobs held no meaning, only the soft groove which the inverted-V in her black jeans offered.

The coolness of the overworked air-conditioner made me forget about the weather. The intermittent pinging, while it might have otherwise been annoying, was not such a bad price to pay for that twentieth-century convenience. I wondered if Cathy had noticed that she had begun to arouse me. I vowed to remain at ease, and continue the casualness of our conversation; then something she said focused the attention on me.

"Your hair is black fleece!" She took that opportunity to glide her fingers through my lamb's wool.

"Like my Father's before me," I said.

"And like my Father's before *me*!"

"Funny thing about hair. We have it on loan for a while, then it turns white, and then it's gone."

"I've got a notion to cut mine off—completely," she said.

"A cut, yes, but completely? In my culture, hair is a woman's glory."

"Well it's the same here, too. Mine doesn't grow too long, though," she said with a tinge of reluctance.

"And if it did grow long, you would probably be like my sister, wear it short." I hoped that my comment would lighten the air again.

"Any pictures of her?"

I showed her one of me and my sister, Isa. The photograph captured us laughing down on *Avenida Central* at one of the outdoor cafes. It was a balmy afternoon, much like the way it was outside the bar, except there in

Panama I was no stranger. It might very well have been the humidity that drew us together as one fabric. Much like moist skin to cloth, perspiration held us together as a people. Even the shade was no escape from the all-pervasive dampness.

There is an odd realization that occurs to you when you are away from everything you know intimately. You never bother to savor it like you ought. There I ate *arroz con coco* anytime I wanted. (Like other women her age, my Mother shredded the coconut by hand for the meal.) Where could I get it today?

The rain, the hill, the guava tree all had their distinct taste, their special hue. *I held once again a guanábana, bit into it and savored its bittersweet white flesh.* I was beginning to feel an ache that only my Mother's cooking could cure; the aroma of my Father's *puros*, those sweet-smelling Cuban cigars and the ellipses he would generate. In Philadelphia, too, I had found a slice of my tropical home. I filled my room with drawings of fishing boats and sunsets.

4

"Roberto!" Cathy called me away from my momentary reverie. "You'll have to sleep on your own time," she said with a light touch on my wrist. "She's pretty." She fingered the photograph. "And her eyes. Light brown, right?"

The coal-colored nest of curls, the mole left of her mouth. Yes, you could call her pretty.

"She works in a bakery in the capitol. Fifty hours a week. Stays busy. Maybe she will own her own one day," I said. "And where do you work?"

"I'm actually between jobs," she said.

Now, why did that *not* surprise me? Was she nocturnal or diurnal?

"I prefer day work. I was cooking in a take-out in Beauregard Town, but things got slow. I liked it, they let me go. I'm working part-time at Godchaux's selling toys."

It sounded plausible. It helped that I wanted to believe her. The fact remained, I met her on the street: *a street on a day that would have exposed a blemish on the whitest muslin fabric or the darkest shade of gray.* That gave me cause to disbelieve her. This was the daytime, true. Hadn't I ever been in need of a ride? Been stranded? In Panamá, it was not uncommon to give a person a ride to town from the countryside. In the city as well someone might ask for a ride—even at night in the university district. I would have to be careful with this one. To become involved with a

23

woman whose man was behind bars carried its own set variables. A woman standing in the shadows with no visible means to support herself. a husband incarcerated with a violent past. a woman living with a young daughter in her mother's-in-law house. If she were a prostitute, I would know soon enough. Everything might well evaporate after that: a shimmering pool seen from some distance on the highway was an invitation to dive in.

"Are there windows in his cell?" I couldn't believe I was asking about that pitiful man again.

"No. He does have a cellmate, though. Someone to play cards with, I guess."

"Does he write you?"

"He writes, but I'm kind of bad about writing back. In the beginning, yes, but after so many years . . ."

I was beginning to believe her. This was the Cathy that prefaced nothing she said.

"It's not like they convicted the wrong man. It might be easier to hold out. To work to set him free," she said.

"Like a political prisoner, eh?"

"Right."

"How did he end up there in the first place?"

"Coco had a bad habit. Doing the quick came easy to him. He thrived on the tourists in New Orleans and Miami. Shaking them down for jewelry and cash at gun or knifepoint. He would disguise himself and afterward slip into the darkness. That's where he got his name from: Coco Joe."

"And the jewelry?"

"Oh, he'd get rid of it. It was all profit to him, so somebody would always buy it."

This woman was giving me an education beyond the college library: Black Folks and the Fast Dollar. Maybe I would write that book. She admitted enjoying the bounty in nice restaurants and hotels. After four years, Coco's ass was now parked on a bench, where he pressed license plates in Louisiana: The Dream State. He acquired a GED, so there was hope that the streets would be safer when he returned to society.

So how did she stumble on such a prize?

"He was cute, chile! With a car and plenty of dough."

Unfortunately, prison was no place for being cute with "Coco" tattooed on your arm. I could not help but notice that she did not mention how smart he was. No, Coco Joe Boeuf was only as smart as she needed him to be.

Cathy seemed more and more like the "pick-up" she denied that she was when we first met. She sounded like *una gitana verdadera:* a gypsy who followed the prevailing wind. (All she needed to complete the picture would be to don the flowing red dress, the gold loops, and a mane of black hair.) With her husband becoming someone she seldom wrote: the shadow of a man, the shell of a cicada, his presence must have slipped away like a crepuscule. And who knew when the sun would shine again?

"Do you want to see where I live?" I asked her.

"What I'd really like to do is take a shower," she said.

A clean woman. I liked that.

"You can do that at my place," I suggested. The alcohol had made me very fluid in both my gestures and speech.

"What are we waiting for?" she said, getting up.

"Spanish Town," she replied when I asked her where she lived. Although it bore little resemblance to any Spanish neighborhood I had ever seen, either Louisiana or Florida, Panamá or Philadelphia. For me it was a parallel series of shanties, much like the circuits I studied, all faded evergreen: time's attempt to render them invisible. These domiciles cast an ever dark shadow on the horizon of those that dwelled within. I wondered what my housemates would think of Cathy, my date. She had really invited me out. She slid her hand along between her thighs. There was nothing subtle about her. She lowered the mirror hidden by the sun-visor, wiping her face with her hands. Beads of perspiration gathered above her full lips, iridescent pearls my index finger wanted to collect. Her smile was the thanks I hoped for. She placed her left hand on my right thigh and squeezed it.

"You're strong!"

"All that standing I do," I said.

"Must be," she said leaving her hand there for a moment, then sliding it away.

* * *

We arrived at the single-level townhouse I shared on Jennifer Jean Drive. A very nice area, it was complete with its shops, restaurants, and manicured front lawns. Cathy was not at all familiar with that part of town. It was where many students at LSU lived. When Papagayo, our black mongrel, ran up to greet us, I grasped Cathy's hand. He didn't bark at Cathy, which perhaps she appreciated, not knowing him.

Euridice was sitting in the living room, watching some show on television. Ginebra, our self-appointed house manager, stood in the dining room setting the table.

"¡Roberto, tienes correo!" said Ginebra. She walked to the dining room table and handed me my mail.

"Gracias," I said. I had two letters: one from Isa, and one from my Tía Sandra, Tío Carlos's wife. I would read them later.

"¿Terminaste los exámenes?" I asked Ginebra. She said she had finished her finals.

Ginebra was in the habit of racing home to catch *The Jeffersons.* I introduced Cathy to Euridice, and then to Ginebra. Ginebra greeted Cathy in Spanish, perhaps as a clever way to discern if Cathy were Latina. Cathy smiled as if flattered by the familiarity: that she fit in our diaspora. In truth, there was no way at a glance to tell for certain where Cathy came from, short of asking. This was Louisiana after all: a cauldron of cultures.

But Cathy didn't display the confidence she showed earlier in the car. When I looked at how fresh and comfortable my housemates were compared to my dusty friend, I thought that was the reason.

"You didn't say you had roommates," she said.

"We don't stay in the same room."

"Well, you do share the house, right?" she asked.

"Right. We get along. It's less expensive like this."

"So, where is your room?" she asked.

"Back here," I said. We walked down the narrow hallway to the second room on the right. I gave Cathy some towels and soap, then showed her to the bathroom.

"You sure this is all right?" she asked.

"I'm sure," I said.

While Cathy took a shower, I walked into the kitchen to see what smelled so good.

"¡Arepas, qué bueno!" I said, washing my hands in the sink. I picked up one of the doughnut-shaped cornmeal patties. They were still quite hot, the olive oil glistening on their grilled crust. I opened a can of *Polar*, fermentation's finest hour from Venezuela.

"¿Y tu amiguita? ¿Dónde tú la conociste?" Ginebra asked with a smile in her voice.

"En la calle," I replied to a series of giggles from Ginebra and Euridice. Euridice did not seem as amused, though. Her expression changed to one of disappointment. Having met her *in the street* engendered the common connotations: A woman standing diagonally in her doorway; a cigarette dangling from one hand; the other supporting her listless figure. I didn't care what they thought, though. Perhaps a week ago I would have, but school was out now.

27

I opened my letter from Isa.

Querido Robe,

A Papá le gustaron los puros. He had received them: Cuban cigars from Miami.

He likes to sit on the patio, listening to the baseball game, puffing away. It is truly a picture of contentment. Mamá loves the scarf. Is it really silk?

I am glad to hear you still make bread, though you cannot have much time. And Euridice? Do you still see her? Mamá asks "Can she cook?" Mamá likes the pictures you sent. She still cleans your room. Can you believe that? No one even sleeps in it! As for me, it's ten hours a day in the bakery.

Termino acá con cariño,
Isa

I placed the now olive oil-stained letter on the table.
"¿Buenas noticias?" asked Euridice.
"Sí. Preguntaron por tí," I said. They had asked about her. We continued in Spanish, "They asked if you can cook."

"Not like they can."

"They liked the cigars and scarf I sent from Miami."

"Speaking of Miami, I want to go there next week. I should have asked you sooner, if you wanted to go."

"Sooner?"

"I mean, you might have plans," she said, pointing with her chin to the hallway.

"Plans? No, no plans." I looked away at the letter then up at her again. I had caught the stare she gave me when Ginebra asked where I had met Cathy.

"Because if you have plans, tell me."

I felt a churning in my stomach. A familiar gurgling I would get when I was nervous. She needed clarity, and so did I. Was I the wolf straying from the pack?

"We still can do things together, right?" She was letting me off easy, at least for now.

"Of course! I'll take off a week." I felt the secure secrecy which speaking in Spanish provided. Still, bringing Cathy home was bad form.

"A week. That's what I was thinking. The water will feel good and warm." The corners of her mouth lengthened into a smile.

"¡Ja!¡Ja!¡Ja!" laughed Ginebra. Euridice and I looked at the TV, though I could not discern the humor. I was about to open the letter from Tía Sandra when I heard the shuffle of Cathy's paces moving down the hallway.

I knew she had finished her shower. It occurred to me that Cathy didn't have any clean clothes to wear. She could put on one of my long shirts with a belt. It would certainly be no shorter than skirts women were wearing. But when I walked into the room, I was not ready for what I saw. There stood Cathy in a white bikini and those black stilettos, looking curiously at the Maxwell equations on my blackboard. What a queer juxtaposition of beauty! She caught my presence and turned shyly away.

"No, don't stop. You might get more out of them than I did."

"You really think so?" she asked, as if the wall scribblings held no further fascination than would a foggy day in London. "It was all I had to put on," she said almost apologetically. She had carried the bathing suit in her pocketbook. This woman was resourceful!

"And don't think about putting on another stitch!" I said. And was I glad I had learned that expression back in the fifth grade. If Señora Bécquer only knew how well she had taught me. "I'll put your things in the washing

29

machine." She gave me her first full smile. Her front teeth were somewhat crooked. Not the distortion of a cubist, rather it was like the modulation from a blue note to a bright one that created a smile. Her nose narrowed when she smiled, kind of like Nefertiti. And she was *all* legs! At that moment she stood at least five foot nine. The cedar-colored elliptic bow that her legs formed held for me a universe, as wondrous as Andromeda, and to believe that all those constellations were under my own roof!

There was a knock at my door, which was ajar. *"Gracias,"* I told Ginebra, who passed me a black linen sheath. She told Cathy she could return it *"cuandoquiera,"* whenever she wanted.

"I'll take mine now," I said, ready to go into the shower. "Go get something to eat. Ginebra is waiting for you." She slid the dress over her head. "Don't slip out on me."

"Where can I go? You've got my clothes." Cathy walked toward the dining room.

* * *

In the shower a funny feeling of strength came over me. It was a feeling I sometimes felt in Vector Calculus class, when I thoroughly understood the homework, and was ready for the test, even if it came that very day. But my knees were rubbery all the same. No more beers for me! Fortunately, the steam was causing the alcohol to leave my body that much faster.

When I returned to the room, I found Cathy standing again, looking toward the half-closed beige curtain that faced the backyard.

"Do you let *that* stay in here?" she asked, pointing to the curtain.

"¡O, la lagartita! She comes and goes as she pleases," I said, pointing to the little green lizard. It must have

sensed our focus, and remained still. Its presence reminded me of Panama. If the lizard bothered Cathy, she showed no other sign of it.

"Who's that?" she asked, looking at the portrait on the wall.

"My Mother."

"You have her nose and mouth. Your sister, her eyes."

"I'm more like my father. When people ask if we are brothers, he says we are. That I'm the older one."

"Is she blond?"

"Well, light brown—and gray now."

She studied the portrait of my Mother, as if there was more to my telling, but did not ask anything else about her. Of course there was more. The Spanish conquistadors had been very generous with their semen, spilling it like coconut milk from California to Tierra del Fuego.

"Your roommates are very nice."

"Oh, they're the best."

"So is Youri, Youri . . ."

"Euridice?"

"Yes. Is she your girlfriend?"

"What makes you ask that?"

"Well, is she?"

"No."

"Well, she sure looked at me a lot, as if I was taking something that belonged to her."

"She's just protective of her friends."

"As any girlfriend would be!"

"She's got a boyfriend, already."

"I noticed."

"No, I'm unattached. You know, single?"

"Okay." She seemed momentarily convinced. Now she was walking around the room. She moved from the blackboard to the bed, where she plopped. She embraced my pillow. "You smell good."

"But I'm so far away. How can you tell?" I asked.

"You're as close as this pillow to me." She stood up, still holding the pillow in her arms and began swaying slowly. Then she began singing the words to a song I might have heard before, but didn't ask its title.

"I'm just about at the end of my rope. I can't stop trying. I can't give up hope."

"That's a sad song," I said.

She walked back to the bed and sat down this time. She held the pillow up to her face and began to sob. What had I done?

"She's so pretty."

"Who?"

"Euridice," she said.

"She is, isn't she?" I said. That was apparently not the right thing to say, because it started to rain in my room.

"Are you sure you're not sleeping with her?"

"I'm so sure that I don't even know what side of the bed she sleeps on."

"Just hold me," she said, lowering the pillow. She undid the straps around her ankles, and her shoes fell away from her feet as pecans from a limb.

My thoughts were confirmed: The tears had nothing to do with how beautiful Euridice was, nor whether she was my concubine. The small kindness Ginebra had shown her did however open the floodgate to important pieces of her past.

"So where were you born?" I asked.

"Chicago. Have you ever been there?"

"No," I said, "I got the feeling you were not from here."

"My mother and father were, though. My daddy was full-blooded Istrouma, you know, Indian."

"And when did you come to Louisiana?"

"When I was twelve."

She stopped crying. I got up and brought back a Coke for her. She told me that her family moved to Baton Rouge, where her father had hopes of landing a job. He found nothing there and instead worked on shrimp boats along the Atchafalaya River until he was drowned during a hurricane; one, which swept through Pass Christian and other Gulf Shore towns.

"I'm sorry to hear that," I said, holding her hand.

Her mother raised her doing laundry and favors for gentlemen in Baton Rouge.

"And when did you meet your husband Joe?"

"Oh, I met Coco when I was seventeen. I really made a mess of my life."

That is when the rogue act began. She would show her doe eyes and a thigh if necessary, and if that were not enough, the babe wrapped in swaddling clothes was a sure bet clincher for eighty dollars a day of tax-free cash. And here I was risking an ulcer on sinusoidal excitation and phasors, while working thirty hours a week, and *Lady Creole* here had found a real cash cow in the gullible public. While there was nothing particularly humorous about her life, it was everything I could do not to burst into laughter. It was how I had found myself alongside her in my bedroom. Who would ever believe it? And if the embarrassment of her confessional had not made her keep her head down, I am sure I would have lost it. It shouldn't have been such an awkward awakening: a pretty girl could always turn a dollar, or trade away sex for a passing grade—and not just a passing grade: an *A*! Of course, there were stories of those who had no time for those games. Hadn't Ulrike Essermann shared her experience with me? It took her five years to finish her PhD in entomology because of the way she answered her advisor's queries: What if, hypothetically, a certain female graduate student noticed that a professor in her department was interested in taking her out, and she repeatedly spurned his advances?

I think you had to be made a certain way, or have fate mold you into Cathy's form to do the things she did. So, I held her. That was the easy part.

I decided it was better to go to a motel than remain in the house, especially after that short exchange with Euridice. I thought of what my Papá would sometimes say quoting Plato, *"Y esto yo lo sé, que yo no sé nada."* Every word of it was true when it concerned what I knew about women. Oh, I could compose a poem about the ringlets that fell to a woman's shoulder, or the sun setting in her eyes, but I knew nothing of how a woman thought. All my books were equally as useless. For all my years, I had few experiences. I had put all my energy into my studies, as if the inevitable afternoon where I found myself would never take place. What was I saving myself for? Asking myself that question made me finally realize that I was afraid of Euridice's rejection. However, if Cathy told me no, so what.

"I'm going to take you out."

"Why?" she asked.

"I want to be with you, but just not here."

"It's Youri, ain't it?"

"I want to go where we can be alone."

"I thought so. Why did you bring me here, to make her jealous?"

"I just want to be with you. Is that so hard to understand?"

"Oh, I understand better than you think!"

Cathy fastened her heels. Her quick movement startled the lizard, which was hiding behind one of the folds in the curtain. Cathy perceived the competition she was up against that I was slow to see. Did I have two women after me? Even now I find it odd to say.

A moment later we were in the car again. The sun was setting, though it was still humid. We rode down Nicholson Drive to a motel. Cathy was quiet during the ride.

"Look, you don't have to take me out, but I could use a couple dollars," she said without the least reservation.

"A couple, sure. But I still want to be with you." I now felt like I was begging, but for some odd reason, I did not feel embarrassed. I felt I had lost nothing. I had certainly gotten her away from what might have been an ugly scene at home. I did not know this woman. Maybe she was right. Just give her a twenty and thanks for the lesson of what *not* to do on a date. There I was, backing away again.

"No, I didn't mean to be rude," she said, switching back to the Cathy I first met.

"It's not far from here," I said.

* * *

Cathy and I walked into the motel. She walked with the confidence of being some place where she was familiar.

The view from the room gave a section of a bridge that connected Baton Rouge to Plaquemine, where Cathy said she would go to pick merletons as a young girl. After she described them, I realized I knew them as *chayotes*, a light green, spiny pear-shaped fruit.

She led me to the bed, where I sat down. She then sat on my lap. My hands found her breasts and she clasped her hands over mine. She turned her head and our mouths were one: hot and liquid. "Wait," she said. Cathy rose and walked over to the chair and table opposite the bed. She slid off her sheath and bathing suit but not her stilettos, which caught slivers of sunlight through the blinds as she walked back to me. Her breasts rose and fell as she did an imitation of a runway model, going back to the window twice more. She walked to the opposite side of the bed behind me. "Close your eyes," she said. She climbed onto the bed and covered my eyes. Her hot tongue slipped into my right ear. She slid her hands under my polo shirt and wove her fingers into my chest-hair and latched onto me as she might the bar of a rollercoaster. I was more than ready for her and slipped on an ounce of prevention. I closed my eyes and swam again in the salt blue water of the Pacific. I held the *guanábana*. I was in the clutches of the panther and wanted to be devoured. Now her teeth were in my neck. Now her legs raveled mine. The room filled with purrs and sighs and rhythmic squeaks of the box spring. We were deep inside the rainforest.

By early evening I found myself exploring Cathy with perhaps the same fascination as those Arabs who traded with *Cathay,* that ancient land. (I would not need an astrolabe to help me.) My fingers tried without success to unravel the ink-black thickets of her still damp hair. I allowed my lips to count every joint on her fingers. Her nails held the taste of lemon meringue. (She admitted having had a slice of pie earlier that day.) Our bodies moved like tangled driftwood, swirling in eddies of the maroon Mississippi. We, too, flowed with undulating easiness, tossed about by the inertia our bodies generated. Our touch awakened curiosities and lunacies. I drifted in and out of sleep. I hacked at the vines until the machete slipped from my hands. A green vine wrapped itself about my legs. It became a snake, locking my limbs. That snake became a woman, an orchid behind her ear, the taste of vanilla in her mouth. The crescent moon cast its tangerine into her eyes; my own eyes now fixed on hers. For dear life I held that image of her, until the snake slipped from my grasp, until the river swept us to a brown clay bank, sometime during the sweet predawn rain.

But with the tapping of the raindrops came a chill that coursed through my body. The oneness with Cathy now filled me. I had reached saturation with her. Where could I take her, except to bed? The nauseous feeling that comes when you no longer want to taste what you were so crazy for hours earlier is what I held inside. *Even chocolate exposed to the sun becomes rancid.* That Mississippi mud: Cathy's flesh covered my body, and I had to get clean before it dried and became one with my own skin; I needed to wash off the slurry that now glazed my thighs and back. Cathy's body tasted of sludge—what is left in a demitasse after the Turkish coffee is gone. *I inverted the cup and saw my future with her: a catfish feeding at the bottom of a Pierre Part bayou.* My intoxication had worn off and I saw Cathy for what she was: a street woman looking for affection, and ready to do whatever it took to get it. Satisfaction had decayed into nothing, exponentially. At *that* moment I could have driven her back to the street where I found her, opened the door and told her to jump! Like an alley cat, she would land on her feet—somewhere away from my door.

I walked over to the window. I could easily see the rear lights of cars and trucks coursing across the bridge, high above the Mississippi. I looked over my shoulder at Cathy. Her body's outline was all I could really make out, like a twisted tree trunk on fallen snow. And like a tree I was going to leave her on the side of the road. I had had my adventure and she her twenty dollars. No matter how many times I thrust between her limbs, I still woke up on a distant shore. She could not rock me back to my homeland.

While at the window I remembered the other letter in my pocket. I opened the thin lilac-scented envelope. Looking down at the words I saw again Tía Sandra's backward slant. She was left-handed. I opened the dimmer to give me more light. It was about Carlito. He was going to get married—but not by his own choice: He had gotten an eleventh-grader pregnant, Claudia Mendoza. I did not know her. Tío Carlos was not going to let him skate out on his responsibility. He was working for The Philadelphia Inquirer as a printer, so he had a job and would not be dependent on Tío. Yes, I would attend the wedding out of respect for my aunt and uncle. Carlito and I were cousins, but had grown apart after high school. I could earn extra money by working doubles at 7-Eleven. It was the summer and no one wanted to work anyway. These extra dollars would pay for the roundtrip and gift. I smelled the letter once again and put it away. Cathy had not moved but it was time to wake her up.

I started dressing. With polo shirt, short pants and sandals on, I woke her up.

"Get dressed."

"Where we goin'?"

"Back to Delpit Drive."

"I want you to take me home, though."

"Fine," I said. That was not unreasonable. She gave me her address. While she dressed she gave me directions.

I got Cathy out of the motel room and found my way to Plank Road. The traffic light stopped me. I glanced over at Cathy's crossed legs. She uncrossed them and raised her sheath to show herself; the black thicket I had come to know. I turned away.

"What are you ashamed of?" she said.

"Not here," I said.

"Where? Under that magnolia?" she said.

I remained silent. Her left hand found my right thigh, tense and bare. Her nails clutched it and I wanted her again. I continued along the road. She directed me to Spanish Town, to the green shanties, hidden among the cypress trees. I had arrived at her house.

She took my hand and walked me to the shed in back of the house. She closed the shed door and hooked the latch. Neither the semidarkness of that space nor cobwebs in the chair stopped us. Our silence was broken only by the squeaking of the rocker that I thought would break under me and Cathy, her legs straddled through the arm rests. Minutes later I was drenched; as flaccid as a rain-soaked willow.

"Now you know where I live. And I know where *you* live," she said. She closed the car door and I watched her ascend the wooden stairs to her place, as I had watched her the day before climb the rickety stairs to the bar. But this time it was without the lust in my loins. That was gone, as fleeting as it had come. My legs were rubber again, as they had been the day before not long after I had met Cathy. This could easily become an occupational hazard, I thought, if I didn't find another line of work: Engineer to Gigolo, or Checkmated in Two Short Moves. Such were the titles for books I might soon be able to write.

I drove away but carried a part of Cathy with me that continued to diminish "as the limit of x approaches zero" as we say in mathematics. Instead of going directly home, I went downtown and parked near the river. I watched a barge drift towards the Exxon plant, buoyed by the deep brown water. I was sure I would never see Cathy again.

It had all been so ephemeral. Why should I invest anymore time in a trip to nowhere? I was with Cathy because I had nothing to lose. I still had Euridice to face. She was anything but pleased with my actions. I knew her well enough to see that. With Euridice I risked losing a friend and perhaps more. She had exposed her feelings, honestly. She had the courage to do that, if only through disappointment. I could have avoided hurting her by going directly to a motel. But maybe I wanted to show my find off to my housemates. It was so uncharacteristic for me to do what I did. Was Euridice like me? Did she want just friendship? If so, this friendship was drowning me. Fulfillment was what I wanted. What good was writing songs and playing the guitar to the walls in my room? I wanted to go beyond the barriers I had built around my timid soul.

I reclined in the front seat in my car and my mind drifted on the wings of a pelican to early days in Panamá. Those were carefree days of soaring; the green hills below and above me cirrus clouds painting their white streaks in the bluest sky. If I closed my eyes and thought hard enough, I could smell the yellow plantains frying in the black iron skillet, could see sliced papaya with its black seeds glistening, hear El Negrote's mellow voice and guitar echoing down *Callejón de la Lechera*, and stand on the soil on Panamá again.

5

I woke to the cawing of egrets flying over my car. I was drenched in the sauna that my car had become. It was almost noon. I couldn't believe I had slept for nearly two hours. I repositioned the seat and drove home. I arrived famished, but chose to shower before getting something to eat. Gerardo and Ginebra were eating a pizza.

I said hello and went to my room. I took a shower and got dressed. I packed my clothing for the trip. I wouldn't need much for we were only going to stay a week.

The phone rang. Ginebra called out, *"Roberto, pa' tí."*

"Hello."

"Hey, Roberto."

"Who is this?"

"You don't know me?"

I suddenly realized who it was. Carlito.

"¡Qué sorpresa! ¡Felicitaciones!"

"Oh, that's why I'm calling. The wedding's off."

"Gee, you're full of surprises."

"Well, getting married wasn't my idea. I convinced Claudia that getting an abortion was the best thing to do. That if we did get married, it shouldn't be under a shotgun."

"What about her family? What did they say?"

"They were against it. Even though one of her sisters has two kids, is single, and is still living at home."

"And her father?"

"He's never been on the scene. That made it easy for me. Her mother is upset, though I was practically living there, buying groceries, spending the night and all. Man, you won't believe this. I really started out with her mom! She's so hot! But when she saw I was interested in Claudia, we had an argument and I left. Soon after, though, she begged me to come back. That she had gotten used to having me around. It was really about money. I realized it, too. I had filled the house with gadgets and stuff: TVs, VCRs, furniture—the works. Her mom loves trinkets, so it was easy to get back in good with her. It got a little messy, though, sleeping with both of them, so I cut that out. I convinced Claudia we should cool it. That we should clean the slate. She got that abortion and man, what a relief!"

"And her mom?"

"Well, you won't believe this. I'm with her again! It's like it all never happened! Claudia's a young girl. And her mom, well, there's nothing she won't do for me. I bought her these scanty hot outfits, and she wears them under a raincoat when we go to the mall! I can't believe it! I never felt more like a king."

"What bothers me is Claudia. You were probably her first boyfriend."

"Yeah, you might think, but girly been 'round the block. This is her *second* abortion. She had one at fifteen. Now she's seventeen. Can you believe it? She's saying stuff like as long as she can see me every day, and I can give her some *de vez en cuando,* she's cool with that. You can't believe it either, can you?"

No, I couldn't. "I hope you're using protection."

"You got that right! They all say they're on the pill but that's just to keep you around. Bitches think they slick!"

Yeah, and you're so smart. "I was looking forward to coming up there."

"And you still can!"

"Yeah, I guess."

"Sure. Look! Forget them damn books! I know some baaad mamis, make you forget all that calculus shit. You haven't seen my new ride either, have you?"

"No, I haven't."

"It's red and slick. A Toyota. A real mami magnet. Look, I gotta go pick up Ruth, Claudia's mom. She just picked out a hot little dress and shoes. We're going out tonight to celebrate. Man, do I feel relieved!" Carlito gave me his phone number and new address. "Let me know when you're coming. Take care."

Hombre! It was like listening to five episodes of a soap opera at one sitting: *As The Cuchifrito Fries.* From mom to daughter and back to mom again? That was a new one for me. I didn't know Claudia, but I felt sorry for her. She was at one with abuse. But she would at least be free of the pain of being with someone who wanted no part of marriage. She couldn't exactly say she was left at the altar. But to say Carlito didn't give a damn about her would be an understatement. And living under the same roof—at least part-time—how could he stand to see his ex every day? And her mother? She was a new breed. So much for loyalty. She was just like Carlito: All about self. He sounded so happy to be free to run the streets again, too. It didn't sound too promising to me. Well, I had my own life to sort out.

* * *

Gerardo laughed out front. It was good to hear them having fun. Without a doubt, Gerardo would be out for the night—alone. He was so predictable: flowers, pizza, a romp with Ginebra on the mattress, and off to the races. It wasn't the kind of love I understood, but then again, what kind of love did I understand?

He and Carlito would have a good time together, comparing notes. While I was in no position to point a blaming finger, I still felt my stomach turn at the thought of Carlito sleeping with the mother and the daughter. Well, at least they were not all in the same bed at the same time. Talk about lower self-esteem on the part of Claudia. Who is that character in *West Side Story*, Anybody's? That was Claudia all right. And there were a lot of Claudias in that neighborhood.

"*¡Roberto!*" It was Euridice, standing at the door of my room in a lime green bikini and flip-flops.

"*¡Vaya!*" Way to go. She had just come from the pool. We continued as always in Spanish.

"Are you ready?" She asked.

"Just about." I grabbed my tennis racquet and bag I had packed.

"Take the guitar, too!"

"Okay."

"Let me dry off and get dressed. I'll burn up in this bathing suit."

"Definitely."

"Rub some sunblock on my back, please."

I walked into her room, found the lotion, and applied it to her back. It was the first time I had ever touched her back in all its bareness. The tan was only broken by the faint thin spaghetti shadows of a brasserie. I smoothed in the lotion almost clinically, not missing any area. She thanked me. She slipped on a white cotton sleeveless blouse. She also wore the red Phillies baseball cap I had given her some time ago, jeans, and the flip-flops she had on earlier.

"You want to take the first leg of the trip?" I asked.

"No, you drive. I'll take over in Mississippi."

"I'll pick up some coffee along the way."

Having had little sleep the night before, I was looking forward to turning the wheel over to her by the time we crossed the state border.

6

We were going through Alabama by the time I relinquished the wheel. Much to my surprise. Something about getting away from the familiar, freeing myself.

"So, when do I get to drive?"

"Anytime you like."

I pulled over at the next rest stop: a gas station with a room for rent sign in the window. Six hours of driving was enough for one stretch. Euridice had napped along the way. She told me she had done thirty laps at the LSU Natatorium. She swam every day and had the smoothly defined body of a swimmer. The summer had painted her dark orange. I had enjoyed the smell of perfume in her hair as she nestled her head into my shoulder while I drove. This was a new experience with her and I liked it.

Euridice nudged me and I gradually came to. "We better pull in for the night somewhere," she said. It was seven and the sun had set while I slept the rest of my languor. What a difference two hours made.

"We'll go to the next motel we see," I said, not knowing where we were. Then I spotted a Florida license plate that had Escambia on it. Next, an interstate that read Florida. We were passing through some country town, just lots of trees against a reddish sky on a bed of cumulus clouds.

"Over there. That's as good as any," I said. The sign was barely visible. One of the florescent tubes was out, not disclosing all of the letters in EVA'S MOTEL. There was a single row of six units under a rain shelter. We walked through the office door and two women greeted us.

"Hello. We would like a room for the night. How much?"

"Thirty-five dollars. Just fill this out," the silver-haired woman said.

I completed the form.

"We've got some videos you can watch if you like," said the younger woman, smiling.

"Thanks," said Euridice. "Anything good?"

"You be the judge," she said, handing her five. They're all Rs and Xs.

"Rx, like pharmaceuticals?" I said.

"What's that?" said the young woman.

"Oh nothing," I said. My sense of humor was lost on her.

We went back to the car and drove to Door 5. I pulled out our luggage and carried it into the room. I turned on the air-conditioner. Euridice went into the bathroom to take a shower. I sat down on one of the double beds. I looked under the night table and found a menu to a take-out restaurant. I called the number and ordered a large pizza and two bottles of orange soda.

Euridice walked from the bathroom, her hair wrapped in a towel, as well as one around her body. I passed her on my way into the bathroom. The fresh scent of watermelon filled the air.

"¡Huele bueno!" I said, commenting on the pleasant smell.

"Gracias." Euridice secured the already tight towel around her tanned skin. I mentioned that the money on the table was for the food I had ordered over the phone; that someone would be there shortly.

After my shower I shaved. The delivery person had come while I was still in the shower. I found Euridice watching television, still waiting for me to join her before eating.

"*No tenías que esperarme,*" I said.

"Well, you did order it," she said politely.

We sat down at the edge of the beds and pulled slices apart and enjoyed the hot, gooey cheese and sauce.

"*¿Quieres ver una película?*" she asked.

"*Sí,*" I said, not caring what kind of film she put on.

"*Young Adam?*" she asked.

"*Sí, como no.*" I had no objections, and had never heard of it.

We sat in our respective beds. About a half hour into watching the film, Euridice snuggled into bed with me. It was at the same time that the film began to get steamy: The barge worker, Young Adam, availed himself of an attraction he had for the woman who owned the barge. This happened the night the woman's husband went into town for drinks. The same sort of liaisons happened on subsequent nights. When the husband came in stuporous, the wife wanted no part of him, having already given herself so shamelessly to the new man on the job. Perhaps forty-five minutes into the film Euridice was asleep, having driven more than she was used to that day. With Euridice's warm body nestled against me, I felt happier than I could remember in a long time. I don't know if I was falling in love with her, but I couldn't imagine feeling better. Just let the natural feelings guide me, or us. Yes, her head on my chest was all I remembered, as my interest in Young Adam faded with the sound of crickets into the night.

* * *

I woke up refreshed, having slept sufficiently. I enjoyed not having heard any doors open and close, any telephones ringing. I looked down at Euridice, caressing the large pillow. I got up and took a shower.

While in the shower I thought of the film I had watched the night before. Adam was not a bad person, but he was to some extent to blame for his girlfriend's death. He had left her in the dark after having had his way with her. Yes, she, too, had made a choice to be with him, but to be left on the docks alone? One could argue that she should have seen earlier that he was not a stable person, certainly not one to choose as her mate for life. His thing was running around for as far as his blond hair and blue eyes would allow. She could not have known that everything came to him as easily as she did. Everything except writing, that is. The evidence that would have linked him directly to his pregnant girlfriend sank to the sea like a sextant (still pointing to him). What was Euridice looking for in me? Euridice was all I could ever hope to be with. Did she feel the same way about me?

"¡Oiga, guárdame un poquito, compay!" Euridice said, cutting into my thoughts with her plea for hot water.

Euridice woke me from my mini-analysis of the film, which I had watched alone for the most part. We continued in Spanish.

"You sound like a Cuban!"

"Cuba, qué lindos son tus paisajes! Cuba, qué lindos son!" she sang out, the lyrics to a popular song about Cuban landscapes.

"Bueno, tenemos Celia Cruz!" I said, teasingly comparing her to the famed singer. I came out of the bathroom, the long white towel wrapped around me. We exchanged high fives as she walked into the steamy bathroom.

7

I returned the videos and settled up with the motel owner. Euridice and I moved on down the highway in search of someplace to have breakfast. A roadside diner not far from the motel seemed as good a place as any, so we pulled in.

"I'll have waffles and scrambled eggs with coffee," I told the waitress.

"And you?" she asked Euridice.

"Maybe a cheese omelet with potatoes. Oh yes, and some wheat toast with butter. Coffee, too. Thanks."

"So how did you like the film?" Euridice asked.

"It was good, but a little strange. It was a sad movie."

"I thought so, too."

"But you fell asleep on it."

"Not before I realized that I had seen it already."

"Gee, so what did you think of it?"

"His girlfriend painted herself into a corner with that guy. I mean, he was a real bum, *verdad*?" She waved her hands to emphasize her point. "He might have been gifted as a writer, but he gave up on himself. He was a smooth talker, and he had a story to tell. Do you remember the story he told about how the woman they fished out of the water was maybe thrown in by her lover and so on. He just went on but of course that was early in the movie, so the barge owner had no idea where he got the idea. And neither did we."

"I couldn't believe it!"

"Yeah, wasn't it crazy? He had lots of imagination. Even his lovemaking was imaginative. The tragedy was, at least to my mind, that he looked for affection only as a substitute for digging inside, working hard."

"Exactly," I said.

"And there was almost no investigation after her death. What was her name, Cathie?"

"I think so. His was Joe, but why was the film named *Young Adam*? He was a complex character. But she was simple."

"I wouldn't call her simple. She knew what she a wanted: A husband for her child. Maybe a family. I agree that he was complex, though. And certainly unsure of himself."

"What about his sexual exploits?"

"I think that's typical. He had a lot of opportunities— and took advantage of all of them! Unfortunately, he left all of his experiences unfulfilled."

"And that electrician who was accused of killing Cathie?"

"How ironic! His only crime was adultery. But it was enough for the film writer to give him the rope—to hang himself."

"Only adultery?" I said.

"Well, the film, as I remember it, was about casual sex. The barge woman slept with Joe every chance she got, and she was married, too! Why, that woman was generous to a fault. She even lined up a *date* for Joe with her *grieving* sister-in-law."

"I mean, Joe was getting it when he wasn't even trying!" I said.

Euridice and I were laughing, but I wondered whether she was making a comparison with *Young Adam* and me. I left our townhouse before things got out of hand, so she didn't really see any of the things I did. Of course, she didn't have to think too hard to connect Cathie in the film with Cathy of a day ago. For me, though, they were one and the same. Cathie on the docks of Scotland. Cathy on the shores of the Mississippi. I needed to segue into a different topic. *Stay with films, then it won't seem like you are changing the subject.*

"When I was in Panamá, I used to love to watch Mexican westerns. Remember María Felix?"

"Of course!"

"We were all in love with her."

"We or you?"

"Well, I was, for sure."

"Now we come to the truth," she said with a smile of victory, as she dabbed the ketchup from the corner of her red mouth with a napkin. "And who else?"

"María Conchita Alonso, Isabella Rossellini, Anna Magnani."

"Anna Magnani?"

"She's dead. A great one, though."

"So, you like the dead ones, too?"

"Just some of the dead ones."

"And what about Halle Berry?"

"What about Angela Bassett?"

"What about Sonia Braga?"

"What about Euridice Betancourt? You could be an actress, you know."

"I've no desire to do that," she said, taking a bite from her toast.

"That was some list of ladies."

She nodded in agreement, looking down at her eggs. "Now you on the other hand . . . At least you sing. Look at Rubén Blades. He's made a lot of films too, you know."

"And still had time to finish law school!"

"And you'll finish engineering school, and build lots of power utilities stations," she said, reaching across the table, clasping my hand. Some of the water in her glass splashed onto the blue tablecloth. The cloth bunched into waves.

"¡*Ojalá*!"

"¡*Ojalá!*"

We finished our breakfast after a spirited conversation. She later mentioned that she had seen the film some months ago, one night when I was working at that graveyard job of mine: 7-Eleven. She and Ginebra had discussed it; they had watched it together.

8

The Florida sun was glinting through the trees. We wanted to make the most of the daylight hours driving. I found my Ray-Bans. Euridice had already donned hers. I drove with the windows down. The sun shone intermittently, playing hide-and-seek with the tall cypresses. Still a bright orange, the sun was hidden whenever we turned the semicircles of curves that made up much of the highway early on. The trees leaned and bowed at an angle toward the morning sun as if paying homage. Euridice's sleeveless arms were already a sienna color and in glistening contrast to the white blouse she wore.

"What are you thinking?" she asked, catching me as I glanced at her.

"How good that water is going to feel."

"Like a hot tub, I bet."

"Probably, and ninety-nine in the shade. We'll cool off with one of those *guanábana* milkshakes!"

"You said it!"

I couldn't wait to hit Miami. Then there was the nightlife, too. Euridice loved to dance as much as I did. I hadn't been to a club since I was last in Miami. Back in Philly, Carlito and I would go to *Iglesia San Eduardo* (St. Edward's Church), which wasn't far from us. On Saturday nights some of the great bands would come to play. It was after listening to one of the local bands, *Orquesta Panamá*, that Carlito asked Tío Carlos for a tenor saxophone. Tío Carlos got it for him and Carlito started taking lessons on Fifth and Somerset. From the start he could play along with records. He especially liked "Chombo" Silva and Ronnie Cuber, though I believe Ronnie Cuber played baritone sax. For Carlito it didn't matter. After he learned a lick, it was etched into his memory. He played in some Latin band in Union City, New Jersey, where he later picked up the flute and was quite something. He especially loved the adulation, as would any teenager. He would take a bus up to Union City, spend the night and return Sunday, exhausted, but full of tales, some of which were true, I'm sure. On a few occasions I went with him and met some of his female friends. He knew some beauties, I have to admit. All were great dancers and I learned some sweet turns from them. It was so exhilarating to still be in high school or just out and having so much fun. It was nice to have some free time away from the hardware store, to which I had devoted so much time in junior high, and to see what young guys could do to have fun without ever getting into trouble. As for me, I continued to play guitar, but never with the interest to do it professionally.

"Is it too windy for you?" I asked Euridice.

"Are you kidding? I could go like this forever."

We continued until we got to Daytona Beach.

"I feel like swimming," she said.

The beach was so inviting. Finding a place to park would be the problem.

"Let me call Francisco Duarte, remember him?" she asked, but I couldn't recall him. I began to think he was one of her ex's.

"Don't give me that look," she added.

I was no good at disguising my doubts. She was more familiar with Florida than I was. She had gone to Florida State University for a year before transferring to LSU.

"He's from my hometown, Maracay. He transferred to Florida A&M after two years at Southern. He's in med school at Florida State now."

None of the things she told me made any difference, until she mentioned International Night at LSU my sophomore year. Francisco sang *Quizás, Quizás, Quizás* and sounded like Tito Rodriguez. How could I forget *that* evening? I can say he made me take notice of Euridice for being something other than a monster mathematician.

Euridice had stood in a group of three lovely ladies: Gertrudes, Pilar, and Euridice. No jeans that night. Dresses and heels were the attire. Euridice wore an emerald-colored silk dress and black satin pumps. All that beautiful hair of hers was up, showing off a pair of thin gold loops that lay against her gorgeous neck. She might have been wearing contacts, because the honey in her eyes melted mine away. And her lips painted ruby. She was poised to strike like lightning. But how was I to know that she would strike me? Was I the tallest tree in the woods, or just the luckiest?

"Are you coming to Pilar's tonight? Why don't you come? It's going to be fun!"

How could it be anything but, if you'll be there, I thought. I hadn't known Pilar for long. Pilar was from Tegus (Tegucigalpa, Honduras), but she never used the whole word. Well, I would be there if I had to walk!

"Yes, I remember Francisco now." Gosh, I felt so stupid. It all came crashing in on me. Euridice had liked me for the longest time, and I was out chasing strumpets. *Panning for pyrite when I was standing next to an emerald.* I needed to have lightning hit me!

"I wonder if he still sings," I said.

"I hope so. He could be working in a nightclub."

I pulled over and Euridice walked to a public telephone. Meanwhile, I took in the sights. Young women in bikinis, and some of them carrying boards on which to float. I could see why these beaches were the attraction. Euridice came back running.

"He's in! I gave him our location. He's not far from here, he said."

He wasn't far because in fifteen minutes a very tanned Francisco arrived—and not alone.

We exchanged *abrazos* and rapid-fire greetings in Spanish amid the hugs.

"This is Isabel Rojas," he said.

We shook hands. She was quite striking: long hair as black as midnight with eyes just as dark. I did not want to stare. The yellow *tanga*, as we call the string bikinis, was really next to nothing. She wore a shear white covering from her waist to her ankles. The sheerness of her *skirt* was merely an allure. Her cheeks were fully exposed under it. She was not unique. That style of bathing suit was the order of the day on that beach. Coming from Baton Rouge, where the women's bathing suits, particularly, are modest, for poolside swims, the contrast here was arousing. No, I might not remember Francisco ten years from that day, but unless I was stricken with Alzheimer's I would *never* forget Isabel.

"It's good that you came on Saturday. We're both off." Isabel spoke looking at me and I averted my eyes to Euridice. It's amazing what the mind photographs in a millisecond: the sunburnt strands of hair, the mole just above the right side of her mouth, the protruding nipples the equilateral triangles did their best to cover, the tiny gold cross and thin chain around her neck.

"Well, we are the lucky ones," said Euridice.

9

The beach was full, but Francisco and Isabel took us to their favorite location, no less crowded. They were admitted sun-worshipers. But Francisco had little time for the beach with his studies. He was entering his third year of medical studies. Isabel was still an undergraduate chemical engineering major, a senior like us, but with an interest in pursuing medicine as well.

I noticed her Spanish accent but could not tell from what country she came.

"Chile," She said toweling her long hair while standing in front of Francisco.

"And I thought I was far from home," I said, finally loosening up.

"Oh, I think I'm the farthest from home, though my mother lives here in the States."

"Where?" asked Euridice.

"Miami, where my father practiced medicine until three years ago, when he died."

Euridice and I expressed our sympathies. Isabel grabbed Euridice's hand, helping her up. Isabel wanted to go back in the warm water. The two of them ran to the shore while Francisco and I watched.

"She's out here every chance she gets. I think it helps her forget," said Francisco.

"Forget what?"

"The pain of losing her father. The fact that he will never see her graduate, or see her go to med school."

"It's odd. My father is still alive, but I never think about him not being around. I suppose I should, though. He has sacrificed a lot to make life better for me." I paused and caught the two women playing in the waves. "Look at those two. Like little girls."

"You're right about that, too," Francisco agreed. "Are you two serious?"

"You know, I've just become so. Our friendship has grown into more than just being together. And you two?"

"Oh, we are. We have grown more so since Isabel found out she might have to return to Miami. Her mother is lonely."

"Why can't her mother move here?"

"I'll have to marry her first, since Isabel and I are living together. You know what I mean?"

"That doesn't seem so bad. You love her, right?"

"Oh, sure. But the thought of having her mother in the same space with us, well, I'm not for that."

"I'm sure she wouldn't plan to stay with you, only to be close to her daughter."

"Sure. I would say you are right, except that she was diagnosed with cancer recently, so she will be staying near us. I'm looking at these skimpy outfits for the last time. Her mother isn't going to go for this stuff," he said, pointing to two young women whose bare rears were facing the sun. "All I'm saying is that it's going to take some getting used to."

"Exactly. And as for the cancer, there are so many treatments now, there is the possibility it could be put in remission. You probably know that, though. And didn't you say her father was a successful doctor? Surely she has means to support herself. You are still in med school, besides. When you talk it over and clear the air, things won't be as complicated as they seem."

"You're right. I'm just being selfish. I want her all to myself."

"As any man would. I'm sure Isabel will still be yours. She knows how you feel about her."

"I proposed to her, and she accepted. I told her that we should not wait, and she agreed."

"You're further ahead than we are."

"Man, women are making plans while we sleep," he laughed. "Here they come."

"Gee, that was great," said Isabel, out of breath. Euridice ran up, on Isabel's heels. Isabel lay face down on the beach towel between me and Francisco, totally exposed to the sun. Euridice sat next to me, her head against my shoulder. Her knees were bent, so that my view of Isabel's near-nude body was partially blocked. Women are so clever, I thought. Francisco was not distracted by Isabel's flirtatious behavior; he decided to go out for a swim himself. In the waves I saw him splashing water with two young women.

"Would you put some sunblock on my back?" asked Isabel.

The question was general, but I chose not to respond. Euridice pulled out a bottle and applied it to Isabel's back. Isabel applied some to her buttocks without embarrassment. As I looked away, Euridice pinched me and pointed with her chin; her okay that I could look.

"Roberto, Euridice told me how well you play the guitar. You and Francisco have to do some songs while you are here."

"I'd like that."

"We can go to the patio behind the apartment. It's cool there." She apparently had absorbed enough sun. "Are you going to stay here tonight?" Isabel asked. "At least for dinner," she added coyly, as if there was no way I could deny her suggestion.

"I'd like to," I said before allowing Euridice to say she would.

"Aren't we eager?" said Euridice, having fun with me. "Maybe I should have let *you* put the lotion on."

"What is this, a conspiracy? Let me put some on your back," I told Euridice.

The two women laughed as if sharing some prearranged joke.

"We're going to get something to wear tonight," said Isabel, "as soon as Francisco gets back."

When Francisco returned, Isabel told him of her suggestion and we went back to the apartment. There on the patio I tuned my guitar and asked Francisco what he wanted to sing.

"Just play something. I can't think of anything right now."

I played some chords and scales, then more chords. "What about this?" I said. And his mouth formed the first full smile of the day. It was the first chords of *Quizás, Quizás, Quizás*. We sang that and several other songs, even one made famous by Carlos Gardel, *Adiós Muchachos*. Isabel taped the session.

After the singing, Euridice and Isabel went out shopping.

10

Euridice and Isabel came back to the apartment. Each of them carried bags from their afternoon of shopping.

Francisco and I were watching a John Wayne western, but were already dressed to go out. It was 6:30 when they emerged from the hallway, first Isabel, then Euridice. The women had showered and gotten dressed. They looked spectacular. Each of them had on a T-shirt minidress and spaghetti-strapped sandals, about four inches off the floor. Isabel now stood five foot ten. Her sky-blue dress hugged her form and made her more alluring then her unclad body some hours earlier. Next to her was Euridice in a black T-shirt dress with a double-buckled belt offset to the right side of her waist. She just as high as Isabel; her caramel thighs were those of a dancer, and were those the same gold loops in her ears she wore the night of the International Festival at LSU?

We left the apartment on foot to go to a Cuban restaurant that Isabel raved about. It was just a few blocks away.

I was so excited by the way the two women looked that I couldn't eat. I left my meal of seafood soup all but untouched. Just a few shrimps and broth was all I ate.

We had decided to go dancing. Again, Isabel knew of a favorite club. The name, The Body Shop, made me think of a place where autos were serviced. I was right. In the lobby was a 1970 Chevy hoisted on a lift. The male workers wore white cotton overalls; the female hostesses wore black body stockings and strapless heels. The Latin music pulsated; the guitars, trumpets and congas alternately taking the lead in providing the tropical music atmosphere. Francisco and Isabel spun together, feeling the spirit of the night, one after another. I held onto Euridice with a like *salsa* fever. Francisco and I later switched partners and I danced the *merengue* with Isabel. She was so uninhibited, pressing so tightly that I would have thought she was from the Dominican Republic, the country of origin of that dance. She danced so close to me I vowed not to drink any more rum and lime that night. After four *merengues* on the crowded floor, I found Francisco and Euridice again, but not before Isabel had planted a kiss on my mouth! I was surprised, though not embarrassed. I had never even kissed Euridice on the mouth! It sure felt good, and I knew that I would take Euridice all the way, if that's what she wanted. There was nothing subtle about Isabel, and she was somehow pulling back the sheets for me and Euridice.

The music slowed to a medley of *boleros.* Euridice's perfume was as intoxicating as the hot summer night there in Daytona. Now getting down to Miami was not as important. Oh, we would get there, but when was the question.

It was a little after 1a.m. when I if asked if we could soon leave. We were going to be on the road again the following day. We had had a fantastic time. Who could have predicted that a casual phone call would give birth to such promise? We danced a last dance, then left the Body Shop, our engines well-oiled.

We walked outside to catch a taxi back to their apartment. We arrived at the apartment. My intention was to say good night, to say that we would meet for breakfast in the morning, but that we would spend the night in a motel. Francisco had to go to work at the hospital at 5:30 a.m.

"We should have left at midnight. You would have gotten a little more rest," I suggested.

"Look, we had a great time, and I don't regret a minute of it!" Francisco emphasized.

We sat at the kitchen table. Isabel made some Cuban coffee and we each had a slice of *flan*. She put on an album by Jose Luis Rodriguez.

"You'll have to come back for the wedding," said Francisco. "It's December 22nd."

"Wow! You didn't mention the date earlier," I said, surprised by the suddenness of the announcement.

"I didn't get around to it."

For some reason I felt he hadn't gotten around to giving a date because he was not eager to end the close relationship with Isabel, having to soon share her with her mother. No wonder he didn't seem to care about Isabel's coquettish displays, her near nudity at the beach.

"Congratulations!" Euridice and I exclaimed. Euridice got up and gave Isabel a hug.

Francisco finished his demitasse, then said, "I'm going to bed, excuse me."

"Of course," I said.

"Look, you stay in touch, and take care of Euridice," he told me.

"For sure."

He gave us *abrazos,* and then kissed Isabel good night. It was almost 2 a.m. He was such a quiet person. He disappeared into his room. His ways contrasted sharply with those of Isabel, who was very demonstrative. At times they seemed happy in spite of the near-end of their coupled lifestyle.

"I'll get your bed ready," said Isabel. She pulled out the futon in the living room. We had had a full day. The only one in the room with an endless amount of energy was Jose Luis. And he could have sung all night! The three of us became quiet after a full night of dancing. I removed my shoes. And said I was ready to turn in.

"Well, you're not going to leave me up!" said Isabel. She hugged us alternately and went to bed.

I went into the bathroom first. As I exited, Euridice went in. Maybe ten minutes passed. When she came out, I was not ready for what I saw. The scene was from some French film: a black satin bra, black waist cincher, two-toned black stockings and black stilettos that lifted her four inches off the floor. She looked at me and smiled, "I know just what you like." She dimmed the lights and approached me with the gaze of a jaguar. Our bodies picked up the whirling red and blue lights on the hood of a parked police car. The silent lights cut like scissors through the Venetian blinds.

"You're exquisite," I said.

"Maybe you'll write me a song."

"How about a symphony?"

"Just hold me, Roberto."

Where had I heard that before? My lips were smarter than my brain for not uttering the name that came to mind. We walked in unison, as I back-peddled her to the futon. She pressed her hands against my chest. My heart raced with anticipation. She was so soft and warm and smelled of honeysuckle. I was getting to know Euridice on this trip to Miami. She was all woman, at once delicate and smart. She enraptured me as her scent filled the room. I could not have imagined that night, locked away in her arms.

I hoped we hadn't made too much noise that night. Euridice's scent painted my body as if I were a canvas. The morning light sliced through the blinds and stripped Euridice's bare thigh. I covered it. Now the diagonal lines lay against the lavender muslin.

The sun was strong, as was the smell of brewing coffee. When I awoke at six, the sun burned my face. It felt good. Euridice lay as still as, well, I hesitate to say, an angel. Her face was covered by her long brown hair. Isabel stood pouring a demitasse of coffee. She was again in her favorite diaphanous black skirt sans panties. This woman had a real fear of being overdressed.

"Buenos dias, Isabel."

"Muy buenos."

I wrapped a sheet around myself and walked to the bathroom. The warm water and soap brought me around. I felt wonderful. I was ready to move on down the road. I could smell breakfast cooking in the kitchen: eggs with peppers and sausage.

I walked back to the living room where Euridice, draped in a sheet, sat with Isabel having coffee and breakfast.

"When did you two go to bed?" asked Isabel.

"Not long ago," I said.

Isabel smiled at Euridice. "Are you going to stay another day?"

"We're going to be moving on, thanks," I said. "Though the hospitality has been the greatest!"

"Just don't forget us."

"We'll come back for the wedding."

"Make sure you do."

"I'm going to miss doing those duets with Francisco."

"I'm glad I had the tape running," said Isabel. "I made a copy this morning for you."

"Thank you, again."

We finished eating and cleaned up the living room. We packed our bags and were ready to leave, when Isabel asked if we wanted to take another swim. We said no. She was in another little swimsuit and wiggled her way to the beach.

11

About an hour into the drive the sky grew dark and it began to rain. It was a thundershower; nothing unusual. An hour later the sun was out and as strong as ever. The rain had been enough to make Euridice fall asleep. With her head against the window, the heat woke her up.

"How long was I asleep?"

"An hour."

"You and Francisco had fun, eh?"

"I really didn't get to know him back when I was a freshman. He's really nice."

"I thought you would like him."

"Did you know about Isabel and her family?"

"I talked to him a few months ago. He told me about her, but that's all."

"Do you think she's pregnant?" I asked.

"No, why?"

"The wedding seems sudden, don't you think?"

"Well, her mother is moving to town, so it's may be time that they get serious."

"What about us?"

"Oh, I think we're serious. Don't you?"

"Yes. That's what I like about you. In spite of the recent fling."

"Well, I had no idea how you felt. I mean, I wasn't sure that you thought about me other than just a friend."

"Sometimes a woman wants to see if the man is interested. I threw out the line a few times, but you didn't bite."

"I really didn't think I had a chance with you. I mean, what would your father say about me?"

"What do you think, we're Rothschilds or something?"

"Well, I only know there is no oil in my family. My father worked all his life at the docks. Hard work is all we know."

"And that is all *my* father knows. Even if it is in a law office."

"I just don't want to be the fish that you throw back into Lake Maracaibo."

"My father already knows about you, even your misgivings. You see, I talked to him about you."

Her candor made me relax, even as I drove down the highway. It was somehow easier to love her, knowing that her father would accept me. With all my industry, I still felt that without any financial wherewithal, her family might not accept me. I knew of cases where the same thing had happened. I didn't want to end up like them.

"What does he know about me?"

"That you are a tireless worker; that you sing and play guitar. That I care about you."

"Does he know that I care about you?"

"I think he does. I talk about you enough."

"This is all a revelation, you know."

"Oh, come on, Roberto. You had to know I have been crazy about you for the longest."

It was when she said *"estaba loca por ti"* that I got a chill. No one had ever said she was crazy about me. It was a superlative expression of emotion that was uncharacteristic for her. And to be the object of such an expression was overwhelming. I pulled off the road as soon as it was safe.

"And how long have I been crazy about you?" I asked. "Maybe two years, with no courage to tell you." I kissed

67

her red mouth; her flushed cheeks. I held her, having shaken myself of the timidity that held me captive for so long.

"We are two crazies who belong together!" she said.

"And I'll always wish I had said it first."

"But I said it for both of us."

Euridice revealed that while her father received any news about me with enthusiasm, her mother was less animated. What concerned her was that her mother stayed out of conversations about me. Wasn't she concerned, or did she hope this was something that would pass like a trembling in night; a driving rain that as it reaches the shore dims to a drizzle? She showed enthusiasm only for her studies. Wasn't that the reason they had invested their resources? A husband, as her mother said, she could find *"dondequiera."*

That, of course, was not true. To say "anywhere," I felt, was said only to diminish the importance of finding, or for that matter, looking, for one. I wasn't aware that Euridice was looking for a husband. For all I could tell, she poured all of her energy into her studies—and the evidence was in the degree to which she excelled. No, even now that Euridice had confessed her love, it was not a foregone conclusion that we would be like Francisco and Isabel marching down the aisle. There were a lot of junctures to face before we arrived at that one.

"I think your parents don't want you to be distracted. After all, I am a distraction from your goal."

"I don't see you that way. I think we want the same things—for ourselves and for each other."

I believed what she said. I had no choice but to finish what I began. I was at the finish line. My job prospects were plentiful—worldwide. Things were no different for Euridice. I was just glad to be with her.

12

The sun was setting when we arrived in Miami. The sun reflected in all of its orange brightness from the business buildings and commercial avenues. The hours of driving had taken the energy out of me. I looked forward to having a good cup of coffee in Little Havana, where we were headed. Our friend Héctor Serrano now lived in Miami, and had made it his home after graduating from Southern University in architecture. After not finding any work in design, he had the idea of doing landscaping. "It's a multibillion-dollar business. I'm sure there's some there for me," I remember him saying. He wasn't wrong. All of his hard work was paying off. He was able to visit Venezuela every year, and it was always fun to visit him and talk about school days. We were fond of sitting on his enclosed patio, enjoying a mango from the tree that grew in his front yard. I pulled over to use a public telephone to let him know we were in town.

"*¿Alo. Está Héctor?*"
"*¿De parte?*"
"*Roberto Dávila.*"
"*¡Roberto!*"
We continued in Spanish.
"We just arrived. Man, is it hot out here!"
"Welcome to Miami. Is Euridice with you?"
"She's in the car."
"Well, we're eager to see you."
"We'll be there in ten minutes."

"Go well then."

I got back to the car and watched the heat waves rise from the street.

"He said they're waiting for us."

"Who are they?"

"I didn't ask."

When we came to Law Street, where Héctor's house was, there were two older gentlemen playing dominoes in the adjacent yard. They reminded me of my own father, sitting there in their white *guayaberas,* jostling the noisy white rectangular blocks.

We spoke to the men as we passed them. I rang the doorbell. The door opened.

"Yes?" The woman said.

"I am Roberto. This is Euridice. And—"

"Oh! Come in. Héctor is in the shower," she said.

"I am Silvia," she said, allowing us into the house.

"What a beautiful rug," remarked Euridice.

"Oh, Héctor brought it back from Venezuela."

"Could I get you something?"

"Maybe some water?" Euridice asked.

"Of course," Silvia said, and she walked carefully back to the kitchen.

I looked to Euridice but her back was to me. She was engaged in the wall paintings and objects suspended from the walls: a small white replica of a hammock; a flag of Venezuela; a *cuatro* guitar.

Silvia returned to the living room where we stood with a tray of four glasses: two of lemonade and two of water. She eased the tray onto the table. "Please sit down. You must be exhausted."

"It's so nice to be out of the car," said Euridice, taking a seat.

"It must be. I've never been to Louisiana, but it is a long way to come."

"What's all this noise?" boomed Héctor, running down the steps.

"Hey, brother," I said, as we embraced one another.

"Euridice. So great to have you here. You met Silvia, of course."

"Yes, we did. The lemonade is great, by the way."

"Thanks," said Silvia, looking in my direction but not making eye contact.

"You're playing piano now, Héctor?"

"No, Silvia plays," he said.

"How nice," added Euridice.

"Maybe she'll play later on," suggested Héctor. "I ordered seafood after you called. I hope you two are hungry."

"I am," said Euridice. "Mmm. Seafood. I can't wait."

I noticed that as Euridice laughed about her own enthusiasm for seafood, Silvia's eyes moved about busily, without focus. I asked Héctor about work.

"Oh, it's summer so I'm as busy, as you can imagine."

"Let me show you the house, Euridice," said Silvia. She held her arm out for Euridice to loop hers through it, and they left the room.

It was most noticeable then that Silvia had a vision impairment. Silvia used her free hand to guide the two of them around the house.

"So, how long have you two been together?"

"It will be six months next week."

"She's very beautiful," I remarked about Silvia. She was the same height and size as Euridice. She was a black woman with a complexion the color of ground coffee. She wore her black hair up in a tuft.

"I was walking down Flagler Street and she was sitting by herself in a Cuban café. I asked if I could sit with her. She said she was leaving soon, but I sat down anyway. I asked where she was from, thinking she might be Cuban because of her accent in Spanish. She said she was from the Dominican Republic, born of Haitian parents. Her parents came her three years ago. She had worked as a secretary. I told her I could use a secretary in my business. Then she told me that her sight was failing; that she might not work out for me. Well, the more we talked, the more I realized I wanted to see her after that day; that she might work out for me after all. I mean, business was getting better and better. I asked her if she could still type and answer the telephone, that sort of thing. Well, that was a year ago."

"And you've been together for six months?"

"Yes."

"And her sight?"

"She got another examination scheduled, but they think it's glaucoma. She's taking some pills that seem to work. We're taking it day by day."

"Sure."

"Otherwise, life has been good. And with you?"

"One more year, then graduation."

"It must feel good to be near the end. I know it hasn't been easy." "You know too well."

"I laugh at it now. It's so different now that I'm working. It's easier now."

"I hope to say the same thing in a year."

The women came back into the room.

"You should see the grapefruit tree in the backyard. Those things are huge! They *do* look like giant grapes," said Euridice.

"Go take a look," said Héctor.

Euridice and I walked through the house. I thought of how the last time we were there Héctor was seeing a different woman, Sandra. Maybe she had gone back to Colombia. Héctor was a busy guy back then. Was he becoming domesticated?

"You're right!" I told Euridice. "They're like cannonballs!"

"They are *big*," she said.

"I wonder what happened to Sandra," I whispered.

"Things change," she said.

We looked around the garden. We walked along the short path and admired the magnolia tree and rhododendrons. The path was laid in flat stones which we were certain Héctor had placed himself. He was very detailed; the house had his signature inside and out.

By the time we walked back into the house, Silvia was setting the kitchen table because the seafood had arrived. We went to wash our hands, and then returned.

They had ordered oysters, clams, octopus and catfish, and rice and bean.

"Who else did you invite?" asked Euridice.

"I don't think Roberto needs any help," he said.

Euridice and I sat down across from Héctor and Silvia. It was great to be able to relax, speaking Spanish as fast as Arabian horses, discussing things that were familiar to us all: the bottom dropping out of the Venezuela economy; political turmoil in Perú; whether Vizquel would take the Cleveland Indians to the World Series; and jokingly which was a better rum: Brugal Añejo or Cacique.

"Well we don't have Cacique or Brugal, but we do have Bermúdez, and I think Cristóbol Colón drank that in 1492!" said Héctor, getting up from his chair. He brought out four glasses along with a bottle of Bermúdez and some limes.

"I like mine straight," I said. "I don't know Bermúdez, though."

"It's Dominican," interjected the all-too-quiet Silvia, now wearing dark glasses.

"To future success!" I toasted.

"It's smooth," said Euridice, taking a sip.

"Sing us a song, Roberto," said Héctor, after throwing back the rest of his rum.

I realized I had left my guitar in the car, got up in a hurry. I told them where I was headed.

"I'll help you bring in the bags," offered Héctor.

There were no trees on the sidewalk to protect the car from becoming an oven. My guitar case was extremely hot. We brought in the bags.

Well, we sang into the evening the favorites we had sung growing up: *"Muchacha Tímida," "Guantanamera," "Sopita en Botella," "Usted Abusó"* and some of my own like *"Euridice No Sabía."* The singing had drawn the attention of some of the neighbors. The two old gentlemen who were playing dominoes earlier were sitting with us; they took us back to the halcyon years in Cuba. The songs they sang were songs my father might have known, but were lost to me. It's a shame my parents were so far away, but here we were doing the same kinds of things we would do in my beloved country. We would sit outside around a fire, singing into the night, as the embers flickered and smoke spiraled into the air.

We ended our fun at midnight, about the same time the Bermúdez was gone. Héctor and I stayed up to talk a bit.

"Yes, I'm busier than ever, but that beats unemployment. I have three crews that I can count on, so I am able to relax once and a while—like today."

"I'm looking forward to just working, and not doubling up on work and more work!"

"And it won't be long. There's consolation in that," said Héctor.

"So are you and Silvia serious?"

"Seems that way, huh?"

"It does," I said.

I think I have found the right one. I mean, she doesn't ask for the world, which was the problem with Sandra."

It was his first opportunity to mention her. She had returned to Venezuela. He had heard nothing further from her, and had moved on with his life, not looking back. Well, he said he had tried not to. He had invested so much emotional energy in trying to give her what he was unable to: She came from a wealthy family, so it was not the right pairing for them.

"Oh, she'll find what she is after. I just wasn't that guy."

He sounded certain and over whatever heartache he might have experienced.

"And you and Euridice?"

"Actually, this is our really getting to know each other tour. Like you, I think I have found the right one."

"She and Silvia enjoyed themselves tonight."

"Euridice has liked me for a long time. I was just too timid to act; to know if she would say yes to my overtures. I wasted time; should have known better, but it's not like mathematics. Or maybe it is. Love can have a multiplicity of solutions."

"Hey, don't look to me for an explanation. I am just as confused by all of it as you."

"And we're two of the lucky ones! So how is Silvia getting around with her vision the way it is? She seems to do well."

"She's a marvel! She's so organized, which is a great help to me. Silvia Diversé is everything to me."

"Diversé! Definitely a French name," I said. "Does she speak it?"

"She speaks it to her family, mixed with Creole. She sounds like a different person."

"You know, I have often wondered why Haiti is so poor," I said.

"Believe me, if they had oil, it would be different story."

"Maybe not. Political corruption—which is a staple there—could create the same disparity," I said.

"Yes, but with so much wealth, the people would revolt. They wouldn't go for leaders living in palaces, while they fight for a crust of bread. Toussaint had the right idea, but Napoleon locked him away."

"I wonder if the Duvaliers are related to Napoleon. They kept the masses in poverty, and they haven't rebounded yet from those years of dictatorship."

"Well, I don't know about being related, but they were not about bringing their people into the industrialized world. They have a shortage of every necessity except sunshine and rain."

"I bet if they were part of the United States, they could build themselves up. Tourism would flourish. They would be able to grow trees and change the ecology of that huge rock of a country."

"I think that Bermúdez has made you a statesman!"

"If I'm intoxicated with anything, it's justice."

"And I would toast to that but we polished off the last of that bottle."

"With the help of those old gentlemen."

I had been holding my guitar and put it back into its case. "I am going to turn in," I said.

"Good night, Roberto."

I walked into the bedroom where Euridice and I were staying. The previous times we had visited Héctor we had stayed in separate rooms. I lay awake that night, pondering the disparity of justice in the world: how we went to bed with our stomachs full, while others just outside the door struggled for a crust of bread, or a manner in which to earn a living.

The answer I was looking for might have been in Silvia's eyes, those small black spheres which I caught myself glancing at while we talked that evening. She seemed aloof, not really in the conversations. But her eyes looked busy, as though following the movement of a fly in the room. She might have brought some light to that conversation Héctor and I had late that night. Where was Hispaniola in the scheme of world politics? Sure, the Dominican Republic was a repository of some of the best baseball players in the world, but what about Haiti? I was ashamed to say that the extent of what I knew about Haiti was that it produced Alexandre Dumas, and that I had read the schoolboy novels *The Three Musketeers* and *The Count of Monte Cristo*. Had Haiti only produced a family of dictators and a father and son family of writers? Hadn't they produced any poets of aspiration? So much poverty must have spawned a class of people clawing for their share of the global pie. While Silvia was quiet, her silence spoke volumes of what her past held locked away. Or were her parents of wealth, foreign-educated, having no care about the legacy of Toussaint Louverture? No, I should not expect so much of our *hostess*. Don't forget, this is a vacation, I told myself. Still, my mind was anything but vacant. I needed to read more if I wanted to answer my own questions. I was tired, though. After sitting on the edge of the bed, I let gravity pull me down to the pillow, and next to Euridice I drifted off to sleep.

13

The morning sun shone red through the white curtains draped in crisscross fashion in the bedroom. I could smell the bacon frying in the kitchen. Euridice was already up, and I could hear Spanish and laughter coming from some morning television program. Now I could smell toast and felt an emptiness in my stomach that I was sure would soon be filled.

Well, the table was set: bread, papaya preserves, orange juice, eggs, and the bacon I had smelled just minutes ago.

"¡Buén día, madrugón!"

"¿Pa'que madrugarme, si estoy en vacacione?." I replied to Héctor. After all, why get up early, if I am on vacation?

"Well, you're right, but I have to leave. I'll call later," he said. "Silvia has a plan for you and Euridice," he added, and left the house.

"Buenos días," I said to Euridice and Silvia.

They spoke and returned their attention to the morning program. José Luis Rodriguez was singing in his typically warm style. I walked into the bathroom, where I took my shower. After shaving I got dressed and returned to the dining room, but this time to tame the lion in my stomach.

I loaded a toasted long roll with lechoza—papaya preserves—and began my feast, albeit alone. The early risers had moved into the living room to listen to the entertainment on television. As I ate I admired the wall hangings, among which was a small flag of the Dominican Republic—almost an afterthought. It hung as still as Silvia's presence in the house. She was a housemaid after all, or was she? She kept the place immaculate. True, it might have been because of her failing vision. The quadric arrangement of furnishings was Mondrian-like: very colorful but a series of rectangles and squares. Like the night before, her presence was almost imperceptible: the fly on the wall. I looked up at Euridice and Silvia and caught their profile on the couch. Their faces held some animation. That reassured me that Silvia was not the housemaid. My misgivings were ill-placed. And the diamond ring I caught a glimpse of: was it an engagement ring?

"Look, Roberto! It's Silvia's father!"

Was it true? Silvia's father was being interviewed on Spanish television.

"Yes, that's correct. The living conditions of the Haitians are better here than in Haiti, but this is the United States: The land of plenty. And we are voicing our displeasure at the inadequacy of housing and health care for those residents whom the governor, by his own observation and admission, said he 'would address and not ignore.' That is why we are here today."

"*¡Vaya, Papá!*" shouted Silvia, in an uncharacteristic display of emotion.

"Wow! You didn't say your father was an activist," said Euridice.

The television screen flashed an identifier under the portrait of this articulate and well-dressed black gentleman: Charles-Christophe Diversé, Attorney.

"I didn't know where he was speaking today. And yes, he is an activist. That is the reason we fled Haiti. Of course, I was so young and don't remember much." As she spoke I thought of the speech Pablo Neruda gave upon receiving the Nobel Prize; how he galloped across a stream leaving Chile, entering Argentina. The Diversé family had crossed into the Dominican Republic, still in the Americas, so the analogy seemed appropriate.

"So where is he speaking?" Euridice asked.

"It looks like City Hall," answered Silvia.

"Look at all the protestors," I said. There were plenty of Haitians, I am sure, as well as people beyond the Latin communities.

"Maybe you can meet him before you go back," suggested Silvia. "I would like nothing more," I said.

"I'll call him, and leave a message," Silvia said, getting up and walking to the telephone.

"Aló Celeste! Oui, Je lui ai vu!" said Silvia, speaking with rapid excitement in French.

They continued talking. Silvia's personality was amplified beyond the narrow scope I had given it. I could only catch the laughter and histrionics. It reminded me for a minute that there were other languages in the Americas: Dutch, Quechua, Portuguese, Italian, and others. I felt so limited in my own scope, having only Spanish to navigate the Southern Hemisphere.

"He has a meeting tonight at seven thirty. Celeste said he will be home at nine," Silvia told us.

It seemed like a great opportunity. This man was making his voice be heard, fighting for a cause. It would be a joy to meet him.

"Do you want to take a walk, Euridice?"

"Yes. I'll be right with you."

14

The heat was rising from the sidewalk. Still, children played on their parched front lawn. I did not notice the men playing dominoes as we had the day before. We walked several blocks. We passed a blind teenaged girl dressed in nothing but a bathing suit and sandals. Euridice spoke to her.

"Buenos días."

"Buenos días."

"¿Dónde puedo encontrar café cubano?" asked Euridice, about the Cuban café she knew was in the neighborhood, not remembering exactly where.

The girl turned in the direction we were going and tapping her long plastic cane said, *"Sigues directo, hasta que llegues al semaforó. Después, cuando ve el rótulo Exxon, dobla a la derecha. Está por allí el sitio que se llama Café Jiménez."*

We both thanked her. I marveled at her presence; at her utter uncanny ability to describe her surroundings without the assistance of anything more than perhaps her own visual photograph. As she walked away I took another look at her. Had I been alone, I would have talked to her. She looked to be at least eighteen, tanned with long dark brown hair. She wore no dark glasses, so I took a look at her face. It glowed light brown. She was stunning. Euridice squeezed my hand, and playfully tugged at me. The girl spoke, giving me another chance to look at her large brown eyes without guilt.

"¿De dónde son ustedes?"

"Venezuela, gracias de nuevo," said Euridice, telling her where we from without allowing me to speak. She sensed I was looking for just such an excuse to talk to her, or for her to talk to me.

"We'll never get to the place if you start chatting," she said with a coquettish smile. Then as she had said several nights before, "I know what you like."

15

There was a crowd in the Cuban café, but we decided to stop in. As we walked in the door we spotted a couple leaving and we took our seats.

"Café negro con azúcar."

"Igual," I said, ordering black coffee with sugar just as Euridice had. This is what living is about, I thought. A radio played just above the head of the waitress who served us. We sat at a counter where men ate *sandwiches cubanos. Yes, I was going to have one of those before we left town.* Euridice smiled at my contentment. It was extra special that someone I cared for was with me to savor the atmosphere of conviviality. It was like I was in Panamá. All I needed was the flag unfurled with large red and blue stars to convince me this was not a dream. Euridice said it didn't take much to make me happy, and she was right. In the time I was in Louisiana I had never felt at home— outside of my adopted family. It had less to do with the fine people I met. It was a longing for the salty air in my nostrils, the beach, and coconut groves in proximity, and someone like Euridice who understood me without a preface of explaining. Two men laughed about money one of them had lost dog racing. This was a different place, for sure.

We were ready to walk back to the house. In the short time we had been in Miami, Euridice had gotten dark, the sun was so strong. While I never used any sunblock, Euridice thought it wouldn't be a bad idea.

Otherwise, she said, I was going to burn. I was inclined to agree.

It was nearly noon when we arrived back at Héctor's. The children we passed on our way to the café were nowhere to be found. We knocked since we had no key. Silvia came to the door and when she opened it she said we had a guest. It was the teenager who had given us directions to the café. I'm not superstitious, but somehow I thought I might meet this woman again, or maybe I just hoped that I would.

"Olga, this is Euridice and Roberto."

"Pleased to meet you," said Euridice, extending a hand to Olga, who was now standing.

"Pleased," I said, also shaking hands with her.

"You are the couple I passed earlier. Did you find the café?"

"Thanks to your directions," said Euridice.

I was surprised that she would remember our voices, though it might not have been so remarkable for her. I mean, she might have done it all the time.

"You're welcome," she said. "Have you been to Miami before?"

Euridice and I looked at each other, and both said yes at the same time.

I had decided to let Euridice be the one to talk. I would answer a question only if directed to me. That way I figured I would allay interest (I hesitate to say any lust) on my past. It was working fine, too. But this young woman quickly exhausted her questions for Euridice: where in Venezuela was she from; had she ever seen a jaguar; had she ever fished for marlins; did she like to read? She could really go a while.

But she was only warming up. I was next.

"But I thought you were from Venezuela?"

"No, just Euridice. I'm studying in Baton Rouge. I'm a senior." I must have seemed timid to her. I know that's how I felt. I wanted to ask her questions, but how could I with all eyes and ears alert to my every syllable.

"Are you studying electrical engineering, too?"

"Civil." I thought I was doing great. I mean, I only looked at her crossed legs when she occasionally ran her hands along them. What else could I look at? Her big brown eyes? Well, yes! That is exactly what I did. I felt she deserved that: negotiating these hot streets in next to nothing. I was ready to walk her back if she had asked. I was a gentleman on call. I was doing well, parrying her volley of questions with the reliance of an expert witness, but did she have to ask about the guitar?

"Silvia says you sing beautifully," she said.

"Silvia is too kind," I said. "Silvia, why don't you put on a cassette of that great Quisqueyana group . . ." I had gone too far. I could think of not one Dominican band. Then, as La Gran Manzana came to mind . . .

"Sing us something from Panamá," she said.

Her voice had softened. Euridice, from whom I was taking all stage directions, raised a hand in the direction of the guitar. I tuned up and played several instrumentals I had penned myself. Everyone liked them.

"But you haven't sung a word!"

And it was the way she said *ni una palabra*—not even a word—that really did something to me. I had warmed up and felt the fire of the night before when the old men sang about the Cuba they remembered. I sang one locked away in my vault of a heart.

> The woman I love works in the kitchen
> Her eyes are green as an apple's skin
> Her lips as red as a cardinal's frock
> A meal starts on a butcher's block
> The oven is where our yearnings begin.
> The woman I love has a heart so huge
> a nation she taught how to love

Her hand and heart were first I knew
And how to dance she taught me, too
And soar on clouds in skies above

The woman I love I have not seen
In far too many her years yet still
The love I have for her has grown
Not just in verses I have shown
But in my heart and always will
But in my heart and always will

This slow song made with three verses was perhaps not what Olga had in mind. I looked away from the space I had stared into while singing, only to find Olga in tears. By their show of silence, Silvia and Euridice were moved.

"Who is that woman?" asked Olga, wiping her eyes.

"My mother."

"What a tribute," said Silvia. "I think any mother would be proud."

"I agree," said Euridice, who got up to give me a kiss on the cheek.

"You can forget engineering. Start a band!" said Olga.

"That's a very nice compliment. But I've been working toward graduation for a lifetime."

"Still, you've got talent!"

"And he'll still have it," interjected Euridice.

"Well, of course he will," said Olga, though less enthusiastically than before.

"Olga didn't mention that she plays guitar," said Silvia.

"And after hearing Roberto, I think I'll pick clarinet or something—anything else!"

"That's kind, but what would our music be without a guitar?" I asked.

"Or drum," added Silvia.

"Oh, without the drum, we'd be lost at sea, or shipwrecked like Cabeza de Vaca," laughed Olga.

We were all laughing at last. A safer place to be than in doubt. "And would you play something for us?" I asked. I had been the center of attention for too long.

Olga was garrulous, if nothing else. And I was eager to hear her play.

I passed her the guitar, sat back, and closed my eyes. Well, she loved flamenco, I can tell you that right away. She had a beautiful right hand. Her fingernails caught the strings and awakened the cedar wood from the melancholy drowsiness of the song for my Mother. This woman practiced daily! That's one thing I was sure of. I wish my old teacher, Don Jorge, had been there to witness it.

My mind drifted to Granada, a city I hoped someday to see. I envisioned Sevilla: the flowing ruffled dresses; the toe tapping and heels clicking; castanets recalling García Lorca words and song. I opened my eyes near the end of her playing. We all applauded.

"So where do you perform?" I asked.

"At Silvia's most times," Olga said, running an arpeggio up the fretboard of the guitar.

She reached out, offering me the guitar. I wanted to ask for more. My better judgment prevailed. Let her offer to play. But she didn't, which was fine. I could get Héctor to ask her, if she were still there later. This dealing with women could be ticklish. Especially talented women. Hadn't it taken me forever to go beyond the casual with Euridice? To say anything to Olga beyond the banal weather question—¿qué tiempo hace hoy?—was going to be awkward.

"Do you teach guitar?" asked Euridice.

"No," smiled Olga. "I'm in law school."

All I could think of was all those tomes—and in braille! If I could have read the expression on my face, well, no I didn't have to, because I looked at Euridice, whose face could only have mirrored mine. For me, law was a cold practice. I would not have thought a person with such artistic fire would practice law. But maybe a trial lawyer was her ambition. Now *there* was theater!

"Someone needs to address the issues of the visually impaired. At least that is my interest. Unlike you, I have two more years."

"You know, Roberto and I thought you were a teenager."

"It's nice to look young. But a teenager . . . Maybe it was the bathing suit."

"Maybe," said Euridice.

I was leaving all conversations about yellow one-piece ounces of silk to the women. Sometimes it's just nice to study anatomy from afar.

"No, I'm legal drinking age. That's all I'll say."

"And that's enough," said Silvia.

"Well, how about some lunch?" asked Silvia. "You must hungry after all that swimming and playing."

16

We sat down to *sancocho,* a beef stew that Silvia had prepared that morning. I enjoyed a tamarind soda along with the meal. I still wanted to know something about Olga's past. So I asked.

"Where are you from?"

"I was born right here in Miami. Cuban parents. But you could tell that from my Spanish."

I tried to imagine how difficult law school was for her. But it was only difficult for me to imagine because I wasn't doing it. For her it was a passion. She was driven to pursue her dream just as I was mine. What did not being able to see have to do with it?

"My parents have always encouraged me, even before I began to lose my sight. I was twelve, and an infection I had contracted affected my optic nerve. I still have some vision in my left eye, but minimal. Since my parents were able to find the right specialist, I was able to retain some of my vision, and shortly thereafter began rehabilitative therapy. I was able to suggest my specialist to Silvia."

"It has helped me, too," said Silvia.

"And how long have you played guitar?" I asked.

"Since I was nine. It was fortunate I started before my sight started to fail me. Now I *see* everything I do. It is easier than walking, if I can use an analogy."

Olga asked how we knew Héctor. We told her we went to college together. I talked about his success. She said her father introduced him to her after he became one of his accounts. That was over a year ago.

"My parents live in Coral Gables," Olga said.

I could see the large front yards, maybe a few mango trees, but definitely a rich green lawn.

"Oh, Héctor has several accounts there, thanks to Señor Llorens, he has said," inserted Silvia.

"My father likes Héctor because he is a 'good man' as he says."

"He's the best," I said.

We finished our lunch and went out on the patio behind the house. The trees provided shade from the ninety-degree temperature. Silvia brought out cold water, which was refreshing, as we toweled our foreheads.

"I am going swimming this afternoon. Do you want to join me?" asked Olga.

Now what man wouldn't have said yes to that offer? The chance to gape at beauties in skimpy swimwear was not an everyday occurrence.

"Sure," said Euridice with a smile for me.

This woman knew me too well, I feared. If this was a trap I was already in it.

"That sound fine to me," said Silvia.

"Let's let our food settle," suggested Olga. "I'll meet you back at my apartment in a few hours."

"By then Héctor will be back," said Silvia.

Euridice helped Silvia with the dishes and straightened the dining room.

When Euridice came back to the room where we were staying, I was stretched across the bed, enjoying the air-conditioning. She snuggled herself into my arms: a perfect fit.

"You couldn't take your eyes off of Olga."

"Well, it was only when she was talking, and she did talk a lot."

"And you did like what you saw."

"Hey, a blind man would have liked that!" A perfect woman: body and brains. A woman uninhibited. Those were the words written in my sealed envelope.

"I think she's gay," said Euridice.

Now, the thought hadn't occurred to me, but why verbalize that? Anything to soften my erection that was growing by the minute. I was so full of lust I could not conceal it. And why should I?

"Is that a crime?" was all I could say in her defense. I didn't care what she was!

Euridice began to massage, and then held me in her hand. "I know you want her."

Why all this talk about Olga? She was gone. I would have been happy just to think about her in the quiet of night, swaying under a mosquito net, back in Panamá years later. The woman I once met. Here Euridice was giving me a lover I didn't even want. Or rather, I didn't even want her to know about. For all we knew, she had a lover. She must have found some time for diversion, if she could squeeze it in between seven hours of guitar practice, or whatever her regimen was.

* * *

Euridice was enveloped in me like a moth in its chrysalis stage. We awoke after a nice nap.

"You go swim with Silvia. I'll stay here."

She just kept setting traps for me. And if they weren't traps, why did I feel another erection rising? I just said all right, and slipped into my Jantzen Olympic bikini briefs. Her monthly had begun just that morning. Oh well, I didn't make the world.

17

Silvia had received a call from Héctor: He would be coming an hour later. He had to fill in for one of the workers who hadn't shown up.

How did I know Silvia couldn't swim; that she was overcoming a fear of water, having once seen a shark circle her boat in the Dominican Republic?

"But there are no sharks in a pool," I offered with Socratic indifference. I could certainly be insensitive at times, I thought. Silvia stayed at the four-foot end of the huge pool. Olga and I played every game but water polo. I swam with her on my back. I did the crawl as she held me at my waist. I did the backstoke as she held onto my trunks, abandoning whatever pool protocol she ever knew. Where was everyone anyway? Why weren't they frolicking like we were? Were we the only pair of river porpoises around? Oh, I looked up and Silvia had found a friend to give her some lessons. She was making progress: She was in the five-foot section. No matter. I was playing lifeguard with my ever-so-willing assistant hanging onto my bikini and its contents. I would have to show this trick to Euridice. No, on second thought, it would only lead to a nasty line of questioning. I would need the services of an attorney, and Olga might not present such a convincing argument. *Just have fun, Roberto!* After killing yourself for Southland Corporation and depriving yourself of even a modicum of fun, just learn to smile for a moment.

Well, that smile must have turned to a grin. Olga and I had ventured off to the sauna, of all places. I was really taking risks. If Olga was gay, she definitely had a straight side. And I really think Euridice just said that to keep me at a distance. The distance between us in the sauna was our clothes, our tongues, and our lips. She put my mouth to her breast. Her protruding nipples were as perfect as those of a mannequin in the French Quarter in New Orleans.

"I want you," she said, bringing back the words and sentiment of the Marvin Gaye song.

"But I'm already taken," I said, suddenly remembering the love I felt for someone else.

"No, not like that. I don't want a baby. I just want you." She took me by the hand and led me out of the sauna. The difference in temperature from the back outside was almost refreshing. I looked back and did not see Silvia, nor was her male instructor around. "Don't worry about her. She knows her way home."

"But I don't want her to go home without *me!*"

"Relax, I told her to wait at the bar for us. She won't leave without you."

Silvia led me to her apartment, 158. A nice one-bedroom place, though I really wasn't there to see her set of Britannica in braille, which was displayed on an expansive set of bookshelves. My reason for being there was reduced to her three words.

"*¡Quítate el bikini!*" she said, ordering me to drop my trunks.

Well, if I thought I was swimming before, it was nothing like having on a life preserver. Olga's sensitive mouth was every bit as delicate as the fingers that laced my own.

"*¡Quédate allí!*" she said.

Where was I going to go? She was right back with joy in a cup: ice.

I went from 98.6° F to 60° F in a nanosecond. This was a summer I would never forget.

"¿Te gusta?"

Well, that must have been a rhetorical question because what man in his right mind would say, Stop! I hate what you are doing to me! When I reached my climax, it was ecstasy I felt I didn't somehow deserve. But I said *gracias*, and kept any undeserving remarks to myself. I felt pangs of guilt; had I stayed back at Héctor's, none of this would have happened.

Olga noticed my inquietude and said, "No reason for guilt. This isn't sex."

"It isn't?" I said, waiting to hear how she defined what we had just done. Because if it wasn't sex, why did I feel guilty?

"Just go to Black's Law Dictionary and see, if you don't believe me."

"I have never looked at Black's. I don't even know people even bothered to define what we just did. It's about feeling, isn't it?"

"Oh, it's about feeling for sure. But it's not intercourse—for which I could appreciate guilt on your part. Isn't Euridice your wife?"

Now why did she have to mention her name, as if I hadn't been thinking about anything else since I walked into her apartment?

"No, she's not." Though saying that didn't elevate me to a person of high character, if I was ever one. Oh, my record was as shiny as a pewter cup.

"You'll find no sympathy here. I'm looking for passion, just like the next woman. The fact that you were with someone else when I met you, made me want you all the more. I could tell how she pulled you away when you were looking for the café this morning."

I wonder just how much she *could* see. She had said she had some vision in her left eye.

Olga thanked me, with kisses all over my body. She pulled me up from the bed and we walked into the shower. We lathered one another, and between the heat of the water and peppermint soap, I was washed anew. *Just enjoy this, Roberto. You're with a lawyer—almost. She says there's no contract between you and the party of the third part. It never will happen again.* And enjoy it is exactly what I did.

18

When Silvia and I returned, Euridice was not feeling well. The cramps were bothering her. Silvia offered her some tablets, which after a time reduced the pain. She had no appetite and remained in bed for that evening and the next day. Silvia's mother had called to say her father would not be in until nine tonight.

I said that since Euridice was not feeling well, it was not the ideal time to visit him.

Silvia prepared Euridice some broth, which I brought to the bedroom on a tray.

"Play for me, Roberto."

I got my guitar and played some random melodies.

"I feel you really love me, Roberto."

"I do, Euridice."

"And that song *Euridice No Sabía*. What didn't she know? Does it have words?"

"She didn't know how much she meant to me. More than words could say. So no, there are no words to it." There, I had told the truth, and that was all she needed to know. Now to live the truth. I loved her, so be with her. Anything else was superfluous.

I adjusted the pillows behind her head. I held her hand. She was weak at that moment.

"I had enough soup," she said making an effort to move the tray away.

I put the tray on the table in the bedroom. She lay down. I sat in the chair next to her. At that moment I wanted to ask her if she would marry me. Better to ask when she is up, feeling herself. *Don't wait too long, though.* She dozed off and I left the bedroom.

"Yes, she's sleeping," I told Silvia after she asked me.

"You don't have to wait for Héctor if you are hungry."

"I can wait, thank you," I said, though I was famished after all of that water-play.

"You are quite a swimmer," she said. "Did you enjoy yourself?"

"Yes," I said.

"Olga had fun, too," she said with a new coyness. The smile out of the side of her mouth left no hint of the fun she meant.

"We both did," I said, not pretending to hide anything.

"Good. Euridice told me how hard you work during the year. It must be crazy, the job and studies."

"Every bit of it, but I'm nearly done now. Others have done it. Look at Héctor."

"Oh, and my father, too. He had a hard time finding work in the Dominican Republic. He worked for a newspaper—going out and getting stories of the people's yearnings. He got roughed up, but it didn't stop him. Then he made enough to come here. I learned English there, so I found work here. Funny, they require you to know Spanish a lot of times. I think it's just a way to keep jobs for Spanish-speaking people. Anyway, we have survived by sheer will."

"*Sí, tenacidad.*" I repeated her words, because it was so true. No one knew willpower like a person with an obstacle to overcome.

Héctor came in, and we both stood up. He removed his baseball cap.

"*Hola, 'mano,*" I said.

"*¿Qué tal?*" he said and gave Silvia a kiss. He then walked into the bathroom.

Silvia set the table for the two of us, as is the custom in our countries.

"¿Y Euridice?"

I told him she wasn't feeling well, that she went to bed. No, it wasn't serious, I said in answer to his question. We continued in Spanish as we always did.

* * *

Dinner was wonderful. Fried plantains, rice, red beans, and fried chicken. Héctor was very tired from having to pitch in since he was working without the help of one of his workers. He had three crews to oversee. He went from one location to another, staying on top of each project.

"These guys never take off. One guy is out for a few days, but he'll come back as strong as a bull."

"Where are the guys from?" I asked.

"Mexico. I can see how they built those pyramids. They just can't work hard enough."

"Come on. Let's go out. Silvia will stay with Euridice."

"We won't be too long, right?"

"Oh, don't worry. Enjoy yourselves," said Silvia.

I had enjoyed myself quite enough for one day. I would suffer withdrawal once I returned to Baton Rouge. Héctor grabbed me by the arm and we were out the door.

We walked down to Café Jiménez. There were some single women sitting who looked at us. Héctor spoke as we passed them to an available table.

"So, are you having a good time? I don't think I'll be able to spend a lot of time with you. I may have to hire another guy."

"I could work for you until your man gets back."

"You know, I think I'll take you up on it. It's tough work, though."

"I think I better do something to stay out of trouble," I said, looking at the two young women who glanced up as I spoke about them.

"I know what you mean. Maybe you should have come alone."

"You know, I'm really crazy about Euridice. But I'm weak for the flesh."

"We all are. And they just keep coming at you. Here, we're not even giving them the time of day, and we're being hunted."

"You're telling me. And the things they wear are all the provocation you need," I said.

"I'll be right back," said Héctor. He walked over to the two women we had just passed and began chatting with them. The one with blond hair decided to let it fall to her shoulders as her dark-haired friend laughed at something Héctor said. He walked back to me. "They're just out to have a few drinks. But they're really friendly."

"I'm not here to pick anybody up," I said.

"Neither am I. Just conversation."

That's how it begins, I thought. Wasn't that how the afternoon began? I am sure that if Olga hadn't played guitar, I would have never pursued her in her game. "No, you are right. I'm just overacting." I paused for a moment. "I met Olga today. She's remarkable."

"Isn't she? I started to say she knows this city blindfolded, but then that wouldn't be fair," he said.

"Well, it would be true. She took us swimming today."

"Watch out! She's a barracuda!" he joked.

"And like any fish, she can swim," I said. "Since Euridice wasn't feeling well, just the three of us went."

"You don't have to tell me the rest. She hit on you."

"How did you know?"

"She doesn't saunter around in that bathing suit for nothing. She's showing off that flesh."

I decided to let Héctor do the talking, which is exactly what he did. He had known Olga first, since he had lived in the neighborhood for a longer period than Silvia. He had done the same thing for which I felt guilty. Except that he went all the way with her—several times. They had continued their relationship during the time he was with Sandra. Sandra left for Venezuela, then came Silvia. He was frank with Silvia, telling her about Olga, but Silvia said as long as she could share him, she could live with that.

"It didn't seem right. I fell in love with Silvia, and she moved in. Olga understood what was going on and said it was over between us. I told her that I would stop my dealings with her father, since our relationship had ended. She told me it wouldn't be necessary. She said that I would come back to her. Can you imagine?"

"No," I said. This relationship stuff was awfully complex. There seemed no end to which some women were willing to extend themselves. Sexual healing led to nothing but complications.

"I can't see myself going back, though. Silvia and I are one," he said.

It was so believable. But here came the blond from the table *who was just there for drinks.*

"Do you want to go to Franco's for dancing?" she asked.

I could smell her perfume. Her girlfriend walked up and stood next to me. These women were relentless trackers. "Not me. I've got to get up early," I said.

"So do I. Remember, you're working for me."

"Right, and I'm turning in. I'll see you in the morning," I said.

Héctor looked at me quizzically. The women smiled when I thanked them, and I watched them walk away. I stayed at the café just long enough to finish my Red Stripe and then I left.

As I walked home I wondered what Silvia would say about my coming in alone. I did not know Héctor's habits. I wanted to check on Euridice. Besides, I was trying to turn a new page in my life.

I had to knock, since I didn't have a key.

"And where is he?" she asked.

"I was feeling tired, so I came in," I said, never answering her question. "Did Euridice wake up?"

"No," she said.

"Do you want something to eat?"

"No thanks," I said. "I'm going to bed."

"Me, too. Goodnight."

"Goodnight."

I was feeling gummy, after walking back in all that humidity, so I took another shower.

While I was toweling myself off, I heard the front door open. Héctor had returned. I was glad he hadn't stayed out all night.

19

I snuggled with Euridice like the parts of an abstract puzzle: two bodies overlapping and twisted.

I awoke several times during the night. Restless, I stood up at the window, as if there was something that would distract me enough to fall back to sleep. I realized I was overstimulated from the full day. I convinced myself that in a few hours I would be up at work with Héctor. Better to lay down under the weight of Euridice than to awake not ready to give a full day's work. Euridice lay her leg over the length of my body and it felt good. Sleep came again.

Morning came in what seemed an hour later with a knock at the door. I kissed Euridice and got dressed. Silvia had made *mofongo,* which I had with a glass of *parcha*—passion fruit. I never have been much for a big breakfast. It was quiet at the table, probably because of the time of morning: five thirty. We finished our breakfast and left quietly.

Héctor had a nice Toyota pickup to which was attached a trailer with work equipment. He explained that I would be responsible for picking up lunches and moving the men from location to location.

"It isn't hard. Miami is easy to get around, as you know," he said.

It was true. Miami is so easy to navigate, because all of the streets use a numbered system. For a math lover like me, it was like sailing the Atlantic with Magellan.

"I thought I would be doing hard work," I said.

"Oh, it gets hard as the day progresses. I will be in one location for most of the day, but what you'll be doing is a big help."

"What happened last night?" I asked.

"Those women just wanted company. Somebody to pay for their drinks. They weren't going to hustle me! I bought them a round, though, then got out of there. They didn't have jobs to go to in the morning, either."

"That *rubia* was on you," I said.

"I had seen her before. She's a little too close to home, if you know what I mean. When you are busy with a job, women find all kinds of time and ways to attach you."

"Even when you don't have time, as long as you have money."

"I think you hit the lottery with Euridice. She's beautiful outside and in."

"You're so right. She has such an easy disposition, which is rare."

"What is important is that she loves you, and wants to be with you. Everything else will fall into place after that."

"I almost went too far with Olga yesterday. She's so talented and hot!" I said.

"She is that! She would have a lot of guys after her, if she were not legally blind. It's bad enough to discriminate, but because you are blind?"

"She doesn't seem blind once you are with her. She's the kind of person you just want to be with," I said.

"She'll find the right person for her, if she hasn't already. She'll be finished with law school and have a career soon enough. But she may have found the right person, if what Olga told me is true."

"Oh, that? No, wait a minute. I told Olga I was taken. She'll have to look elsewhere."

"Well it's nice to have choices. If I didn't have Silvia, I'd be out there looking for the right one, too."

"Olga is fabulous, but I am going to stick with Euridice. It amazes me, though. I have been in Baton Rouge for four years, and didn't get any play. Euridice was there all the time, but I only saw her as an engineering marvel with no interests other than spinning out solutions."

"And all the while you had little *Miss Electromagnetics* by your side."

"Fully charged," I laughed, and we slapped fives.

We pulled to the location where three Mexicans were waiting to get in the truck.

"Ricardo, Teo, Miguel, this is Roberto. He is helping us today."

We shook hands. Then the three men climbed into the back of the truck as they probably did every day. The men probably enjoyed the breeze of sitting on the truckbed. The two with hats pulled down tight on their heads. The third, Teo, had long black hair that swirled around his face. Fortunately, the bed was cushioned with a foam mat. They were well-tanned, given the amount of work they did in the oppressive Florida sun, though they wore long-sleeved shirts which they would no doubt shed during the course of the day. They laughed and talked loudly over the din of cars that passed us.

I marveled at the tall buildings we passed along the highway. Edifices of steel and tinted glass, much like ones whose structures Héctor studied back in school, were an impressive exhibition of wealth. The early morning sun sliced patterns of light from building to building in an indiscriminate display for us. It might be the only joy the Mexicans would know besides a paycheck. This place had money. Jobs were plentiful and Héctor was smart to come here, I felt.

We arrived at a large mansion in North Miami. They had already begun to manicure this estate the day before. It was an impressive endeavor from the start. Even my single pair of hands would make a difference. I let Héctor know I was willing to do more than just deliver lunches.

"These guys are the best. They can manage," he said, reassured of their ability. "Their fathers built Yucatán!"

He was right. If their ancestors could construct the likes of the pyramids which still stood today, a little grass clipping would present no problem. I could see the excellent rapport Héctor had with his crew. He helped them disengage the machinery from the trailer. Then he directed them to continue from where they had left off the previous day. In addition to hauling lunches, I would load the bags of cut grass onto the trailer and tie them down.

By seven thirty it was already ninety degrees. My polo shirt was more than a little damp. Ricardo, Teo, and Miguel stopped for a Gatorade, and were back at it right away. They worked with the fervor of people fighting against the sun. Landscaping is the ultimate fat-burner. When the sun was at its zenith, they took a well-deserved half hour for lunch under a magnolia tree.

Twice during the day I loaded the large bags of cut grass on the back of the truck and trailer. I drove to a location where men were making compost and unloaded the bags, where I was given a receipt for Héctor. The proprietor was one who sold mulch to Héctor during the winter months.

While the work was arduous, Héctor enjoyed it. There was nothing like having your own company he said, especially one where the only limits are the ones you put on yourself.

It would be another day before work on the mansion would be completed. We loaded up the equipment and rode back to where we had picked up the Mexicans. They were relatively quiet on the return. I glanced back and saw Teo nodding. I was no less tired than he was. I was used to working, but not in the heat. The Mexicans seemed impervious to the weather. I, on the other hand, needed something to pick me up. Next, I nodded, and didn't wake up until we arrived at Héctor's.

* * *

"So how was your first day?" asked Silvia.

"Enough to say I want to do something else for a living," I said.

"Héctor said he, too, had to get used to it, too. So don't feel bad."

Euridice rubbed my shoulders after I sat down. Héctor jumped in the shower first. I asked Euridice how she was feeling.

"Better," she said. "I got my appetite back."

I lifted her left hand from my shoulder and kissed her palm. It felt wonderful against my lips. The sweet scent of lilac filled my nostrils. She looked much better than just a day ago.

"I have good news, Roberto. My father is coming over tomorrow evening at seven."

"That's great, Silvia. I am eager to meet him," I told her.

Mentioning that her father would be there the next day gave him a boost of energy. This was a man of conviction, who had seen some rough times—and survived.

"We're taking you two out tonight," said Héctor, emerging from the shower, black hair still dripping. "So don't make any plans."

I had no plans, except to eat, I thought. It would be nice to get out together, since we had not yet done that. Silvia had done nothing but wait on us, so hopefully it was something she was looking forward to as well.

* * *

After my shower I joined everyone at the table for salad and chicken and *arepas*. Euridice had made a flan which we enjoyed with coffee after dinner.

"I was thinking about Franco's. The have a live salsa band every Thursday night," said Silvia.

"I want to go then," said Euridice with enthusiasm.

"I'd like that, too," said Héctor.

I wondered if we would run into the two women we had met at Café Jiménez. Apparently Héctor was not concerned, or he would have offered another suggestion.

20

Well, the women were stunning. Euridice had found another sheath in her wardrobe, this one white. She wore it with white spaghetti-strap sandals. Silvia had on a tight brown dress that accentuated her round rear end. When she walked near Héctor he took full advantage of her, fondling her bottom with both hands, something she did not seem to mind. If that kept up, nobody was going to get to Franco's.

"Let me get my shoes on at least," said Silvia, raising her voice in mild protest. She slipped on her strapless brown suede heels, and we were out of the house.

* * *

We went to Franco's in Héctor's sedan. It was a sleek black Toyota. He said he didn't drive it much, since he worked all the time. It felt good to be out together. Euridice looked stunning, as did Silvia. Silvia liked to go out, but did not do it alone because of her failing eyesight. She was, however, eager to get on the dance floor with Héctor, who was no stranger to nightspots. He rattled off several that were no longer around.

"There was Río de Plata. Now *that* was my favorite!" he said. "It caught fire. Fortunately, it happened when it was closed or there would have been many casualties, like the club in New York that a guy set fire to, with only one exit. Nearly everybody perished."

"Do we have to talk about that?" said Silvia. "You're making me nervous." "That house was something else, eh Héctor?" I said, referring to the place where we had spent the day.

"Immense! It must cost a fortune."

"Which house?" asked Euridice, holding my hand.

"The mansion where we were today."

"It belongs to a bank executive. He must be third-generation money?" I said.

"No question," said Héctor.

Euridice and I held hands. Her hair tickled my face when the breeze blew that way. Being together like this was something I could get used to.

We pulled into the lot, where we parked. Even though it was a weeknight, people were out to have fun. The women were looking fabulous, and the guys were looking as hungry as ever. We walked up to the door of Franco's, where somebody checked IDs. I didn't remember anyone doing that at the Body Shop. It gave somebody work, though.

The music pulsed at a feverish pitch. Silvia moved her shoulders to the syncopated rhythms. Euridice eyes opened wide with anticipation. I held her by the waist and we were on the dance floor immediately.

"Roberto!" someone called out.

"Ghani!" I said, shocked to see my Nigerian classmate so far from Baton Rouge. In the din I introduced him to my friends. He had never met Euridice. He was there visiting his brother, who worked for a chemical firm in Miami. He introduced us to his brother and two young women, Nigerians, I think. I forgot their names as fast as he told me, since I was so amazed to see him so far from our campus. They danced and moved about, soon lost from view.

It was almost senseless to continue talking while the music played, so we didn't. I lost sight of Héctor and Silvia but Euridice called my attention to Olga.

"Over there," said Euridice pointing, and now pulling me toward the siren, where I was sure to have a shipwreck.

"¡Olga! ¡Soy yo, Euridice!" she said, helping Olga recognize her, since distinguishing her voice would have been difficult through the music.

The two women embraced. Olga held a man's hand.

"This is my fiancé, Guillermo Finlay."

We shook hands, though I did not say anything.

"¿Y Roberto?"

"Está conmigo," said Euridice.

"¡Felicitaciones!" we said, congratulating Olga at almost the same time.

Euridice was happy to hear the news. I feigned an expression of happiness which the dim lights and euphoria of the dance club may have concealed. Why she had not mentioned that she was engaged was a mystery to only me. It would have kept our water-play within limits. Was she really lusting as much as I was?

Euridice told me later that Silvia had told her while I was out sweating at the big house. Héctor had known for at least as long as she had. It was only I who felt ignorant—no, stupid! Ignorant implies no knowledge, like naïve. I was stupid for falling for the blind girl with the gray eyes that saw me for what I was: an animal lusting after her Venus de Milo body.

"¿De qué te ríes?" Euridice asked, puzzled at my laughter.

Oh, I think you know why I'm smiling, Euridice. You saw my fawning over the blind guitarist-lawyer-to-be, too! You just wanted to see how far into the vortex I would be sucked!

"This place is crazy!" I said, twirling her around as we danced a *merengue*.

"Isn't it?" she said, laughing all the while.

After ten fast songs, finally there was a bolero. The female vocalist's voice melted away the residue of surprise of discovering that Olga had a fiancé. Just enjoy it, were her words. Now I held Euridice; soft and perfumed. I kissed her with enough passion to fill the room, while the twirling lights above us shone like a galaxy.

* * *

When it was time to leave, Silvia asked if I would drive.

"No, I can drive," protested a plastered Héctor.

"Sure, into a palm tree!" joked Silvia. She wrangled the keys from the defenseless landscaper. We both propped him up on our shoulders as Euridice walked behind us.

"He looks like a scarecrow," laughed Euridice.

"I heard that!" called Héctor, stirring from his stupor for an instant, then sliding like an eel between us. Silvia was quite strong and held up her end. I was hoping that he would not throw up. That was always such a messy affair. I had seen enough of that in my youth, working in the brothel. Just the thought of it brought back memories of scrubbing toilet floors: red beans stagnant in a putrid green pond.

People passed us and looked back on us with varied expressions of wonder. This condition was unusual for Héctor, but I wasn't around him anymore. I had never seen him drunk. All that spinning, I guess. It had been fun, though. This carrying him home would be something to laugh off later, but not that night. He seemed heavy, even against our sober selves.

We arrived at the car in the lot. Silvia passed the keys to Euridice, who opened the doors, front and back.

Héctor had enough strength to climb into the rear seat. His heavy head fell on Silvia's lap.

"*Me siento que voy a vomitar,*" Héctor said and I propped him at 180 degrees. He and I would have swung further, had Silvia not held onto his waist. Héctor splattered Euridice's heels, which she later unlaced and tossed in the back seat with Héctor. After he had heaved up that expensive rum, Euridice closed the door and Silvia let him lean against the window. I drove back, leaving the remaining three windows down, in an effort to remove the stench of our seasick sailor. I glanced back at him through the rearview mirror. He looked so pitiful, mouth opened and smeared like putty against the window.

When we were back, Silvia laid Héctor on the sofa.

"Oh, no! I'm not sleeping with him until he takes a bath!" she said.

Euridice walked to our room, and we removed our clothes. Within minutes we were in the shower together, washing the smell of the return trip from our bodies.

"*Te compraré sandalias nuevas. No te preocupes.*" I told her, promising that I would buy her new sandals.

We were fresh again. We toweled each other and slipped into our robes. They were on only long enough to close the door. Euridice hid her head in my shoulder. I was getting used to that feeling and the scent of her body bathed in lavender. As she lay on her stomach I massaged her shoulder. She hunched her back bones into two crests and I licked their peaks. Goosebumps formed on her body and my hands glided across the fine hairs on her back, waist, and buttocks. There was no part of her that did not fill me with exhilaration.

"*Me toca a mí ahora,*" she said.

I turned on my back and felt her silken touch against me. The headlights of a vehicle slipped into our bedroom and splashed against Euridice's breasts like a brushstroke.

It was dark in the room again. The bed swayed like a pendulum until she fell asleep in my arms.

21

Héctor was quiet the next day, and understandably so. He had put on quite a performance the night before. He stayed in his room when Euridice and I went for a walk down to Café Jiménez.

"Do you think we'll run into Olga?" she asked.

"Maybe," I answered with indifference.

"Yeah, maybe."

"I wouldn't have guessed that she was engaged," I said. "So much for your gay theory."

"Well, I wouldn't dismiss it entirely. She still came off that way. It's something a woman can feel. Didn't you notice how close she sat next to me? She was self-assured, but almost, well, asexual."

"Maybe that's it," I said, wanting to end this conversation into nowhere. Hadn't I made a fool of myself enough with her already? Of course, I had noticed. But I had wanted to be where Euridice was sitting. Let her be whatever she was: the cute little carpet-muncher.

"Anyway, Silvia says she's just using that guy. He's a lawyer, you know."

"*¿Sucede?*"

"Okay. I'll drop it," she said, grasping my hand.

I looked down at her orange T-shirt. Her nipples were protruding, and that was the first thing I liked about that day. She caught my glance and gave a reassuring look of *I know what you want.*

She was probably right in her observation. I preferred to believe her anyway. When had I ever been right about women? Use the guy. Get your degree, then drop him and he'll be so shocked he'll never feel the torts book land on his head. If I took inventory of my short life, I could truthfully say that no one ever used me. I had gotten plenty out of the relationships, and more than I had given. That fact was not completely my fault. My choice of women up until recent history had been women of low self-esteem. They gave their body and that met our mutual needs. True, I had fallen in love with Bella. Cathy was physically perfect. But I needed more. Euridice was that person. Life was repeating itself. First, Carlito and the revolving door of mother and daughter. (I really didn't want to know how that ended.) Now, Olga and her fiancé. Héctor and his roving eye. You couldn't tell me that he wasn't chasing *tangas*.

And what about me? But I was at least—after Olga—turning a new page. Euridice was as good as two women.

* * *

We sat at a table in Café Jiménez. The two women Héctor and I met earlier were there. While waiting for our *sandwiches cubanos,* I chatted with Euridice.

"Let's play a game," I suggested.

"What's that?"

"If the sum of three numbers is twelve, what is the reciprocal of that number?"

"Gee, give it a rest, Roberto! One-fourth!"

"That was too easy," I said.

"All in all, it was fun last night. It got pretty hot in that place."

"And you looked great!"

"Héctor may sleep all day. He works so hard. He's planning to marry Silvia."

"Funny, he never mentioned that to me."

"They haven't set a date, but they are making plans. She said her father wanted to give his daughter away, but legally."

"I hope to meet him tonight," I said.

A waitress arrived with our food and coffee. The steam of the strong coffee streamed in the air. I was going to miss the good sandwiches I had gotten used to enjoying. Baton Rouge had nothing like this, but it was tops when it came to seafood.

"What do you say we go back in two days?" she suggested.

"And give some privacy?"

"Exactly."

"How about three days?"

"Three is fine. We can go to the beach tomorrow," she said.

22

When we returned Héctor and Silvia were gone. There was a note that her father would be coming by that evening at seven thirty.

"You'll get your wish," said Euridice.

"I hope we have time to talk."

"I am sure that is the reason he is coming."

"Let's go to the beach now!" I suggested.

"We won't be able to tonight," she said.

* * *

The water was warm and the sun was as strong as ever. Still, it felt good to be on vacation. The spume collected on us as we splashed one another. Over and over we dived into the green waves that buoyed us like the occasional jellyfish that floated by. I took every advantage of being together with Euridice. We played a game of Frisbee. There was another couple with a volleyball who invited us to join them. We exhausted ourselves with full knowledge that we had only to return to a cool swim.

The couple was Cuban but seemed to have forgotten their Spanish. They were friendly and offered us soft drinks. We had sandwiches to share with them, so it was a pleasant afternoon.

* * *

I exchanged addresses with the fellow, Manuel. That was a habit I had gotten into and I continue it to this day. Funny, I have never reacquainted myself with any of the people I have met on these chance occasions.

I drove back to the street where we had stayed for a week. There were two cars in front of us. A trash truck was moving in its staggering pace down the street. I saw men who looked like the Mayans of Chapultepec. These men lifted boxes and bags that may have equaled their own weight. Their bodies in sleeveless shirts gleamed in the sun that blackened their backs. These men of small muscular stature removed the refuse and broken toys; the appliances whose warranties were no longer valid; bicycles missing a tire or handlebar that would never again light the eyes of children, at least not in this country. Back at home I can remember taking an old motorcycle tire, slipping it over my head, and sliding it down to my waist. I rotated it for as many repetitions as I could. What a joy it was. My Mother scolded me when I walked in the house with the black rings on my shirt. Still, I remember the fun it was. Who knew how many more lives these old toys would have before they were reclaimed by the earth?

* * *

When we walked in the house Héctor and Silvia were straightening things up. Héctor had rearranged the furniture, and there was now a large carpet in the living room.

Euridice commented on how lovely it looked. "There is nothing more beautiful than a Persian rug," she said.

"I have wanted one for a long time, too," remarked Silvia.

The bright red and blue colors must have cheered Silvia. She smiled broadly when she spoke, as if her sight captured the vivid geometry displayed in the wool. She stood on it in her bare feet, her toes curling as she spoke.

"Look, I apologize for last night," Héctor began, but I broke up his apology.

"Hey! Didn't we have fun? Sure we did."

"Still, I ruined Euridice's shoes."

"No, they're fine," said Euridice, coming to his defense. "But you can buy me a new pair of stockings."

"Let's go out and pick up a few things," suggested Silvia.

"Okay, I'll only be a minute," said Euridice.

"Let's go play some tennis, Héctor."

"I haven't played in so long, but all right. You're feeling full of energy!"

"Just making the most of this vacation."

We walked down to the courts. They were well kempt, with what looked to be new nets.

Héctor still had fluid strokes. He stayed at the baseline, as did I for the workout. The occasions I did go to the net he sent me back with perfect parabolas. He had an excellent lob. We had long rallies, and worked up a sweat in five minutes. After fifteen minutes of hitting, we changed sides. We hit for another thirty minutes before we walked off the court, dripping with perspiration.

"Nice hitting," I said, extending my hand.

"I'm sure I lost a pound just then."

"Are you kidding? In this heat you lost ten!"

"You looked like Lendl out there," he said.

"If Lendl were left-handed."

"Exactly."

There was a branch of a mango tree suspended over part of one of the courts. It must have been there years before the recreation area had been a thought. The bright red fruit hung from stems which must have been two meters each. Some of the fruits had fallen to the court, leaving it stained. Bees took advantage of the feast. Héctor climbed the tree with agility and dropped one down to me.

"¡Aaa, fallaste!" he said as I missed it.

He dropped two more, and I caught them. The first one had splattered, and the bees hovered over it with instinctive directness. The mangoes were as hot anything left in the plain sun. I took a bite into the warm flesh and the juice trickled down my chin and arm. The towels we had served dually as oversized napkins. As warm as the mango was, it was refreshing, giving me some of the energy the sun had depleted.

We walked back to the house, exhausted and eager to wash the salt from our bodies.

23

Dr. Charles-Christophe Diversé arrived with an elegance uncommon in the United States. In his arm he carried a bouquet of red roses. He was a tall, thin man with tamarind skin. His hair was more white than gray, brushed back in a sea of soft waves. He wore a white boutonnière on the lapel of his dark blue suit. He had on a red paisley bowtie, which I could see was tied by hand, not the clip-on variety that I had worn as a youth when I first arrived in the States. Every detail of this man was impressive. His black Italian wingtips were polished as if done by a bootblack.

Silvia greeted her father with kisses on each cheek and some words in French, thanking him for the roses. She walked him into the kitchen where we were now standing and waiting to be introduced to him. As always, we all spoke in Spanish.

"Yes, I am pleased to meet you as well, Roberto."

"This is Euridice, Dr. Diversé," I said.

"Encantado, Euridice," he said, kissing Euridice's hand. "And are you an engineer, too?"

"Almost. I don't have a job yet," answered Euridice with a smile.

"But you will soon. Graduation is not far off, I hear."

"That's true."

"Oh, allow me to introduce my legal partner, Señorita Caroline Faust."

We shook hands with her. She was an attractive brunette, and stood about five foot eight in her pumps, which made her breasts more prominent. There could have only been one reason she wore a pink brasserie under a white silk blouse. She embraced Héctor as if she were his sister-in-law, planting kisses on both of his cheeks. She shook my hand, as she did Euridice's. She was American, I figured by her accent in Spanish, though she spoke well.

We walked back to the living room and found seats. Caroline sat in a chair and crossed her legs as if getting ready to take shorthand. I cut a glance at Héctor and read his expression: Dr. Diversé was romantically involved with Caroline. It was not something I expected, after seeing this articulate man on television only days ago. He spoke so resolutely on behalf of the Haitian refugees. Was he no different than the rest of us? I really wanted to believe otherwise.

"How are you doing with housing efforts for the Haitians?" I asked.

"Thing are moving forward, though not at the speed we would like," he said.

"We are organizing. That's what counts!" interjected Caroline.

"Exposure. That is what is lacking. If we get half of the attention that Haiti got when the media were trying to blame the AIDS epidemic on Haiti, we would have the housing we need."

"But AIDS affects everyone," said Silvia.

"And everyone doesn't need housing?" asked Dr. Diversé.

"Of course," said Euridice.

"The one fortunate thing is that Haiti, Florida is in the hurricane belt. When the big ones hit, they knock down the big houses and the shanties alike, reducing them all to cinder. Equal justice for all," said Dr. Diversé. "The unfortunate thing is that in Haiti there aren't the resources that there are in this country."

"What if there was agrarian reform?" I asked. "If you could initiate some loans to reforest the country. Make it virgin again, the way it must have been when Colón landed there."

"I read a poem by Neruda that described just that sort of thing. What was once a whore was finally washed pure again? I wish I could remember the words he used with such rhythmic elegance. The sentiment was what might be if that great day were to come. If only justice would prevail."

"God is just," said Silvia, her eyes roaming the ceiling as if for some divine presence.

"Yes. Now I want to experience some of that justice, too. I'm a believer, and so is ninety-nine percent of the Haitian populace."

"Justice is very relative. I came to realize that when I studied law," said Caroline.

It was peculiar to hear a white person in America talk about the relativity of justice, as if she had experienced some injustice in her lifetime. I looked at this woman with perfect teeth, healthy hair, and skin like a model in Cosmo. Her jade-colored eyes seemed to negate the very notion. What an alien concept, I thought, though could some injustice have ever happened to her?

"Believe me, unless you're rich, you *will* experience some injustice in this world," said Caroline.

She was speaking in vagaries: vacuous sound bites of the privileged. But she went on. "There was a time in this country when women could not own property; could not vote. That's changed now. The struggle continues! It will change for Haitians in this country, too."

"Maybe Héctor will be the one to start the forestry reform in my beloved Haiti. Plant *robles*," he said, using the Spanish word for oaks, "and eucalyptus, mahogany, and citrus groves. He has the skills, but the politics there are putrid. What can grow on such sullied land?"

"Compost is rich in minerals, Doctor," I said.

"And the sewers are full of caiman!" he shouted, reiterating the point of the political climate to the extent I could see the fetid stream of refuse at my feet.

Certainly the struggle did continue, and would forever. Caroline held Dr. Diversé's hand. Was it in solidarity, or a passion of a different kind? She was passionate all right. Her breast heaved when she spoke. And she spoke with confidence. If she fought as hard for indigent housing, it would not be long before the homeless would be out of the rain.

Silvia served us white wine. It was pleasant-tasting, cold but not sweet. She sat next to Héctor, their knees touching. Then she decided to sit on his lap.

As we finished our wine, Héctor offered us more. Euridice said yes, but the rest of us declined.

"Doctor Diversé, son las nueve y media," said Caroline, after looking at her Rolex watch. It was nine thirty. She had a flight to catch for Minneapolis in the morning. She took the occasion to fondle his chin and kiss him.

"But she drove you to the house," Silvia mentioned.

"He'll keep the car until I return next week," said Caroline.

"What are you driving?" I asked.

"A green Audi sedan," she said, holding Dr. Diversé's hand once again. They stood up as they walked to the door together.

We exchanged smiles, handshakes, and kisses on the cheek, wishing each other success.

"What time is your flight?" asked Héctor "At six. We're going to turn in early," she said.

To ask any more questions about the logistics could have gotten sticky. At no time during our stay had Silvia mentioned her mother. Only her sister, Celeste. So I assumed that her parents were divorced.

"Have a safe trip," I said.

Caroline's cheeks were now flush from the wine, if not the anticipation of her doctor's house call.

She was in her twenties and in love with this handsome, successful man. Silvia had to have noticed that long before I had. I held Euridice's hand as we watched them leave.

We came back in the house and sat in the dining room. Silvia had prepared a flan which she forgot to bring out when Dr. Diversé and Caroline were there. She served us slices with coffee.

"Your father is very genial," said Euridice, "and quite handsome."

"I am so glad to see him happy. He suffered for a long time. After Mamá died, he retreated inward. Not the garrulous man you met tonight," said Silvia.

"May I ask how she died?"

"Euridice, tal vez no debas," I said, cautioning her that maybe she shouldn't.

"We were still in Haiti, and therefore quite young. Infants, really. As you can see, Papá is politically involved, and always has been. Just out of law school and as fervent as L'Ouverture, he started mobilizing students against the dictatorship. Well, Mamá was returning home from the market when a fight broke out, or at least that is what the journal said. She was bludgeoned to death, two cans of Carnation evaporated milk crushed and spilled under the weight of her body. Papá wears a carnation in his lapel to this day because of that incident. He says I have my Mamá's face. Her large dark eyes. I don't know why he says that only to me and not Celeste. We have the same face and eyes, except I am much darker than my sister."

Silvia had opened up on our last evening in Miami. She finished her flan and poured herself more wine into her coffee cup.

"Supposedly, the police rounded up the perpetrators: three law students, whose shirts were clean, save the blood from their own bodies, Papá said. These young men were associates of Papá, so they had no motive to kill Mamá. Papá refused to believe that the accused had anything to do with the murder, but the authorities would hear nothing to the contrary of their fabricated findings. Papá did not press charges. We were too young to understand why Mamá had died. Even with my failing sight, I now see what we were up against: the sorted politics of a dictatorship, interested in palaces and Paris fashions while the people live in squalor with nothing to eat. Papá knew that our lives were in danger and with the help of a Dominican patriot and poet he was able to flee to Santo Domingo."

While Silvia showed all the eloquence of her father, she shared with us the details of what must have been a difficult experience to relate. Her chest heaved with a sigh, as if expelling the last heavy breath the memory of that fateful day her mother left this life. We sat there at the table transfixed. I had nothing in my past to brace me for such a life story. We had led protected, privileged lives by comparison. With all his knowledge of architecture—the masters of the past and present—what kind of edifice could Héctor construct to protect this woman who had witnessed so much as an infant, albeit through the eyes of her father? By comparison, architecture seemed only an ivory tower study, as did engineering.

Euridice looked at Silvia, then got up and sat next to her, holding her hand in condolence.

Silvia wiped her eyes, though she smiled with the beauty her coffee-colored skin was able to find that evening. Euridice and Silvia clasped hands, then almost the same complexion, baked under the same Miami fire.

"It makes me feel good to see a man still reaching for all there is in life, as he does," said Héctor. "Caroline is a great match for him."

"Are you kidding? They are inseparable," said Silvia, finding laughter through her tears. "Law is their affinity."

"Yeah, the Law of Gravity," I said.

Everyone laughed. I was glad to have put a smile on Silvia's face. It had taken tremendous courage to share the pain of her past. I had the fullest of fond memories of my own Mamá, with hopes of seeing her face still.

"Play something, Roberto," said Héctor.

It was only appropriate, being our last night together. I got out my guitar and tuned it. I thought immediately of *Soneto a Mamá*, by Joan Manuel Serrat. It starts with in a minuet that reminds me of Bach. Then it takes on the quality of a ballad. The words are so beautiful in Spanish.

I have never sung them in English. But if I did, the translation would be like this:

> It isn't because I have forgotten you I have
>   not returned
> Nor the smells wafting from the kitchen
> From afar they say you can see clearer
> that no two people walk the same path the
>   same way
>
> And I found out that love has green eyes
> that there are four suits in a deck
> that what you once had never returns
> that seasickness comes and later goes
>
> I found out that what is simple is not foolish
> that you can't confuse value with price

and a mouthful can be any morsel
that the horizon is light and the road a kiss

It's not because I have forgotten you I have
    not returned
It's because I have lost my way home, mamá

I quietly returned my guitar to its case. Héctor held Silvia's hand. They disappeared behind the wall and I listened to the alternate squeaks of their footsteps on the hardwood floor. The width of light from the bedroom narrowed to nothing after they closed the door to the bedroom. Euridice finished the wine in her glass. Her cheeks by then fully flush, her hair in ringlets from the humidity. Her look was lovelier than any composition I could pen. In the quietude of that moment I was reminded of summer nights spent on our patio back in Colón, the mosquitoes testing the netting for an entryway, but unable to find one; and the symphony of frogs and katydids, tanagers, and crickets surrounding our house that seemed at those times the stage of an amphitheater; sounds within measures of rests on manuscript paper, where single dashes of black ink streaked across the moon on nights that held us captive.

Our own stay had come to an end. The sunrise would not catch us sleeping.

24

I awoke once that evening with anticipation, thinking it was morning. It was still dark out and there was no predawn traffic. The heat of Euridice in my arms was reassuring. A sense of belonging overcame me and, under her gentle weight, I fell asleep once again.

A knock at door seemed to come only moments after I had closed my eyes.

"Roberto, tengo que irme. Son las seis menos cuarto," called Héctor. It was five forty-five and he had to go to work.

"Quise levantarme temprano. Perdóname."

"No te preocupes. Te llamaré despues."

I had wanted to rise early. Héctor stood at the door, not wanting to come into the room. He asked me to give Euridice his best, and that I stay in touch with them.

"Gracias por todo," I said.

"No fue nada," he said. It was typical of him to say it had been nothing, having hosted us there in his house better than any hotel could have done.

The predawn sky held its lavender light and brushed itself against the walls and windows of the houses on the street. I decided to stay up, so I helped myself to some of the coffee Héctor had prepared.

Silvia came out of her room, her hair in a red silk scarf, her body covered by a white silk robe.

"Buenos dias, Roberto."

"Muy buenos, Silvia."

"No hay que partir, lo sabes."

"Sí. hé de regresar al trabajo." She had invited us to lengthen our visit, but I had to return to my job, I told her, thanking her for their kindness. *"Han sido demasiado amable con nosotros."*

Silvia walked to me and poured me another cup, then filled her own cup. "I am going to fix those sandwiches cubanos that you love so much."

I thanked Silvia for remembering. My blurry vision was awakened by the diamond on her finger.

"¿Y este anillo?"

"Estoy comprometida."

"¡Felicitaciones!" I kissed her on the cheek. Héctor had proposed to her after we all retired. She was overjoyed. I could only imagine the contentment her father would have, knowing that his elder daughter would have someone with whom to share her life; he would have grandchildren, something my own father wanted from me.

"What was Héctor like back in school?" she asked.

"Very serious about his studies. While his favorite architect was Oscar Niemeyer, the guy who built Brasilia, he spent a lot of time drawing space stations. Have you seen any of his models?"

"There is one hanging from the ceiling in the bedroom." Silvia smiled.

"He hasn't lost his love for them, I see."

"I wondered why he would spend time on them, so I asked him one day. 'You've got to keep one foot in this century, and one in the next!' he told me. With the landscaping he has one foot firmly in the firmament."

"It has really taken off. The fellow he started with is doing well, too. He works in Jacksonville now."

"Once we get married, Héctor will be able to get a green card, and eventually citizenship, if he wants."

"Of course he wants! He won't have to work under the umbrella of his friend, Stephen Gallagher. He will be free."

I hoped that Héctor was sincere about his intentions to marry Silvia. I was sure he loved her, physically, but the chance to acquire Yankee citizenship had served so many before him as an incentive to riches in a burgeoning economy. I had read that there was 20 billion dollars made in landscaping yearly. Héctor was certainly aware of that fact, if I was. Silvia was aware of the earning potential Héctor would have. And if things did not work out for the two of them, she would still be entitled to a share of the wealth he would amass. If Silvia considered these ideas, she did not show it. She looked down at her ring as though it held magic. It was quite beautiful. The diamond set in the gold band. She held it up to the light that passed through the kitchen window. Flecks of light danced on the walls: prisms of joy.

"Euridice is going to love it," I said, wanting to fill the air with words that might somehow make the moment last. Silvia walked over to the telephone and made a call. She spoke in French to her sister, Celeste. I had some toast and butter with my coffee, now warm, though I drank it anyway.

Silvia was animated, as I had seen her the day her father had appeared on television. She walked around the house as if giving the walls a view of her new possession, repeating Héctor's name in the process, as if he were in earshot. She was a schoolgirl again. Together with her sister they would make wedding plans. They would scour bride magazines for months, and look for a church in which to have the ceremony. I had known no one to do those things before. Everyone I knew got married as a result of pregnancy, and hopefully before the bride-to-be started to show. Most had just begun to set up house: not so differently than Gerardo and Ginebra. Now those two seemed like a married couple, complete with the arguments brought on by allegations of sleeping around. Héctor had his vices but maybe now that he was engaged, he would give up his flirting, though I did not think he would.

Euridice emerged from the bedroom, hearing the voices. She had on a new robe which she had gotten on her trip into town with Silvia. It was short and emerald green and she wore a pair of green sandals that clopped when she walked.

Her eye widened when Silvia turned, facing her with her hand extended. Silvia ended her conversation and the two of them embraced. I don't know who was more excited. Euridice showed surprised, as I expected. The pressure might very logically be on me to make so lasting a gesture. I wanted to, but not just yet. We were still new in our relationship, though I felt confident enough that Euridice would say yes to my overture. Everyone around us was making commitments. Even Olga had sprung a surprise on us. Was it desperation? Was it the weather that had us latching on to each other, clinging to one another lest we be without a prom date? Except this was not for a night at Franco's or a coffee at Café Jiménez. This was for permanent partners. As for me, I was sure I could find no one more compatible than Euridice. Whether she felt the same, I would know very soon.

Euridice sat next to Silvia. I stood up and smiled at the two of them. I returned to the bedroom to get dressed. This had been a full two weeks. I was feeling overwhelmed by the pressure. But why should I be? I had really nothing to offer Euridice. Working in a convenience store certainly paled against medical school in the case of Francisco, and having a landscaping business in the case of Héctor. And I had the issue of being accepted by Euridice's family to address. Why was I not worried similarly about how my own family would look at Euridice? Well, how could they not accept her? She was so different from the usual women with whom I had fallen in love: the two harlots. I was quite good at dredging the cesspools for mermaids. At that I was certainly just as good as Carlito. What a standard to uphold! I was suddenly feeling gritty. I decided to shower.

25

Silvia had fixed our sandwiches and packed them away in the carrying bag we had brought with us from Baton Rouge. We sat down for breakfast and by eight thirty the sun was blazing through the patio where we sat.

"Bueno, Silvia, dame un abrazo," I said embracing her. She and Euridice held hands as they walked to the car. We were loaded down with certainly enough food to last a few hundred miles. We waved, and I watched Silvia's slight figure diminish through the rearview mirror.

* * *

Euridice removed the cap she had been wearing and applied some sunblock to her face and arms.

"Silvia was full of smiles when we left," she said. "Her ring was beautiful."

"What would you be if I gave you a ring like that?"

"I would be all smiles, too."

She glowed when I looked at her, and not just because of the lotion. "I want you to be a part of me, but I don't have much. Not yet anyway." It wasn't coming out right, but I kept talking anyway. "I never took the chance of going any further than I had because of the difference in social class. My father drives a truck for a living. Yours works in an office."

"They both work. They both support a family. And they are living their own lives. We have our own choices to make, just as they did."

"Will you marry me after graduation?"

"I will marry you after graduation."

"I am relieved to hear you say that." I held her hand as I continued to drive. I knew I would have to give her a ring to confirm everything. But that detail would have to wait. My finances did not allow for any luxuries. But I started talking marriage; her father would be expecting some demonstration of wherewithal on my part. That was understood. He was not going to watch his daughter of means be with a *nobody*. Why did I keep thinking of myself like that? Because I had struggled for so long, it was all I had to remind myself of what I lacked. I became nervous, then remembered she loved me. Just as quickly as my attack of nerves came, a terrific calm began to come over me. What was there to fear if the daughter was willing to marry me? As she said, 'they are living their own lives'. Ours were ahead of us, just like the road we traveled.

* * *

I had driven for ten hours and was exhausted. We pulled into a small, modest motel where we spent the night. I began to doze; Euridice's warm hand sealed my lips when I started to speak. I had nothing to say, except how much I wanted to give her the world, and I realized that I had the world in that small room with me. The tepid night clung to our bodies like Velcro.

Sometime during my sleep that night I saw myself writing solution manuals for cash. The solutions to problems came effortlessly. It had to be a dream, for nothing should come so easily. But it was knowledge, and after you know something that's all there is to it.

135

Everything was vivid. Every problem I approached was waiting for me to apply whatever theory or axiom was required. Knowledge was the key that opened every door. Then I faced Euridice's father. He stood there, a granite wall of a man seven feet tall. I remarked that he was even taller than my own father, who was a big man. He replied that he, my Father, was not the biggest man in the world. I asked him where was his proof; that in the absence of proof, he could not say that. He could not even say that he was bigger than my Father, a man he had never met. He wanted to see my proof. I told him he was looking at it. I still remember the words I used.

"Aquí estoy, hecho y derecho." For I was standing in front of him. He is as I am, standing as straight as I. He was not convinced, but then from behind him my Father appeared. But he was not as I remembered him. He stood hunchbacked, his hair white, his hands arthritic, holding one of the cigars I had sent him. *"¿Qué te pasó, papá?"* He replied that I had been gone so long that his back had lost what it once had. He could no longer support himself, much less a son. I told him that I was standing in his place. I introduced him to Euridice. *"¡Qué bella!"* he said. I agreed, as did her father, whose granite face now sported a smile chiseled into it. Euridice asserted that my proof failed, but that my will was strong. That is what I remember from that night.

"I think you better start soon" is what Euridice said upon hearing about my solution manual dream. "Where will you find the time?"

"The future holds all the time we need."

It was true then as it is true now.

26

We returned to Baton Rouge in the evening and were welcomed by a driving rain. We were both glad to be back, excited about our commitment to each other. I had decided to buy Euridice a ring. I had convinced myself that if I had money for a vacation, I could afford a ring. *"Un casa de empeña,"* said Euridice. She would be happy with a ring from a pawn shop. She was rare indeed, I thought.

We pulled up in the driveway. The house was dark and there were no cars parked. Euridice and I looked at each other and decided to make a dash to the front door. I fumbled with keys and dropped them in the puddle. The rain soaked my back as I reached for them. We walked in the house and Euridice turned on the light. It was after eight, but still early for it to be so quiet. Everyone was out of school. Maybe Gerardo and Ginebra were out of town. I followed Euridice down the hall then slipped into my room. There was a bath towel on my bed, so I got out of my wet clothes and dried myself. I was almost dressed when I heard a knock on my door. It was Euridice. We were not alone. Ginebra was in her room. Alone. We walked in to see how Ginebra was, to tell her about our trip.

Ginebra looked like she hadn't eaten in a week. Her eyes were swollen, as if she had been crying.

"Gerardo se fue," she said, then hid her face in her pillow. Gerardo had left. But more tragically, He had left

137

her. He will be back, I told her, without any assurance. He had always come back before. She had always accepted him with anticipation. Besides, the car was missing. That meant he was coming back. No. *"El coche está en el taller."*

The car was in the shop, so Gerardo may have indeed not been coming back. She said he left shortly after we went to Miami. So she had been alone since then. She looked like she wanted to die. His running around had not prepared her for this moment in her life. I thought that it might have, though. But I had been alone for so long, how would I know how she felt? Euridice and I looked at each other with helpless expressions on our faces.

"We're taking you out," I said, speaking for both of us. I had no idea where. "We're going to Godfather's Pizza." She looked like she had lost twenty pounds. I went back to my room while they got dressed. I would have enjoyed sharing our engagement with Ginebra, but that would have to wait. I did not think Euridice would choose this time to break the news to Ginebra. She had been through so much already. I could only imagine what seeing a ring on Euridice's finger would have done to Ginebra.

We climbed into the car and headed for Godfather's. The rain had not let up, though it didn't matter now. The flooded streets parted as we found our way to Tigerland, where the shops were located. The area was only half-lit. The rainfall had undoubtedly caused many electrical outages. This was a common occurrence in the summer there.

Euridice and Ginebra sat side by side, like the day I arrived home with Cathy, only there was no amount of TV to amuse them. This was life in its cruel, lopsided dimension. Gerardo had left everything except his books, baseball glove, and some of his clothes. He apparently was *not* coming back, though I kept that thought to myself. Euridice didn't, though. Her Spanish accelerated, tearing into Gerardo's less-than-sterling character. She could find nothing redeeming in it.

"What kind of dog could leave you here in a foreign country—alone? No. It's something even a dog wouldn't do!"

And that was one of the nicer things she said. Most of the remarks are beyond my ability to translate, but I will try. "Go down to the river, and find the filthiest catfish feeding on cow pies and dog feces and you will find him: *Gerardo del Alcantarillado*—Gerardo of the Sewer. Go down to Maracaibo on a hot summer day. Any fetid latrine will bear his name. Open the door, and the stench that reeks from it will be his breath, after he has belched up his dinner of goat vomit." I mean, Euridice was brilliant in Fourier analysis, characterizing metallic crystalline structures, and distinguishing the Carnot and Rankine cycles, but all that knowledge paled when compared to her ability to deface Gerardo. Euridice was as sharp in a pair of four-inch stilettos as the dagger between her lips which, once exposed, could draw blood. It put me on notice to treat her with the greatest respect, less I be debased like Gerardo: to the level of a motherless maggot.

The pizza came and Ginebra found her appetite again. The conversation drifted from the man who had kept her mind in a straitjacket for two weeks. We convinced her to take the course in microbiology she had been avoiding for a year. I found as much therapy in Euridice's words as anyone. I was eager for the summer to end so that I could begin my senior projects, graduate, and return home.

I had yet to negotiate with Euridice where we would settle, since that depended on job offers. And I hadn't asked Euridice how she felt about my becoming involved with projects in Haiti. It was, without a doubt, the most neglected nation in the Western Hemisphere. I wondered if race had anything to do with it. If I discovered a way to extract oil from its shoreline, I could restore dignity to that nation. I would need a graduate degree in petroleum engineering and a PhD in mathematics. They were within reach. I had a lot going for me. There were plenty of opportunities in the southern states, although I saw the need to return to Panamá, especially after meeting Dr. Diversé. Panamá and Haiti were neighbors. Our outstretched arms could touch each other easier from that distance than from the States. In the States to find a sponsor was an obstacle to hurdle. But I had no doubt that we would achieve a successful outcome, as we faced the fleeting sun.

27

Baton Rouge, Louisiana—1990

All that time lost. I was floating on a vapor as if my sail would never stop billowing. I had built an imaginary world where I would be accepted. Her father didn't care that I had graduated with honors. Something that surprised even me. Hell, all I *knew* was hard work. Honors had no place in my mirror. When the letters for graduate school came in, I showed little of the joy my Mother did upon hearing about them. Where is Valparaiso? Cornell? Rensselaer? she asked. I smiled at her childlike innocence.

"I just want to work," I said. I needed more than ever to get cracking at a job.

"Claro quieres trabajar, Roberto. Pero hay tiempo para eso," were my Father's words, and he was right. Who had worked any harder or longer than he? Driving the highways of Panamá, his handshake filled with calluses. Like Braille embossed upon his skin, which I felt when he slapped his hand against mine in high-five fashion, or when sharing a handshake. He had passed the baton and I already knew the course. It was the high point of graduation day. Oh, I missed him so. I could forget that Euridice would not be coming with me, if only for a moment. All of the kind things my Mother said to her. Things she surely memorized, sounding like Queen Sofia of Spain. Still, I was proud of her to have taken the time

141

to make such a splendid speech at the place I called home for four of the five years in Baton Rouge.

"I lift this glass as a toast to the hard work and years of sacrifice spent in this land of so much." My mother didn't say America, less people give all the credit to the States as the "land of so much," and not pay tribute to Latin America, a true bounty in its own right.

"To our sons and daughters who are here today," she said, finding Euridice in the crowd, unlike most of us still in our gowns. LSU had already had their commencement ceremony several days earlier.

"I'm going home with my Father," Euridice told me. It was not that she was going home that felt strange. It was the thought I would never see her again. "Don't be silly. Remember, we are one." One what? I wondered. "We're leaving tonight." Oh, her father wasn't wasting any time. He had reservations arranged before his arrival in the States.

We found time to take a slow walk through Tigerland for what would be our last one there.

"Oh, come on. Don't you miss Panamá, too? Of course you do."

She was all questions—and the answers. When we got to the Colombian bar in Tigerland, I wasn't thirsty. I raised a half-filled glass of water and clicked her bottle of Budweiser. She tilted it back: Reflections of Cathy.

28

It's amazing what you can accomplish without distractions. Three years at Cornell and I had my PhD in Mathematics. I laugh at the fact that I went on few dates, to no parties, and made no calls to Euridice. I had developed the callous mind of a proof-ridden mathematician. Didn't Newton go crazy? Oh, that's where I was headed: to a padded cell with a blackboard and dustless chalk. I found a job at a small college in Wilmington, Ohio. It was green there and I loved the quiet. But all was shattered when news arrived that someone I knew needed to be picked up at the bus terminal.

"She didn't give her name, but she had an accent?" said the secretary in the Math Office.

My heart raced at the thought that Euridice had sought me out. No, I was going to be cool. I was the missing ingredient, the rudder to right her ship. Oh, I felt like pulling out the guitar that I hadn't touched in two years.

I drove down to the bus station and looked around. Was her hair long or short? She was no doubt dark from the sun.

"Roberto!"

It was not her voice. I turned to see Isabel.

"Isabel?" I was so glad to see someone from the past I had tried to forget. We spoke in Spanish.

"Why didn't you answer my letters?" she asked.

"I did answer the first one."

"But the others?"

"I really had nothing to tell."

"What about your work? Your new friends?"

"I just slipped into these woods, just another evergreen," I continued, not caring where the conversation was headed. "How did you ever find me?" My words were awkward. "No, I mean—so good to see you!"

"You left your information at Cornell. When I told them I was your cousin and a physician . . . They don't know one accent from another—they gave me your information."

"Congratulations. But I still don't see what brings you here. And Francisco?"

"This will come as a surprise to you, but Francisco and I were together for me to keep my residence. And the other piece is that he has returned to Venezuela."

I was afraid to ask another question, because I knew the answer. "I bet Euridice figures into this somehow."

"She and Francisco were married two years ago. I didn't attend but it was a big wedding."

"So Francisco was always in the picture. Gee, I was too blind to see it. Do I feel stupid!"

"No, I was the one. All that talk of marriage and arrangements. I hoped that something would grow out of living together with him. They had made their own arrangements!"

"Her father must be happy," I said.

"Don't be bitter. It won't help."

"Oh, I'm over bitterness. My heart has turned to granite." I wasn't holding back my feeling for what had never materialized. I somehow felt the ease of letting myself fall to the bottom of the sea.

"And what about you?" I asked.

"Oh, I'm in Philadelphia at a Catholic hospital. I'm in radiology."

"Still, it's good to see you." We walked to the car and got inside. My gaze eased as I looked into her eyes. Was I actually engaged in a conversation with a woman I cared about, or was this just another game?

"On Monday I have to be in Columbus. A radiology conference. It's three days."

"I have been there a few times, but not recently."

Isabel and I climbed into the car.

"This is nice. I didn't know you were into sports cars. An Audi?"

"The green matches your eyes."

"Ever the poet. Do you still write?"

"Only equations."

"You must change that." She was holding my hand as if to bridge the time an absence can create. Her eyes held impetuous curiosity.

"And your family?" I asked her.

"They're all gone now."

"I'm sorry to hear that. Your father must have been proud."

"Unfortunately, he never saw me graduate."

I held her hand. I understood why she had sought me out. I was close to her and the memories of good times together.

"You must be exhausted."

"I'm a little hungry."

"Of course. We'll be near campus in a few minutes. I hope you can stay the weekend."

"I can. I am just so glad to see you!" She pressed my hand again.

The semester was over. A two-week break was time enough to catch up. The weekend would be a beginning for whatever outcome we arrived at. I was no mind reader but I was willing to bet I would we tracing her bikini line before the night was over.

* * *

The half-eaten eggs and toast remained on the table. The blue napkin was tossed on the chair, the cups of Brazilian coffee cold. Meanwhile, Isabel murmured *locuras* in my ear.

"I wanted you for a long time," she said, "way back in Florida."

"Whatever happened to that black bikini?"

"You remember that? The salt water devoured it."

"And the mole above your navel. There wasn't much to devour."

I was letting her chip away at the granite rock my heart had become. Hadn't the Egyptians heated stones for the pyramids before pouring cold water on them to later watch them crack? Did Isabel have that talent?

"Do you still have family in Philadelphia?" she asked.

"My aunt is still alive but the rest are gone."

"Even the cousin you mentioned in your letter?"

"Carlito died five years ago, but I forgot I mentioned him to you. Before that, he watched his girlfriend and her mother die. All of them from AIDS."

"I'm sorry I asked. It is so tragic."

"It's the times we live in. But tell me something."

"What's that?"

"What disintegrates faster, a relationship or a family?"

"A relationship," she said without hesitation. But before I could ask another question, she had straddled me and slipped her tongue into my ear. I felt the rough edges of my heart drop away and the soothing water from her mouth warming it.

* * *

"I find it hard to believe you are still single."

"What about you? It's even harder to believe."

"I'm married to my work."

"No, that's my line," I said, meaning every word of it. "Who in his right mind would be thinking of doing another PhD in mathematics?"

"What's wrong with that?"

"It's easier than getting involved with someone."

"Still, you haven't answered why you are single."

"Oh, I was involved with a Jordanian for a few years in graduate school until she returned to Jordan."

"What happened?"

"She told me she needed more than a 'trampoline act'," I said. "But she was the real acrobat."

"See how freely we talk?" She caressed my temples.

"Something I wouldn't have done years ago. I held back as if the truth would not someday stare me in the face like my gray hair."

"We both have gray hair."

I held her soft buttocks, and wished for nothing more than to be where I was.

"When were you in Philadelphia last?"

"Five years ago for Carlito's funeral. He had melted away to ninety pounds. What a waste!"

"You'll have to come back now."

"Why don't we go down to Panamá?"

"I'd like that."

"My parents are still alive. I was able to buy them a house."

Isabel stood up and draped the sheet around her nude body. She poured two glasses of white wine and passed one to me.

"To a new day," she toasted.

She sat on my lap as we emptied our glasses.

"Do you think we could make something work?"

"We're together for a reason," I said.

"I mean something that lasts." She let the sheet slip from her body and stood before me. She found her pants and slid them onto her nude body. She put on my white shirt and her sandals. I dressed as well.

"I want to show you the campus, it may be the last time you see it. These conifers are quite special. I would miss them if I left this place . . . if I found a position somewhere else."

"I'm looking for some place to call home, too."

I watched Isabel walk ahead of me to the door, the sound of her heels against the hardwood. I could get used to that gait in my life.

29

The news came to me like mortar rounds: Isabel had received the approval she had not even mentioned during her stay in Ohio: Her application to Doctors Without Borders had come through. She was off to Iraq. Well, she might have mentioned it! She didn't think she would even be called seemed the weakest of reasons. I might have gone with her. Didn't she see that I was crying out for a friend in this world of feelings so casually discarded? Oh, the loneliness her absence engendered! But the second blow came three months later: a newsletter came that her jeep had hit a land mine. She lost an arm and later died from a loss of blood. Talk about an emptiness. It was the darkest day of my life.

Part 2

Home, Well Almost

30

Philadelphia, Pennsylvania—2003

I kept asking myself why I had returned. Because of the funeral, I said. But was that really enough? I mean, I didn't really know Aunt Rebecca. She was my Uncle Carlos' sister-in-law. Carlito, his son, had long been cold in the grave. How many generations of grubs had fed off his cadaver? Maybe I just wanted to bring back the beauty of the memory of having chocolate cake on her back steps; the sun melting the icing into the palm of my hand; my licking the sweetness of a time almost forgotten. The memory of her smile was worth a return visit, even if she wasn't there to greet me. The plane descended onto the runway, the tires touching the tarmac all too smoothly, and I wondered if the falling snow had turned to ice, if we would come to a halt by colliding into some fixed body. No, there was plenty enough runway. No cause for alarm.

Lillian's smile melted my heart when I caught sight of her at the end of Gate D. I was surprised to see here standing alone, holding an overcoat. She embraced me in a way she might not have if her husband had come there, too. There I was: reading something into nothing.

"Tom said this overcoat should fit you."

"He knew I wouldn't have one coming from Baton Rouge. Thanks."

"You know Tom. Details."

153

"Where is he?"

"He's got a lecture this afternoon. Said to just take you for something to eat and we'll have dinner together tonight."

"Maybe just some coffee," I said.

We found our way to Lillian's gray BMW. Its hood and roof were partially snow-covered. January had really pounded them with a foot, she said. For us in Baton Rouge the winter had been mild. I hadn't even brought inside the avocado tree I started from a seed.

The backseat of the car held a box of school papers, no doubt Tom's. I only had one suitcase that I placed in the trunk.

"Don't bother to clear the snow," she said, stopping me as I brushed some of the snow from the trunk. "We're going to a carwash anyway."

"Just wanted to touch it again."

Lillian took advantage of that moment to grasp my hand and place it to her cheek.

"It's still warm." She smiled.

"Just turn the heat up, thanks."

We exited the airport and were on our way to City Avenue and Sixty-third Street, where I had reserved a bed-and-breakfast room for a week. We could have some coffee there.

"Tom said there was plenty of room with us, that—"

"You two have already done too much. I need a little time to reach my cousins."

I had no intentions of reaching anyone who hadn't reached out to me. Where was Carlito anyway? No, just pay your condolences, and get back to work.

"You know who asked about you?"

"I have no idea."

"Her name begins with a Y."

"Yolandita 'Monge' Martinez?!"

"*Esa misma*! You got it in one guess."

"I don't know anyone else whose name begins with Y. What's she up to?"

"Well, you'll be able to ask her yourself. She's coming to dinner tonight. She's only recently returned from Italy."

"And in all this snow?"

"She'd rent huskies to see *you*."

Yolanda was easily one of the smartest people I had ever met with perhaps the exception of Euridice. I had to qualify my judgment because of the emotional attachment for Euridice that took a long time to get over. I plunged into my studies with a verve I couldn't have imagined possible after my love went south, figuratively and otherwise. Euridice shared with me once that her mother wanted nothing more than that she marry a European. I was certain that I could overcome that small hurdle once her family had met me. That occurrence was never to happen. As for Yolanda, I met her when I was in San Antonio for the weekend with Jorge Martinez, a fellow engineering student. He was the cousin of Tom Olivet, a friend living in Philadelphia. Jorge lived in San Antonio, Texas. He invited me to stay with him and his family. Yolanda, his cousin, was there on her holiday and had just started school in New York, at Cooper Union, so the opportunity to talk to someone who was familiar with that part of the country seemed a reasonable fit, and nothing would be lost in meeting her.

I was not interested in making any new acquaintances, but we went to a dance and I had the best time I'd had in years. It had nothing to do with the rum. I had all but given up alcohol as it reminded me of times and faces I wanted to forget. Then Yolanda told me she wanted to stay with me that evening, that she liked my company. I said okay, but it was easy to lie in the blue lights of the room, and the dark light of the infrequent headlights of the cars passing outside. Something remarkable about

Yolanda was the shortness of her hair. It was black, she said, but there was almost none on her head. She had these earrings she had made from coral shells. She said, "I only wear black because it goes with everything. The earrings wear me!" I thought that statement was a new way of talking, or maybe something she had picked up in New York. We danced the merengue every time one was played. Yolanda pressed her 130 pounds—what I figured—into me until the blackberry dress became juice.

Lillian pulled into the parking lot.

We went up to the room.

"Quaint," she said, examining the living room. "Even a piano!"

"Well, you did find it for me. You know what I like. Would you like some tea?"

"I'm going to get the car washed and get back," she said glancing at her watch. "Tom will pick you up a five thirty."

I walked her to the door and she kissed me.

"See you tonight."

I pulled out my sketchpad and charcoal pencils and sat at the window where there were several sycamores: lifeless and branch-ensnarled. I made careful strokes on the off-white paper.

I was pleased with the rendering. I even caught a sparrow as it went by. It was a sad landscape, if only brightened by the thought that Yolanda would be at dinner, too. I took a shower, dressed for dinner, and watched the snow accumulate on the sill until the weight of the flakes on my eyelids closed them and I fell asleep on the soft blue couch while holding a green silk pillow.

There was a knock on the door. I was about to answer it, but she let herself in. She wore a long black parka, a pair of Sorels, and an irresistible smile. She had on goggles as if to keep out the glare of the sun.

"May I come in?" she asked with superfluous immodesty.

"Only if you take off your coat."

She took off her coat and I didn't even care if she didn't take off her goggles, because the white Lycra bodysuit told me she had to be an angel.

"So, are you ready to go?" she asked.

"I'm just trying not to come," I thought.

She stood there waiting, then finally said, "The huskies are outside. Bundle up. Here, I'll help you." She walked over to me, and my nostrils absorbed all the lavender in her body. She helped me up, and her body was as soft as cashmere wool.

"I thought Tom was going to pick me up. He isn't coming, is he?" I only hoped that he wasn't.

Why had I even mentioned his name? First Lillian, now this masked lady in white.

"Just let me help you into this snowsuit, and we're off."

"And you don't even remember who I am, do you?" She paused and said, "This will help you." She pulled down her Lycra suit to expose her light brown breasts. "And now? You said the taste of them took you to the Isthmus."

The dimple in her right cheek was a clue. The black shoulder-length hair was another, but neither enough. She had white teeth like Lillian, the coyness of Euridice, and the slender fingers of Yolanda.

"Of course I do and I'll tell you if you take off the goggles."

"I will, but I hear someone coming."

"Ding-dong." It was the door.

31

"Who is it?" I said, as if I had just been doused with cold water.

"Tom."

I opened the door, and there stood Tom, his shoulders broadened by his brown overcoat.

"Hey, what a friend! And in all this weather. How've you been?"

"Great. And you?" I said.

"Life is good. Lillian said your flight was on time."

"You guys came through as usual."

I walked over to get the coat-on-loan, and said "Now you can't tell me Yolanda is still coming."

"Forget that! She's already there, Lillian told me. I am coming straight from school."

"Yolanda the jetsetter. How was Italy?"

"You'll have to ask her."

Tom walked me to his Range Rover and we climbed in.

"So how is your research at Rougetec?" he asked.

"Sometimes I can't believe they pay me what they do for accumulating data. I run mathematical models, month after month, displaying and explaining the results, and they give me another project to take part of. In another month I may be in Kazakhstan exploring the Aral Sea for lithium," I told him, though I was trying to get back to that dream, and the woman in white Lycra.

"Lillian knows how you like your desserts, and has made a special one for you."

"On a moment's notice?"

"Well, it's a way for me to get something special, too."

"And Yolanda? How's she?"

"I'll let you be the judge, but now that she's graduated from school in Milan, she'll have plenty to talk about. She'll find a nice design job in some architectural firm. At least that was her aim, when she called once from Italy."

Tom crunched his way through the icy streets. The wider ones were salted, and in some places exposed the asphalt, though not much. The snow had stopped. The wind swirled around the mercury street lamps like little tornadoes. I noticed a line outside of State Store on Sixtieth and Manning, the way men usually did when they readied for a holiday of drinking. Although Martin Luther King Day was coming up, that didn't conjure he same sentiments. Still, the weekend was reason enough for tilting spirits skyward.

"I'm surprised this place is still open," I said.

"Remember how the young tough guys used to hang out here?" Tom mentioned. "This was the incubator for the cirrhosis that eventually claimed them. Stubbs died last year. I read it in The Tribune."

"I never liked him anyway," I said, surprised at my own candor.

"I had nothing against him, you?"

"Yeah. He pissed on me in the schoolyard once. I hated him and his mother ever since." I paused. "I do regret never telling him so. It doesn't matter now. He's got rigor mortis as a companion."

"Most of those dropouts were destined for the skids. And to think that guys like Stubbs joined the Army and died in Bosnia, or Afghanistan."

"Look at this street! All these boarded-up properties. Some developer will turn all this around, once the trains on Market Street are renovated."

"Is that the latest project here?"

"There's a lot work for a civil engineer."

"I can't see coming back this way," I said with no reservation in my voice.

We pulled up to Tom's home, a Victorian twin of six bedrooms on the 6200 block of Carpenter. This series of houses was a pearl in West Philadelphia. Tom mentioned it was still a wonderful neighborhood three seasons of the year; however, in the summer the ethnic barbecues could get loud. That may not have been the only reason he and Lillian would find their way to Menorca for six weeks. It served the opportunity of visiting the home of Lillian's father, a villa with a vista of the Mediterranean. Lillian's father, Don Joaquin Joan Olivet, still kept himself busy in his vineyard, and produced a fine madeira. Tom, Tomas de Lloret, was well on his way into writing his third novel, for which the weather off the coast offered the ideal atmosphere. His present work was a 1,000-page manuscript on the life of the Golden Age poet, Luis de Gongora. The first two novels were based on the lives of Juan Gris, a cubist painter, and the eleventh-century Muslim astronomer from Spain, Al-Zarqālī , respectively. Al-Zarqālī was known for his production of instruments, the astrolabe was one, then later for his contribution to mathematics related to astronomy. I was fortunate that Tom shared much of the latter manuscript with me because of my love of mathematics, and that he valued whatever insight he felt I might lend to his work. I would be the first admit that Tom put the "p" in painstaking research. It is a wonder he was able to complete his work given his penchant for parenthetical phrases. "Six hundred pages is my absolute minimum," he once said.

As Tom put the key in the multi-paneled glass door, I heard Danilo Perez playing "Bright Mississippi" from his CD entitled *Panamonk*.

"You must have taken the scenic route," Lillian said with a laugh.

"Well, we did go down memory lane," Tom offered.

"Ecco le cual! Si eso e' Roberto?"

"That could only be Yolanda! Italian and Spanish in the same breath!" I said, but had hardly gotten it out before she planted a kiss on my cheek, and then one on my lips.

"Bienvenido!" she shouted.

"I should be the one welcoming you! *Y Milano?*"

"Loads to tell about that," she said, swinging her head toward Lillian, showing off her black braid, which was every bit of six inches past her waist.

"And all that hair!"

"I said I wouldn't cut it until I found a job."

"Where are you looking?" I asked.

"Everywhere!" Seeing the quizzical look on my face, she added, "No, I have sent my resume as far away as Istanbul."

"Really?" said Lillian. "That's the adventuresome spirit for you!"

"I'm ready to spread my wings—again."

"And there isn't a person in this room who hasn't been on at least two continents," Tom added. He was now in the kitchen washing his hands. "We can get dinner under way. Lillian was so gracious. She had the food caterers drop it off a little earlier. Let's stand here and hold hands for a moment of thanks to the Creator, *el infinito.*"

We held hands: Tom held Lillian's, Lillian held mine, I held Yolanda's, and she held Tom's. We stood in semi-silence, because each of us in spontaneous turns thanked *el Infinito* for the fortune we had found in each other and the world. Holding hands there I had a unique sensation:

Lillian's hand was cold, and Yolanda's was warm. I had no reason to give it any thought before since the only time I had held their hands was at a dance, or at Tom and Lillian's wedding reception they had here in Philadelphia. They had their first one directly following the wedding ceremony in Menorca, which I was not able to attend for financial reasons. I could hear Yolanda murmuring things in Italian which I did not speak. My own prayers were among other missives) asking for forgiveness for the angry and ugly words I had said, and thoughts I had harbored for Stubbs all those years, and for not being completely selfless about coming to Philadelphia for Aunt Rebecca's funeral. True, I did not know her well, but she had shown me a brand of kindness I seldom saw in other relatives, save my Mother and Father and Tio Carlos. I would seek out her now adult sons, whom I could imagine would appreciate a thought of remembrance. Gee, I felt my soul lightened already.

I might have said something about Yolanda's long thick braid, had her body not taken me right back to my dream: Instead of a white Lycra, she wore a black bodysuit and thigh-high black boots, and a thin gray wool sweater that hung gracefully. And if that were not enough, her stilettos brought her five foot seven frame up eye-to-eye with me. Forget the dream! I want a love I can see!

"Okay. You can let her go now. She's back on this side of the Atlantic!" Lillian shot out.

"I wasn't aware I was still holding her. It felt so natural." Lillian seemed to have orchestrated this symphony. I just wanted to make sure I didn't miss my solo on tympani.

I watched Yolanda walk across the oak parquet floors, clicking the entire distance, and she returned to me with two glasses of white wine. Lillian also held two glasses of wine.

"Here is to friends from far, and not as far!" Tom toasted.

"Well, I'm ready to eat," said Lillian.

We began peeling away the plastic lids. It was a canopy of Latin American delights: *arroz con pollo, frijoles negros, arroz blanco, platanos maduros,* and an uncommon visitor, broccoli.

"If you only knew how I have longed for all these wonderful dishes," said Yolanda.

"I hope you're not disappointed we don't have pasta," interjected Tom.

"Let's just say I'm not disappointed." And she chuckled.

Tom asked Yolanda to talk about her thesis, which was a rapid-fire sharing of research she had made discussing Santiago Calatrava's classical influences in his modern-day structures. She pulled out a black Pentel, and with a deft left hand began sketching on paper that Lillian had made appear from under the container that held the broccoli.

"Do you see how he takes a form we are familiar with, and elongates it into a bridge? Then another time he takes an eye in its lid, and transforms it into a structure, say a museum or a fountain; a spinal column into an apartment tower."

Yolanda drew and never stopped talking. She didn't seem to have much of an appetite for food. Her work kept her and me afloat in the studio into which she had turned the dining room. Yolanda wrapped up her presentation with, "Well. Do I get the job?"

"I have a study that needs a facelift," said Tom, who was already stacking the dishes.

"If you let me do the dishes, I'll get started on the sketches tomorrow."

"Somehow that doesn't seem fair, but you're on!" said Tom.

Lillian and I were left having coffee and cake, and listening to Milton Nascimento.

"You two have a fine selection of CDs."

"It's about our only indulgence besides books, as you can see."

Shortly after entering the porch room, you were in the library. The ceiling was ten feet high and on the west wall was a desk. To the left and right of three walls were books. What would have been the north wall was the walk through the dining room. Beyond that was the kitchen, the laundry room, a bathroom and the backyard.

They had no children of their own. They had adopted twin boys from Vietnam who were biracial, Vietnamese and African-American. They were both attending college as premed students: one at Princeton, one at Michigan, both on full scholarship. They were both in accelerated BS-MD programs.

"Who's to say what we would have done if we hadn't had such good fortune with the boys: had a couple of ingrates; maybe pregnant teens. Enrique and Rene have been the mortar of our marriage."

As Lillian spoke I felt a level of calm, acceptance of fate. She had met Tom at the university. He completed his doctorate as she was finishing her BS in economics. Nothing interrupted their studies. Not even a miscarriage, because by the summer she had returned to complete her degree. When she presented the notion to adopt, Tom was in total support. She thought of adopting Iraqi children, but their government did not allow such adoptions. There are plenty of children in Vietnam available, suggested Tom, so they went there and started the process. Now the boys—young men—are in college. Listening to her made their lives seem so complete, and mine lacking.

"Hey, what are you two whispering about!" called out Tom.

"We were just discussing Calatrava, and how the name just trips off the tongue," I said.

"Exactly. How he, Milton Nascimento, and Danilo Perez should do a CD together," Lillian added.

"And I can't take any of the credit. It's a concept of singular genius, Lillian. And it all goes to you!"

"You are too kind, Dr. Davila."

"No, you are the kind one, Lillian de Olivet."

"You two are having too much fun!" said Yolanda. "Let's see what the snow is doing." She took my hand and walked out to the front porch room. "My rental is completely covered."

"And I didn't bring pajamas," I joked.

"Tom might have some that will fit. I'll take the top— and you the bottoms," Yolanda whispered in my ear.

The scent of lavender was what gave it away. She was the one in that abruptly ended dream that afternoon. That temptress in white. With her it wasn't the cat-and-mouse tag of Euridice. Or was it? I had been set up before. Way back in Colon when I craved the woman in the Saltamonte Hotel; in Baton Rouge with Euridice; the deaf woman in the mall in Godchaux's who I wanted so badly that she held my palm and kissed it, then pulled a small pad and wrote: "Daddy said no blacks!" Then she disappeared with the auburn sun. I was at my lowest ebb, or as Edith Piaf sings: *Une ombre de la rue.* I was a shadow of the street. This time what did I have to lose? I wasn't the poor Panamanian on a flight to the Promised Land. I was now Dr. Roberto Davila, engineer-mathematician, earning a nearly six-figure income. I was standing next to the most beautiful and accomplished woman I knew, and she was whispering in my ear; careless with her caresses, and stabbing my back with her breasts.

"We're going to turn in," said Tom. "Everything you want is in the room downstairs in the rec room."

"Good-night," said Yolanda.

I said good-night, too. Lillian smiled.

"I need some help with my boots," Yolanda said, holding my hand and leading me to the basement. We descended the steel staircase to another library wall. But I was not interested in books at that point. Yolanda took off her sweater and the glory of the night light embraced her heavenly body. With light behind her I could no longer see her face; only the onyx sculpture into which she had now transformed. I helped her with her boots. They stood up on their own, then flopped to one side. She then turned her back to me. The zipper went just below her shoulders, and she slipped the body suit off. I breathed in another lavender flower bouquet, and was thoroughly intoxicated. No, I was inoculated! I had found a cure for something called loneliness. I stepped into the bathroom, brushed my teeth, and returned to Yolanda, now under the sheets and blanket. Yolanda had already used the vanity and was quiet.

"You got away from San Antonio right after the dance."

"I still remember Camilo Sesto singing *Donde estas? Donde estas?*"

"And I wondered where you were."

"I left a note, though."

"*I wish I could stay,* it said. That you wanted to see me in Baton Rouge."

"You were off to Cooper, then to Milano. What has it been, four years since we last saw each other?" The distance we were away from each other was shortened by fleeting affairs and flirtations with the notice would see each other in Barcelona or in sweltering Panama. Neither place saw us, at least together. Yolanda saw lots of European cities, including Barcelona and Vienna. I could tell her about remote towns like Pierre Part, Jeanerette, and Mamou: places where French was still spoken, as if Napoleon

Bonaparte would buy back the Louisiana Purchase any day.

"Let's not waste any time," I said. "Take me to the country of marvels!"

"Who's that? Neruda?" she asked.

"Aznavour."

The night increased with the intensity of two that might never see each other again. It was a night that made the huskies howl like the wind.

32

I woke up to the smell of peppers and apples. I reached for my wristwatch, to have another hand lay itself on mine. Her arm encircled my waist, and held me in a silken embrace. I looked at the luminous dial. It was a little after eight. With her free hand, she tugged at my thigh. I was easy prey. I gave in without a thought to the contrary. She climbed onto my back and straddled me. She buried her head into my neck, then her teeth into my shoulder. It was not painful. It only proved to stimulate me. She acknowledged my approval and rolled over. The glorious sun painted an orange diagonal ray across her body. I followed the sunbeams with kisses from her pink toe nails up to her neck and back again, more times than I could count. At one interval she held my head in her garden, where I was lost in a chamber along the silk road. She pulled me from my delirium to her mouth. She wrapped her bikini underwear around my neck and held me fast. I laced my fingers through the black string and pulled her down, and she said, "Don't be afraid to let go!"

I managed to make it back to the bed and breakfast, but I was not alone. Yolanda wanted to see my place. I called a taxi, and it worked its way back through the sleeted streets. Cars were plowed in on both sides of Cobbs Creek Parkway. A Rottweiler frolicked in the snow, jumped out onto the street, and skidded into an oncoming car that was moving too fast. The dog, traveling on its own inertia, hit the front of the cab, and by then was sure to die in the street. The driver might have stopped but, perhaps drowsy from being up all night, moved on slowly, without the intention of stopping. Yolanda looked up from my shoulder at the death and gripped my thigh with both hands. She didn't utter a word for a minute.

"Do you think it's dead?"

"It has to be," I said.

"At least it was quick," she said.

Now she was holding my hand up to her mouth, planting kisses.

"In Milan, dead dogs just stayed on the street and flies had their fill."

When we arrived at my temporary home, I paid the cab driver and walked Yolanda on my arm.

She held a bottle of white wine in a plastic bag, as we made it up to the door of my lodging.

33

Yolanda washed out her undergarments and hung them in the bathroom. She now wore the sweater and, since the wooden floor was cold, her boots. I Listened to Ornette Coleman's *"Una muy bonita"* and wondered if the title—a very pretty one—referred to a woman. Certainly, Yolanda's figure fit the description for me. Even after the composition ended, I asked Yolanda if she wouldn't mind continuing to walk up and down the corridor, just so I could hear the clicking of her heels.

"I've got an idea," she said. She decided to tape the sound that reverberated against the wall. She was so creative; she put on a CD soundtrack of *L'homme et une femme* and recorded herself clicking her way through it. I thus had a half hour of her pacing the hallway. That kind of stimulation was perfect for the winter.

"I wonder if this is what they do in Finland," I said.

"If they don't, they should."

"It might reduce the suicides," I added.

"Or increase the birth rate."

Yolanda had the uncanny ability to please me in ways I had given up on people being able to do. I was not one who followed astrology, but Yolanda's birthday was November 15th. Mine was November 12th. That was sufficient for me, at least in that instance, to believe in the stars.

"Did you draw this?" She was holding the charcoal drawing to her breasts. Her mass of black pubic was all I

170

could focus on. *Had she ever shaved?*

"No, this!" she said, drawing my riveted attention now to her green eyes. She sauntered to me, as if I were nearsighted.

"Do you like it?"

"Everything about it. Draw me!"

"Now?"

"As I am!"

I got up and found my charcoals and eraser. She leaned against the wall, diagonally. Her gray sweater hung perpendicular from her shoulders to the floor. There wasn't a lot of light, so the silhouette was the dominant feature—her strong legs, which had bound me for a day, and her stronger mind that made me think I was in a down-filled bed in Finland, had me creating a figure from her waist down to the floor. It was a signature body that I could have drawn over and over. If I'd had the training one gets in an academy, I might have produced a Modigliani. She was long: a feature an artist could exploit. She had a full mouth, as full as the moon, as orange as a the sunset—and I had exploited her perfection from midnight to crepuscule with an insatiable lust that made me turn her around to see if I had missed anything: her lower back, just right of the spine revealed a dark mole. I would have that another time.

She approved of my drawing, found a magnet of a chili pepper, and displayed it on the black refrigerator door: no denying she was here.

It was three in the afternoon. The sky was still. A bit of light shone through the curtains. Yolanda went to the bathroom. She had to shave, she said. There was nothing unusual about that.

Minutes later she walked to the bedroom. She was completely bald, from her navel down. She climbed into bed—boots still on! Was I in for more acrobatics? It was time for our afternoon nap. I wasn't that sleepy, but when was I going to get rent like this again?

"Can you draw me *after*?"

"I won't need as much charcoal."

Yolanda pulled me to her, though we were nearly one already. It was a new sensation. Very new!

"I'm never letting you go again."

That sounded good. I didn't want to be anywhere else. I slipped into the saddle with little effort. The afternoon was a rollicking journey, from the Alps down to Corsica; from Milano up to Napoli. I had Italian on the tip of my tongue with all of Yolanda in my mouth. The room was quiet, except for the ambulance siren I heard once. I fell asleep and woke up with Yolanda still holding my stiffness. It was night but I needed to get up. I checked my messages: two from work. There had been no inclement weather in Baton Rouge. "How are you doing?" came a message from Barbara Ness, a coworker. "I need to talk to you." My cousin Renee, Rebecca's daughter.

I walked into the shower. When the water hit my legs they started to sting. I looked down. There, scratches. Streaks of red: Yolanda's boots. As the hot water splashed against my legs, Yolanda's body was against mine again. Showers do awaken you. It was time to do what I came to do: get the funeral arrangements established.

After I sent Yolanda off in a cab, I waited for another one to Renee's apartment. She lived in North Philadelphia, Tenth and Wingahocking. It was a drug zone now. Back when I lived in Philadelphia it was a decent working-class neighborhood. It, like much of Philadelphia, had spiraled into nothingness.

Inside the building, there was a striking difference from the deteriorating outside. It was clean with freshly painted white walls. It was spacious and inviting.

"We are going to view the body tonight. Do you want to come?"

How could I say no? What could she have meant by the question?

"I had to ask. Some people are squeamish about such things." She was matter-of-fact. All business. She changed the subject and asked about work, my flight, how long I was staying. "And what are you doing anyway in Baton Rouge? I can count the times I've stayed in that city."

"There's one research project after another. A lot of data collection," I said. What would the details have meant anyway? She had enough to work through. "How are you for cash?"

"I can't believe you're broke, too!"

"No. Actually I was asking if *you* could use some financial help."

"I'd appreciate anything." When she spoke she lost her composure. "It'd not as much the money, as I feel all alone."

I held her closely. She was a big woman. Maybe one hundred and seventy pounds, but on a five foot eight frame, she was attractive. She looked like she worked at keeping in shape. There were a pair of weights and a rowing machine in the living space.

"Will five hundred dollars be all right?"

She was still gathering herself, so I pulled out a checkbook and wrote a check payable to Renee Cardozo. I never carried much cash, and certainly not that amount.

"This will really help," she said, wiping the tears with her blouse collar. "She'll be buried tomorrow, but you already knew that." She walked into the kitchen and brought back a tray of coffee and cookies. "You look so nice. Do you always wear a suit?"

"When I'm traveling. Something I learned from my Father."

"You talked about him a lot when you were a boy."

"He's still very dear to me."

"I remember how you talked about him making smoke rings, after he puffed on his cigar."

"Some things you don't forget. Like Aunt Rebecca's chocolate cake."

"You always liked that! Why so?"

"It was one of the only things that reminded me of home."

"When were you there last?"

"Last spring. I go once a year, now."

I had a second cup of coffee. She told me how her son had died in a helicopter in Iraq. Better that than on these streets, she felt. Now she had a grandson, Paul. He was with his mother in Milwaukee. The wake was at seven. It was almost six, so we got ready to leave.

We arrived at the funeral home, also on a desolate block in North Philadelphia. There were just a few cars in front of the Dauphin Street establishment. Two of Aunt Rebecca's female friends were there, as well as a man Rebecca had lived with but never married and a young man who was the man's son by a marriage.

We were not there very long. I departed after a time, saying I would see them at the church.

I turned down a ride from the youth at the funeral home. I thought he read me as an easy mark for money. And even after I told him I had an appointment, he wanted to know with whom at nine. I didn't even answer him and left with the question looming.

I arrived at the bed and breakfast after ten. It was strange not to have Yolanda there. She had filled my days in an unanticipated, enjoyable way. I had been at the place three days, and had yet to have a breakfast.

My mobile rang. It was eleven. Yolanda: If I wanted, she would catch a cab right over. It wasn't a good idea. I had to be at the church at nine in the morning. She understood. Also, she had an interview at two in the afternoon. Why wedge in another engagement? By having interviews over the Internet, much was accomplished. I was feeling that Yolanda was setting me up for the inevitable drop. Hadn't the pattern repeated itself enough? She was a sex addict, for sure. But hadn't she had her fill in Italy? I wasn't going to let her manipulate me. Any day she was inclined to get that call for a job in who knew where. I was going back to Baton Rouge and then to Kazakhstan. I was through with the games. I wasn't interested in more than a night or two. I had had that. No more gypsy woman, and her trail of men.

The mobile rang again. Yolanda?! I didn't want her anymore. I didn't even answer it. She had worn out whatever I had for her.

I checked out after breakfast. Boysenberry yogurt, two slices of wheat toast, and green tea.

I left for the funeral. It was a small service. If there were one hundred people there, that was a lot. The preacher told of how sweet a person she was, and her two best friends related how she was in a better place. Some woman read a card of sympathy, and they closed the casket.

The funeral procession passed by her house and we were off to the cemetery. In the funeral car I didn't say anything, just held Renee's hand. At one point she lifted it and kissed it. I did the same to hers, and we were connected again, if for only a moment when at such times you do the spontaneous.

I left immediately afterward and drove to the airport. It was four and I was in the airport. The next flight was scheduled at seven forty-five. I opened an article in Engineering News on fracturing and began reading. My mobile again: Yolanda. Did I want to get together for dinner? How could I leave without telling her? Was I grieving? I told her yes, but not the reason why: Better to let her think it was because of my aunt passing. It was because I was going back to Baton Rouge where there was nothing but work, and more work. She thought the interview went well; that they were offering her a position in Montreal. Had I ever been there? That the money sounded good to her; and what did I think? Great news, I said. Let me know if you say yes, I told her. I had to go, but would call as soon as I got home. She was so sweet over the phone, but I had gotten over all the long hair. I'd be all right. I was already thinking about Ophelia Roselli, the blind secretary in the office. I wondered if she would go out with me. If she said no, that was all right, too.

I arrived at eleven fifty-five that night. I rented a car to my house on Bilboa Road. I had one tenant: Elena Suarez, a grad student in chemistry from Honduras. She was quiet and we often had dinner together. She said she was engaged, so I never had any inclinations other than owner-tenant. She paid on time and that was all that mattered. She was going to finish her master's, and would return to Honduras or go to Europe. She asked why I didn't call her when I arrived; that she expected me, since I had made the flight arrangements in her presence, and she had driven me to the airport. Why did I hear a certain sensuousness in her voice, coupled with a T-shirt that rose and fell when she plopped on the sofa, and the blacks shorts that I wasn't even aware she had on, until she sat down? Well, I had enough material for a supposition, at least. I could say for certain that all women were predators, just that they knew how to camouflage their intentions so well.

There was no need, I said.

She was going to be up; did I want some coffee?

I said okay and had a cup with her. In the instant I walked to turn on the radio, I heard a short scream. I turned to find Elena's face and T-shirt wet, having inadvertently sprayed herself with the faucet from the sink.

"Are you all right?" I looked for a towel in the kitchen. I tried not to laugh but she started and I followed. "You're completely soaked!"

"Just my front," she laughed.

Well, she could have been nude for what the moment revealed. *Were her breasts really purple? Perfect form.*

She went upstairs to find another top.

I left my phone on the table; if it rang the voice mail would do its job.

34

My alarm clock-radio woke me at six. I showered and went downstairs. When I went into the kitchen, Elena was standing in front of the refrigerator in an oversized white T-shirt and nothing else. She turned and smiled, "*Buenos dias.*"

"*Buenos.*" I said. She had to know I would be aroused by the protrusions my eyes caught. The words Honduras on the shirt would be great for tourism. "You're going to turn me into a fan of your football team."

"Any way I can help them," she said.

"You mean every way!"

"Your friend called twice last night."

When I raised my eyebrows, she continued.

"Yolanda," she said. "She was surprised you had a roommate. I told her that I was a tenant. She paused and said she had called earlier on the cell, then thought she would call on the home line. She sounds nice. Very talkative."

"Maybe curious."

"Oh, definitely that. She asked how we met, how long I had known you, where I was from. It was an interview."

"She's been taking them lately."

"So she said, and that she just got back from Italy. She sounds lovely. So when are you going to drop her?"

When I didn't say anything, she brought over a cup of coffee: our morning ritual.

"Where can I get a tee like that?"

"I can give you this one!"

"I don't need it right away!" When she walked over I watched her breasts rise and fall.

"No? You're taking it off with that look!"

"Is it that obvious? I need a new prescription. There glasses aren't doing their job."

"You know, you can have it whenever you want." And with that she raised the T-shirt, exposing the fullness of her breasts: those small purple circles, swollen like violets. My eyes had not deceived me after all!

She straddled me in the chair and I slipped off her T-shirt. She kissed me in a way that said she could hold back no longer. What had she been doing for so long, not seizing me in all the opportunities prior? My trips from the shower wearing a towel and a smile; her going in right after me, grazing each other's shoulders; my wanting to run my fingers through her short black hair, but not wanting to overstep my bounds. She was a free woman. Since when did an engagement stop her passions? She pulled me into her bedroom on the first floor. The telephone rang. She answered it. I was busy, she said, matter-of-factly, not bothering to relay the message.

"It was for you, but I said you were busy."

Elena dropped to her knees and took me in her hands, manipulating me. Her teeth and tongue were warm and I swelled in her oral cavity, a place that bathed me in mouthwash.

The telephone rang again, but it stopped after several rings. By then I was traveling through the galaxy with my co-pilot on the throttle.

"You never answered my question."

Knowing what she meant I said, "I already did."

That brought on new embraces, as she drove her nails into my back. Oh, this was a chemistry I could get into! I could only hope I still had my first aid kit, and my *doctor* could patch me up. I might have been embarrassed for the way we were rocking that bed. But Elena didn't care, and don't you know that phone rang again! We both laughed when she asked "Should I answer it, or just let the building burn to the ground?"

Elena had a dark sense of humor—and I liked it! "Let's play back the messages tonight after dinner," she said with a glint in her eyes. A smile came with a slithering tongue in my ear. I was deliriously lost in the afternoon with her. "Maybe I shouldn't have been so nice to her on the phone. Then again, I can't wait to talk to her again and lead her on; that yes, you mention her all the time; she must be beautiful. Is she beautiful?"

Sure, she was. But I wasn't thinking about her then. I only cared about the thighs that throbbed against mine; the thin scissors that sliced me at the waist. Elena was five foot seven and only 120 pounds. She had the round breast of a woman who consumed protein—at least she gave that impression. She kept her weight down by playing racquetball. She was fit for any endurance race.

This beauty had found a special place in my heart. The same place where Euridice had driven a dagger, a serrated dagger. By now I had the T-shirt around her waist. As I pulled her toward me, she held onto one of the bedposts; the bed now squeaked like a piglet ready to die. Oh, it was loud! Or was that Elena? I felt *I* was going to snap! The bones of Elena's hips sawed at mine, and she was winning this new game. I had to turn her on her side. There, I was in control again. Elena said she was thirsty. Who was I to deny her: I gave her all of my tongue, and she sucked it dry!

35

I went to work the next day. It was a Saturday, so I was the only one there. There was a note on my desk:

It looks like you'll be going to Kazakhstan after all.
Bart

You think he might have called me. Then again, I was away for the funeral. It wasn't urgent.

I leafed through the memos I had missed: meetings I had missed, where my project was mentioned only once. There was a unanimous decision that I go: I was a senior member of the company and I had spearheaded the project from the start. We wanted to find out if we could capture lithium reserves from the interior of Kazakhstan. It was a new market to explore. No one else was doing it. There was an abundance of natural gas, but what about lithium? It seemed like an extreme expense to find a new market. What if the findings were that there was none? Was that the reason I was going, or being sent? It was not my decision, ultimately. I might have been a senior engineer, but I was a researcher. I would bring back evidence to further the financial interests of the company, and Rougetec Consultant Engineers would take things wherever they wanted. Get that in your head, I told myself. You are a salaried employee. That's all! Still, it seemed like quite a distance to go. It would get me out of the environment there, and make me less of an obstacle for others with ambition to negotiate. Hadn't Peter the Great sent his adopted black son, the promising engineer, to Siberia to build a fortress against the potential invasion from China? The energetic man exceeded his father's expectations, but was effectively removed from the political climate. He was too close to Peter for the jealous power brokers of St. Petersburg!

Maybe I was taking things too far, but I was prone to exaggeration. Hadn't I thought Euridice was mine, and that her family would accept me? *Does your mamá know about me? Does she know just what I am?* I sang that song to myself as I looked out the window and watched the rain that had begun to pound against the window. I opened the drawer and pulled out my white hardhat and put it on the desk. I was pursuing what might make the company millions. True, I wouldn't be in the immediate surroundings, but I would only be a teleconference away. It was not the same as being sent to Siberia centuries ago. Kazakhstan was just as far, but I was ready to leave. I could see myself side by side with Raskolnikov, eating a bowl of soup, but unlike him, I wasn't crushing any cockroach in it for protein. There I was, blowing things out of proportion. True, I didn't know what kinds of foods they ate. Didn't they eat worms in Africa? Rats in Panama? Nutria in Louisiana.? One of the guys from New Iberia talked about having nutria hindquarters. "The meat tastes like rabbit! Best gumbo you can get! *Ave Maria!*" I wasn't even hungry now! I did want some coffee, though. I cleared my desk and left.

It was still coming down, so I got wet walking to the newsstand café. I bought a Times-Picayune for protection against getting more soaked.

"Nice suit," the salesman said.

"What about the tie?" I added.

"Nice green. Goes well with the dark blue suit!"

"Salesman and fashion police! Who knew?" I wiped my face with my handkerchief. "A cappuccino, please." I sat down, and opened the paper to the puzzles in the back page.

1 down. The capital of Bulgaria: Sophia.

8 across. Pepper, but hot: mint.

16 down Umbrellas of —. Easy. Cherbourg.

The coffee was good. The rain had slowed down and it was four fourteen. I decided to leave, get out of those wet clothes.

When I got home, the house was quiet. You knew a woman lived there. It was a nice thought. One that I knew Yolanda wouldn't share, but it smelled so nice. All of a sudden I remembered I had left the drawings of Yolanda at the bed and breakfast: one on the table of the dining room, the other on the refrigerator. I went into the shower, and there were Elena's black panties and camisole hanging on the back of the door. We had moved in together: eating together, using the same shower, sleeping in the same bed. It was as though I had never had another life, I had never known anyone else. She was easy to be with. I liked her: the way she would sneak up behind me and slip her hands under my shirt and say, I'm ready! She had a way of standing at the door and smiling, showing that dimple in her right cheek, looking so tantalizing in a turtleneck and bikini bottoms that revealed her dark legs. I was going to miss her clicking through the hallway, announcing her feminine presence. That was what Yolanda was doing, parading up and down the hallway: reminding me of Elena, without my realizing it then! Elena was the one missing ingredient! The wedding of the real with the imaginary, the $a+bi$, if you will. Oh! Elena would understand that, it no one else would. In the day, she was all laughter. In the evening, barefoot and T-shirts. And at night? Well, tonight I would see her in those garments and black satin heels she wore on occasions such as this. I wasn't going to be near her for much longer. And I was going to have to leave these new comforts for the unknown cold and mysterious Kazakhstan! I got a chill just to think of it! I couldn't even find the kind of clothing in Baton Rouge that I would need for that weather. But how would Elena weather the news? Better not tell her too soon. I didn't want anything to mar the swell relationship we had developed. *No, just keep the good news to yourself.*

36

Two weeks had gone by. By now Elena had really become relaxed. She had taken to walking around dressed in only a white T-shirt and sandals. The formality of clothes had become an encumbrance that she could do without. I had really gotten used to her wearing a certain tee that partially revealed one of her breasts, by way of three dime-sized holes—just enough to whet my appetite for the evening to come. It was like living with a woman out of some fairytale that I might have written. Something else remarkable was that on occasion Elena would bring out dinner, but only on one plate. The first time she did it, I asked her where mine was.

"I want you to sit here."

She walked over to the answering machine and said, "I want you to listen to this." She couldn't keep from smiling, it seemed.

I walked over to the chair she usually sat in, and she sat on my lap. The tape began, after my voicemail asked whoever was calling to leave a message.

"Roberto. Will you call? I have some news to tell you."

"Roberto, llámame!"

"Roberto? Why haven't you called? I miss you."

"Roberto? It's that woman, isn't it? Why didn't you tell me? You really were living with somebody? And not like she said!"

"It's so pathetic," Elena said, with laughter.

"Roberto! What about us?"

Elena chose that moment to raise her T-shirt and looked down to say, *"Porque e' de nosotros,"* and put my hand on her thigh, and gave me a wiggle and a sinister look. "It gets better!"

"Roberto, I need you. Even if you want her, you can still have me. Don't forget that."

"What did you do to that one? Wait! I already know, because you're giving it to me now. Every night!" She kissed me, and slid my hand to her center. I thought I was in a Honduras rain forest, thick with fig trees. She fed me. I noticed that she had achieved something that I had worked on accomplishing: I began to lose weight, but my sexual appetite increased, inversely. I had one more week before I left.

"You should really call her."

I didn't know if she meant it, or really didn't care.

"I have to go to Honduras," Elena told me.

Where did that come from? I was in a quandary. I was supposed to be leaving her!

"When?"

"Soon," she said, as I fondled her breasts. "The day after tomorrow. My father is ill."

Why should I tell her about my own trip? Then again, I had better, I thought. "I have a trip of my own as well. I have to go to Kazakhstan."

"No way! I don't even know where that is!"

"Just think Russia. It's a new research project. They are sending me."

"Will you be gone long?"

"Three weeks at the most."

"I only plan to be gone a week." She nudged her head into my own. That meant dinner was officially over. The plate would remain on the table; the napkins on the floor; the rap music pounding against the window, as the deaf driver passed the building. Nothing would disturb us. My hands had already taken their places, both under the T-shirt, one high, one low and my head was into buried in the peach-sweet nape of her neck. She had lost her shoes—those satin heels—but she found them again, and led me upstairs to her room, clicking all the way. Her room, which tonight was our room, because she liked an unmade bed: her own—the symphony of disorder made right by the rain against the window and pounding sound of hip-hop as a car drove by the apartment.

I drove Elena to the airport. She was so quiet that I didn't even ask her why. Oh, I knew this was our good-bye. No speeches, prepared or otherwise, would avert the inevitable plane schedule. I had successfully done it again in a month: broken off the potential engagement to another excellent choice of Mrs. Roberto Davila. Didn't I want a life partner? Yolanda was an even better choice, and one of the brightest people I had ever met, and she cared for me. How long was I going to harbor the pain of Euridice? Did I think no one after her was good enough? Or was I content to chase the dreams of the already rich, and make more millions for them? No, there was something in it for me: A large bonus and great research. Still, I had left these two recent women hanging. Well, perhaps not Elena. She had declared herself ineligible, though she (in recent weeks) had taken full advantage of living with me: after we slept together, she never gave me another dime toward her rent. The timing was perfect, too. It was almost the end of the semester, so she took everything she owned and boarded a jumbo jet. I stayed for some reason to watch it puncture the clouds. It was raining, so fitting for a final departure. And with her gone I felt an overwhelming joy: no expectations to fulfill. I had succeeded in carving out another living organism from my being. No reason for anesthesia. My freedom was a panacea! It felt so refreshing that I stood out in the rain in my new blue suit. I stood against my green BMW

535i, getting soaked. Some woman pulled up and asked if everything was all right. I just smiled and said great. The smile on my face must have indicated that I was nuts, but I felt so euphoric that I am sure I looked like I was crazy. No one should feel that good, I thought. I climbed into the car. I turned on the tape of Kashif. I just sat there and rocked to the pulsating drum machine, the windshield wipers swishing in counter-syncopation.

I arrived at my apartment and quickly got out of the soaked suit, which I had all but ruined. *Good thing it's cotton.* I looked around the place and said that Elena was a lot of things, but neat she wasn't.

Some of her jeans were still in the hamper. Her underwear stuffed in a pillowcase, a coffee cup with its mold, green and ready for a petri dish. *What a pig!* Something I wouldn't have said days ago, but she was gone now, and I was soon to be, as well. I located the business card of a woman I knew with a cleaning/ laundry service. I arranged for her to come over and give the place a thorough cleaning. I got the answering machine, and left a message. In the meantime, I started bagging things of hers up as refuse. Funny though, when I got to the shirt from Honduras I paused, held it to my nose, then threw it in the trash bag with the soiled underwear. *What would the memory of that do me?*

The phone rang: Zatamae Cleaning Service had called back. They could come by the following day to do everything in the house: Sunday at ten in the morning. Sunday held no special meaning for me. The town was deader than usual. People were either in church or sleeping off a hangover. It was my favorite day of the week. I used that time to buy a newspaper at a German restaurant down in Beauregard Town. It was a place of low frequency—just people from the neighborhood, lawyers for the most part. I had been there with Euridice once, but never again with her. I liked the place for its potato salad and stollen. The coffee was another draw. I had been in the habit of pulling out a notebook after reading the paper, and doing problems from coursework. I remembered one from Vector Calculus: as the limit approached infinity, the solution to the equation approached zero! I had never seen anything like that before, so it fascinated me. As abstract as it was, it resembled life so clearly, in retrospect. Why did the simple become so complicated, and what is complicated have several solutions, all of which gave satisfying results? The point was not to become so convinced that any one result was more favorable than the other. They could all be favorable at any given time and location. Yolanda was best at one point on a graph and Elena on another set of coordinates. Each was a point of tangency of equal merit. Descartes had made it so simple; only I had complicated things. People might have wondered why I spent so much time at the café doing graphs. I liked it there because no one was concerned with me. I was as invisible as I wanted to be.

37

The telephone rang. Maybe the boss with some detail about not drinking the water.

"Hello."

"Did you plan to leave without a word?"

"No."

"Gee. You just dropped me. I'm not even a friend, am I?"

How did she know I was leaving anyway? I had left her out of everything.

"Look, Yolanda. I thought you were in Montreal by now."

"I am, but I thought we were going to get together—like we were in Philly."

Why did a surge shoot to my thighs? I couldn't believe I wanted her again!

"So how is work?"

"Great. So when are you leaving?"

"I thought you were a call for flight confirmation."

"You are really unbelievable. Is your roommate going, too?"

"She left the country."

"For good."

"She'll be back, I guess. But not here."

"You burned her, too?"

"Yeah, but not at the stake. How did you find out I was leaving?"

"Secretary gave out the information because I was your sister."

"So you should have told me sooner. I wouldn't have knowingly committed incest."

"I know. That's why I kept it a secret!"

"You are devious!"

"And I'm your type. Admit it!"

"I admit it. Why don't I come up there when I get back?" I said, as a diversion.

"Why don't we connect somewhere—like Istanbul, on your way back?"

"That's a possibility. I'd like that."

"Don't lie, Roberto! It's unbecoming."

"Why should I lie? Have you been there?"

"You'd love it. I've been twice. I spent a semester there with other internationals."

"Then you're on. How much lead time do you need?"

"Family emergencies can't be predicted."

"I better make sure we're not related."

"It's too late for that."

"Seriously, though," I said.

"I've got to go now. But while you're there, pick up something nice for me."

"What's your shoe size?"

"I thought you knew. Seven A."

"Do you like stilettoes in black?"

"Five-inch heels?"

"You do love me!"

"Forever."

We hung up. Somehow I knew Yolanda had let me off easy. I packed some khakis and white shirts along with my suits. If nothing else, I did have the remnants of a conscience. The things that Elena had done—playing the messages back for her and my amusement—were something I enjoyed for those moments, but were not so funny now that I was without either of them. I am sure neither had lost any time with the bodies they had. Nor was it that either of them was not going to reach the star they sought in their fields. While I didn't care where Elena ended up, I would like to do more than just see Yolanda again. I would send her a message from Kazakhstan. Send me to Kuala Lumpur, but not Kazakhstan. Maybe next time, my boss had laughed.

38

I was on my second flight, out of Chicago, when out of my fit of slumber I caught sight of the Turkish stewardess. She took my breath away. What was so refreshing was the smile, the quiet eyes free of the agitation the airbus turbulence invoked. I wanted to know her. She walked up to my aisle seat and asked if I would like a pillow.

"What comes with it?"

"Sweet dreams, I hope," she smiled.

"Oh, they'll be sweet!" I said, watching her continue on her way down the aisle, offering pillows and blankets to the passengers, her red suit caressing her hourglass figure. I glanced across to the center, where I saw a silver-haired woman looking at me with disapproval. I looked away, dismissing her curiosity. *She has more suitors than she can count.* Still, she was going to be the last thing I thought of when I closed my eyes, and took sail on the cumulonimbus just beneath us.

Do you like what you see?

But how could "like" suffice in the presence of perfection? Ankles elevated by black heels, embroidered silk, Mediterranean blue, exposing the mole on her left foot: a droplet of burnt honey. I kissed it. She did not stop me. I did it again until time became irrelevant. I was delirious with joy. She asked if I wanted more red wine. She did not wait for an answer, but took a sip and let me taste it from her lips. A strange way to sample a bouquet; her lips were as delicate as a rose petal. She touched my beard, so I buried my lips into her palm, and again I became intoxicated: this time by frankincense, by the memory of dreams reborn, and the topaz eyes that fixed themselves upon mine. Would I ever find my way out of this maze? Did I even want to? Are you Dulcinea? Only if you want me to be, she said. Now I sat on the haunches of Rocinante. Then you are Don Quijote, she said. I adjusted myself in the saddle, I backed up Rocinante, had him lower himself to one knee, rise up, then turn him around and I rode away as Dulcinea stood admiring the gallantry. I was as much Don Quijote as the Turkish stewardess was Dulcinea. Then I lost control of the steed when a dog, with the face of the silver-haired woman, began yelping. I regained control of Rocinante, lowered my lance to drive it through the cur, and only caught her leg. Why is there always something between me and happiness? I—

"Sir." There she was right in front of me. "You were dreaming—aloud," she said, as if not knowing the word nightmare.

"And using the most colorful language!" She blushed.

"I apologize for whatever I said. Could I trouble you for some tea?" I did not know what to say. It was the first thing I could think of. She disappeared. Then she returned with tea. After saying thank you, and while holding the cup, the plane had begun to rock, and the seatbelt sign came on. I had no chance to say anything to her. She went about admonishing everyone to buckle up. I looked up at the map on the monitor: 350 mph, 20,000 feet, wind 20 knots. We would be in the air at least three hours longer. I finished my tea, with the intention of finding Dulcinea—one way or another. I adjusted my pillow and lay on my left side—there was no one in either of the two seats to my left. There was no way of seeing the pooch. The chamomile tea relaxed me. I clutched the pillow as if it were Dulcinea's waist. I counted sheep backward by threes . . . 999, 996, 993,..., 866,..., 531,431, 3.14159, pi, pi r-squared, 4/3pi r-squared h, x squared divided a squared–y squared divided b squared equals 999 ... *I have something to show you. Dulcinea! Why do you keep calling me that? I'm Sedef Topkapi. All right. I'll play along. I like games. We walked through downtown Baton Rouge. Old Beauregard Town, but it was next to Spanish Town. They were now that close in Baton Rouge! One was a shantytown, neglected by years of inactivity. Why haven't they knocked these wooden shacks down? That's your job, Dr. Davila! But I need a demolition plan! Who's the architect for this project? You are! Here's your envelope! I opened it: crisp 100s! At least $14,000. I don't want any part of it! But Cathy, the project manager, said you have to or you'll be fired! Cathy's no architect! I don't think she even finished high school! Isn't she still turning tricks on Delpit Drive? That was ten years ago. Now she even has her own restaurant. Dinner is at eight. Look! I just want to be with you, Dulcinea, or Sedef. I don't care about Cathy or anybody else ... just you! Just me? What about Yolanda and Euridice and the blind secretary? You just take advantage of everything in a skirt! I'm only doing what my father did. He said variety was good! And it is! Oh! And Cathy said they'll be serving something you really like: pig's feet and hog maws. I don't eat that shit! And morcilla! And nutria, freshly killed! You know you want it. I don't eat that either! Look! Who put you up to this? You've got the wrong guy. So you don't really want me. I'm just another on the menu. Cathy said this would be your last job. Then you're off to Kazakhstan. That cur knows everything! Does she do counterintelligence or something? She sleeps with the boss now, so she has access—to everything. Look! To lay me, you'll have to follow instructions— to the letter. Well count me out! Wait, where did that dog come from, again? It's my pit bull, isn't she cute? I pulled out my lance and whacked off its hind legs! When I went for its head, Sedef reached down, and caught a blow in the ribs! But she didn't bleed. Only the dog! The flies were quick to swarm. I reached down for Sedef, and she was as light as a newspaper! It started to rain, and she melted away. Still I felt sad.*

"Sir," Sedef was back, alive. "What will you be having? Chicken or lamb?"

"Lamb, thanks."

I lowered my tray, automatically, recused from the nightmare of Cathy and memories better left forgotten. I had recovered and Sedef was there to serve me. I had to talk to her. But how? *Just write her a note, and take it from there. I'll ask her real name then.*

39

The response came with a smile in the form of a folded sheet of airline stationery, twenty minutes before we were to land.

> Dr. Davila,
>
> I am flattered you find my way attractive. We try our best to be courteous. I am, however, going to be married in three months. Where you are headed there will be many eligible women.
>
> Best regards,
> Gül

I had to smile, for all of the energy I had put myself through. Did I really think a woman like that would be sitting at home every night knitting sweaters? Not a chance! I decided at that point to plow into my work and not let any dark-haired beauties distract me. Or at least not until I saw Yolanda again.

We landed in Istanbul, where I remained on the plane. I had not spoken to anyone except Gül for more hours than I knew. It was morning there. The pilot announced the temperature—42 degrees Fahrenheit. It was March, but it was still winter. I was dressed for brutal cold that I would no doubt encounter at my next destination. I peered out the window and was struck by the minarets that dotted the cityscape. I wondered what the people there were like. Those who descended the plane gave no clue. They were orderly and quiet to the point of being eerie.

I stood up to stretch in the aisle, then helped a woman with luggage that was too high for her to reach.

There would be an hour more to wait before the plane took off again. People began boarding slowly. I found the crossword puzzle and busied myself, anticipating another long, silent flight.

12. down: C.D. was no monkey. Okay, Darwin.

37. across: Kathleen of opera: Battle.

9 across: The original spelling of Chicago: Chicageaux.

5 down: The next number in the series 5,8,13,...:twenty-one.

"Afedarsiniz," said the woman standing over me with a bag. I stood up to put it in the overhead bin. As I put the bag in the compartment she continued to speak, but I understood nothing of what she said. Her speech was laced with nervous laughter. I smiled and moved aside; she had the window seat, leaving one vacant between us.

She said something else, at which point I said, "Sorry, I don't speak your language."

"Oh, that was Turkish. I thought you were—"

"I'm from Panama. Roberto Davila."

"Sarah Takva. So you speak Spanish?"

"Yes. And you?"

"Actually, Turkish has some Spanish words: *playa, baño,* for example."

"I wasn't aware of that. I wonder why?"

"I think the Moors brought them with them when they were made to leave Spain."

"The Inquisition?"

"It proved good for us, because they sent away all their doctors and engineers as well."

"Imagine doing that today. If a poor country would have an influx of brain power, it could really change life for them."

"Unfortunately, some leaders would rather their people remain in the dark."

"And, unfortunately, I have never understood politics."

"It's not too hard to understand. Forward-thinking people threaten the power elite. And it doesn't matter your political inclination. Democratic, Labor, Islamist, Communist. Each persuasion has infighting that ultimately works to destroy it from within. There is almost no need for an opposition party."

"It's not so clear to me. If you could give an example?"

"Would you accept several?"

"Please," I said, for this strange woman had my interest.

"It is always easier to see the problems of another country, and not your own. That way no one accuses you of starting a revolution, or attacking the corruption that is evident to you, but not to the majority of the population."

"Do you remember Peter the Great?" I nodded, as would a child, not believing she might relate one of my favorite stories. "Well, he adopted a son who was an African slave that had been stolen from the Ottoman Empire. Now people will argue that he would have gotten better treatment under the Ottomans because they were Muslims, but the fact of the matter is he was a slave, and therefore, property. Now Peter saw that the boy was gifted and needed someone he could trust to bring knowledge from Europe to Russia. The slave became quite valuable to Peter; while in Europe, he learned several languages and earned a degree in structural

engineering. When Ibrahim—that was his name—
returned to Russia, he was repaid by being sent off to
build a fortification on the border with China."

"I fail to see the connection to politics," I said.

"And if I may ask, what is your field of interest?
Business?"

"Actually I studied civil engineering and later
mathematics."

"Then you have no doubt heard of Gottfreid Leibniz."

"Perhaps the true father of Calculus."

"Were you aware that Ibrahim and Leibniz sat
together to discuss mathematics, and that Leibniz thought
highly of the young man's views?"

"No. That's remarkable."

"His threat was so great to those who longed to be
closer to Peter the Great that those same people most
probably backed the need for Ibrahim to build a fortress
that would prevent China from invading Russia. At the
same time Ibrahim would be out of sight and far from the
seat of power in St. Petersburg. And who is to say Peter
himself didn't feel the tenuousness of his power with the
brilliant young man around?"

"What was the threat? He could not take power from
his adopted father. He might have been bestowed it
eventually, anyway."

"That would have been a leap of fairytale proportions.
You are not aware of the racial climate." She noticed that
I flinched. "If you don't acknowledge the racial
implications, you can surely acknowledge jealousy that
exists in every human heart. If Ibrahim is busy building
his fortress against foreign threats—real or imaginary—he
is no longer in the picture. If he is no longer in the picture,
interlopers can fill the czar's ear with lies that only
jealousy can feed."

I paused to digest the meal-sized history this
woman had begun to share. That history was very

old. I didn't see how it was relevant to present-day events.

"You don't look convinced. What about South Africa? There's an example in apartheid. Do you remember how the United States vilified South Africa for its racial inequities? Churches were still segregated at that time, and may still be. People say a lot of things about Islam, but integration has never been an issue, from the beginning of its practice. Why? Because the Prophet Mohamed—peace be with him—practiced what he preached, to use an American expression. This is not throwing stones at those with other beliefs, just an observation of history at large."

I had to admit I had never given these issues any thought, so I really felt inadequate to offer any more than questions. If nothing else this was an opportunity to learn.

"You see, the United States politicians could more easily see the faults in another country than face the ones of their own. Or better, they could point the finger, do you say, at others, as a diversionary tactic."

"This is practiced in sports as well. Everyone has heard of the great Michael Jordan. Once, when the coach threatened not to play Dennis Rodman, because of his antics perhaps, Michael Jordan said that if Dennis doesn't play, he doesn't either. Even the coach had to acknowledge the distraction Rodman provided, so that Jordan could dazzle the world with his prowess. And I don't have any particular affection for sports, just the lessons about human nature they provide."

After such a brilliant essay on history, I wondered what this woman did for a living. She seemed rather young to have acquired so much knowledge. Maybe a writer, I thought. "So what do you do?"

"I teach economics at Istanbul University."

"That's another area I know nothing about. I thought you were a writer, or history teacher."

"When you teach, you read a lot to stay current, to have something to stimulate the students. I have found that reading biographies and autobiographies stimulate the students to do the same—especially about sports figures. I don't understand the game of baseball, but I did find the biography of Elston Howard interesting. Do you know him?"

"Baseball, now that was my father's game! I only know that he played catcher for the New York Yankees."

"It is a lesson in fortitude. Not only did he have to fight racism from his manager, he experienced overwhelming obstacles just to play for the Yankees. He might have done better had he gone to another team, and this is the story written by his wife."

"That makes two illustrations from sports, and popular American ones at that!"

"Basketball is international, if baseball isn't. After reading Elston Howard, I told myself I would read more about the position of catcher. I read the biographies of several. See if you recognize any: Roy Campanella, Yogi Berra, Johnny Bench, John Roseboro, Manny Sanguillén, and Earl Battey."

"I find that amazing! I have heard of them, but do know that Sanguillén is from Panama."

"Well, I'm glad I read about him. He may have been the only one to play what we call football."

"I played it in my youth, but when I went to the United States as a youngster, I almost never played again. I wish I had, now. Did you play?"

"I suffered from emphysema, so I stayed inside most of my youth. Running was not something I could do. Reading I could, though. One year I read one hundred books. Now that's somebody with no social calendar!"

We laughed together. She ran her hand through her black mane, which grazed her shoulders. She had a dark complexion. She was the same complexion as Gül and the same height, about five-six. Now I wanted her to go all the way to Almaty with me. I hadn't known anyone from Turkey. I knew nothing of her culture, but she knew so much about mine. I couldn't get over her having known about those catchers—even Sanguillén! She said she didn't understand the game, but that had to be because she perhaps had never been to one.

"Have you ever been to a baseball game?"

"When I was in graduate school, I went to a quite a few games. Each time I sat near the backstop. That way I could see the entire field. What fascinates me is the social dynamics of the game: the tension on the pitcher to throw things that look like strikes, but are not; the threat of the base runner to steal; the batter's ability to direct a pitch to the opposite field."

"It sounds to me you do understand the game!"

"It is from afar. Maybe I would make a good scorekeeper."

"A statistician, with your background!" I said, being totally convinced that she could pull it off, and with the hint of Turkish in her accent, it would give baseball the international taste that it had acquired in Japan. "Could baseball fly in Turkey?"

"Fly?"

"I mean, could it become popular?" "I rather doubt it. Football is enough of a diversion. People are more concerned with having something to eat. The gray market thrives there. People find a way to help themselves when the government seems slow to respond. If prices are better in Iran, people cross the border."

"What are your students like?"

"Hardworking. They want to go to America to study. Those that do finish, often stay. They get married there and life goes on."

"Do they return?"

"When they can, but there are Turkish communities there, so the urge wanes."

Sarah looked away, into the clouds. I was no longer talking baseball. I had touched on a topic too sensitive, too soon. It reminded me of when I was a freshman. I remembered asking a tutor from Iran about her name. It was the name of one of Prophet Mohamed's wives. She, too, did not want to talk, not about her name but Iran. I understood the longing. Panama was always there to remind me: the guanabana tree in our backyard, the hammock slung between the two almond trees. I wondered if they were still there. That was so many sunsets ago. I just let it go, for Sarah was the talkative type, and we would find a suitable topic.

"So, are you interested in music?" I asked.

"You know, I have become interested in a musician named Jason Moran. Do you know him?"

"No. Tell me about him."

"He came to Istanbul recently and performed as the leader of a quartet, The Bandwagon. He is so accomplished. He plays piano. He played a piece by Brahms. But the most fascinating work was when he took a telephone conversation, and played a duet with the woman's voice!"

Sarah had rediscovered the animation that had left her only moments earlier. If I talked about Jason Moran, she might open up. Besides, she had not asked *me* any personal questions.

"Do you play anything?" she asked.

"I have a guitar. It has been my closest friend."

"Do you like jazz? Have you ever heard McCoy Tyner?"

"I only know that he played with John Coltrane, and that he was born in Philadelphia."

"I did a research paper when I was in high school about Americans that were also Muslims, and came across his name. I bought a cassette of his and that piqued my interest in jazz. I was just getting acquainted with American culture, and had no idea that I would one day do a doctorate at NYU. My roommate in undergraduate school added to my knowledge by taking me to a club in Manhattan: the Village Vanguard. Do you know it?"

"I have heard the name only. You know more American culture than I do!"

"Anyway, I started listening to several musicians after that experience. I was happy to find out that a Turkish family started Atlantic Records, and that they produced the works of Ray Charles, The Modern Jazz Quartet, Yusef Lateef, and you must have heard of Aretha Franklin? Well, when you explore the autobiographies of these musicians, you become aware of the economic struggles they faced. Quincy Jones talked about the financial difficulty of keeping a band together in Europe; Ornette Coleman wanted to know why he was paid so little, when the club in New York he played in was packed every night for a week!"

"What is the answer?"

She looked at me with a smile. "One of Coleman's titles is *What is the answer?* I would say the musician would have to have his own business, which means, he or she has to account for his costs, frugally."

We changed subjects.

"I'm going to Kazakhstan on business, and you?"

"I am looking to recruit students to come to Istanbul. There is a lot of interest in the history of our region. What about you?"

"My company is exploring mineral deposits there."

"Are you a geologist, too?"

"A mathematician, but one must eat."

"I would love to hear about your work."

"I like that idea."

The thought of sharing my work with Sarah was refreshing. My work involved churning out numbers; not the most exciting of endeavors, unless you loved it. Women have the ability to feign interest in something, if it takes them closer to their ultimate goal. Men are generally not willing to put in the time, if the goal isn't visible. I was an anomaly. I still chased the dream, because pursuit of the unknown was so rewarding.

"So where will you be staying?" she asked.

That's forward. In the Grand Almaty. Do you know it?"

"No, but there is excellent transportation. When we figure out schedules, they will be some free time." She hesitated a moment. "So are you married?"

"No, and you?"

"It was for a short time. I was very young."

"Excuse me, but you're not old!"

"How old am I?"

"How could I know, after what you just said?"

"Take a guess. I won't be offended"

"Unless I get it wrong, you mean."

"Exactly."

"I think age is overemphasized. I mean, Bertrand Russell was still mentally sharp in his eighties."

"And what about Eubie Blake?"

"I'm afraid I don't know him."

"I was married to a jazz musician, so I have learned a lot about them because of the music he had. Still, you haven't guessed it. My age, that is."

"Okay. I could be wrong, but you don't look a day over fifty. I am wrong, right?"

"Yes. I'm fifty-one!" Color rose to her cheeks. "No, I'm twenty-eight!"

"See, I told you I was wrong. I am no good at guessing age." I paused because this age discussion had.

Our conversation was leading nowhere I wanted to go. Better to ask about the black hand-knitted sweater she wore. "I love that sweater. Where did you find it?"

"My ex-mother-in-law knitted it. I can say our friendship has out-distanced the one with my ex-husband. Never fall in love with a saxophone player."

"I promise not to. How did you two meet?"

"Through my roommate and ex-sister-in-law. Are you sure you want to know?"

"Only if you want to tell."

"Remember when I mentioned I would frequent clubs? Well, he was playing at a small place in Manhattan on Spring Break. Students do a lot of drinking in clubs and otherwise. For a Muslim woman that was something I was at odds with, and didn't indulge, still the music was the attraction. I heard that Ahmad Jamal had a club in Chicago that failed because it didn't serve alcohol. Well, he played something called *Mysterioso* by Monk. It was beautiful. He told me later he selected it when he saw me come in with his sister. I had to believe that he did, because every time I was there he played that one. I liked it, too. The attention was new for me, being in a foreign country."

"What did your parents think of your husband?"

"They were not concerned that he was black, which would have been an issue as it had been with other college women who dated men of different ethnicities. What concerned my father was the fact that he was a musician. So I stretched the truth: I asked my ex once if would minor in pre-medicine, so he did. Then I told my mother that he was going to be a doctor. I didn't care, but that was enough to make them accept him. An artist does not have much status in my country. There are too many, and to feed a family, at least as my mother felt, would be a risk."

"So you divorced for economic reasons?"

"No. He wasn't ready to settle down. The phone rang a lot at night. I saw someone give him a card. It was a guy that gave it to him. The card was blue. I didn't give it a thought. I picked up his clothes from the cleaners once. The Chinese launder was so sorry for the ink stain in the pants. He had gotten all but a trace out. He gave me the blue card with the information still intact. Ink from the card had been the cause of the by now slight blotch. The card was of a woman's business: *Rita's Salon*. Since the address was not obliterated, only the handwritten portion, I looked it up. I made an appointment. I would have a haircut, if for no other reason than to glean information, if you will. I found her to be quite garrulous. Her skin was the color of gingerbread and though her face was thin, she had a figure that got increasingly large from her shoulders down. Not a great figure, unless you are looking for a pear-shaped woman. She had a derriere that would knock over things it was so wide. I don't know if I am being sarcastic, but it isn't my intention only to describe her."

"You've described a cow!"

"Have I? Well, maybe so. A cow with a pretty face, in all fairness." Sarah chuckled, as did I. She liked describing Rita. It was cathartic, probably.

"Well it was on my second visit there. As I sat waiting for my haircut—my hair was short at that time—I overheard the conversation between Rita and a patron:

"Yeah girl, he played for me last night."

"What did he play?"

"Well, he likes me to put on a white teddy. And he walks around me playing his saxophone until I am aroused!"

"I didn't stay to hear what else he did, because I had already figured out who was doing the playing. I had been serenaded the same way in our apartment."

"But you couldn't be one hundred percent sure without more information."

"Rita had provided the first part of the puzzle on my first visit: A promotional card in her mirror with his picture on it. I didn't want to find a third piece of evidence. I told him I was moving out. He didn't even put up a defense. Only a long silence, and an 'I'll help you move.' "

"I was speechless but relieved at the same time. It was only fifteen months, not fifteen years. So I'm twenty eight and single again!"

"So am I," I said, not letting her continue. "I've never been married."

"I wouldn't have guessed that."

"What would you have guessed?"

"That you had a wife and three children, though you might still have three children!"

"None of the above."

"You'll find the right one." She looked up at me, smiling. She switched to a serious look. Her dark eyes widened, then she motioned to Gül, who was walking in our direction. Sarah wanted the newspaper. When Gül returned, I pretended not to notice her as she passed the newspaper, but Sarah chose to touch the sleeve of my jacket, perhaps as a subtle way to establish a boundary.

That caused me to smile, which signaled that our conversations would continue. She perused the newspaper and asked if I wanted to watch a film.

"What's playing? Let's see," I said.

"What about *Spellbound*?"

"Put it on," I said. So she and I put on our monitors. We adjusted our headsets. I found it riveting: Gregory Peck opposite Ingrid Bergman. I could see the striking resemblance to her daughter Isabella Rossellini. My sister was crazy about Isabella, as was I: all those Lancôme commercials. A half hour into the movie Sarah had fallen asleep, and leaning on me. I couldn't tell my dark blue suit and her raven hair apart, nor did I want to. Was that frankincense, again? Talk about a dream come true! And what an arousal it gave me as Gül walked by. This time I did not pretend anything. Don Quijote had rescued Dulcinea, but this time on an iron horse. If my knowledge of the Ottoman Empire had been then what it would later become, I would have strolled the streets of Istanbul in my mind, and not the sometimes dusty and more often muddy roads I knew from my childhood in Colon, where I would run in shorts, where the oppressive humidity, and the sun that made everything grow, blanched our clothes and baked me brown. Where I was now all but holding her hand, I sailed on a cloud, nestled next to this Seraphim, mesmerized for this moment in paradise.

40

The announcement came to fasten our seatbelts. Sarah had only recently awakened and returned from the restroom, looking no less lovely than she had the entire trip. We exchanged hotel addresses and telephone numbers. I explained that a Dr. Armanova was my contact in Almaty; that she would meet me at the Gate 34 exit. We parted company as we went through different lines for foreign visitors with our passports in hand. After retrieving my bags I went outside. This city was dazzling with its space-age skyscrapers of glass and steel. So clean it was scary. I coursed through the gliding sidewalks to the exit, where people were meeting their intended contacts. I searched a green and orange logo that read "Borgi Solutions." I did not see anything green and orange—prominent colors enough, but nothing yet. Then I saw someone holding a sign. Dr. Roberto Davila, and my misgivings were allayed. The man who held the sign was robust and shorter than I, with Asiatic features.

"Dr. Davila?"

"Yes. Hello."

"I am Ismael, your driver."

He wore a heavy wool coat, with the Borgi logo on its breast pocket. As we walked to the car he was curious about the flight.

"In a word, long!" I said. He would never know the pleasure of Sarah's company. The company which I hoped to share again.

"You are, smiling, sir."

"It was long, I didn't say boring," I told him. He was content with that answer, and grabbed my bags and carried them to the van. No sooner did I hit the seat in the car, did the weight of the long trip make me feel as if I were wearing a lead suit.

"Where are from?"

"America."

The one-word answer seemed insufficient, judging by his glances through the rearview mirror.

"Were you born there?"

"Look, I was born in Panama. Do you know where that is?" I snapped before I realized the weight of my tone. It was too late, though. I was tired and that was evident, at least to me. I was not in the mood for inquiries, least of all from a driver. There was a pause long enough for him to find a radio station with music in English: Eddie Rabbitt's *You Can't Run From Love*. Still, I apologized for my curtness, and I took his smile to be satisfaction. Since my fatigue was shaken to life, I amused myself by the dazzling lights of this new city. It was after eight at night and the streets bustled with shoppers. We were moving quickly through the tree-filled boulevards the neon signs announced technology everywhere. This was no Third World republic. The oil revenues must have accounted for the space-age edifices of steel and glass so attractive even to my tired eyes, slits became widened by the sheer newness, of the iridescence which played against the black sky, and streaks of clouds which arched above us. Where were the poets to paint these shapes into words? What would Pablo Neruda or Jason Moran do in the presence of such splendor? The reflections of neon, halogen, and mercury against the buildings bore a luminescence of some new world. I was indeed an alien in a stranger sense than my passport prepared me to be. What was this juxtaposition of architectural periods?

Islamic against Eastern orthodox, modern against minimalist? I would soon enough be delving into mines where darkness would yet be a newer companion. Did they still use canaries?

41

We arrived at what had been described as a four-star hotel. It was bright to be sure, with mirrors in gilded frames of gold. The was a white marble staircase, which one couldn't help but pause in front of, and a large chandelier suspended above a serpentine sofa. There were two circular tables opposite each other in front of the sofa.

After I arrived at the reception desk, the driver announced that he would be back at eight in the morning. I took my door key: a card the size of a driver's license, and asked about room service. My options were to have a waiter bring a meal up to me, or to attend the festivities in the large hall. I, on second thought, told him I would retire, but would appreciate a wake call at six.

I took a shower that I was more than in need of, jumped into my flannel pajamas, and found comfort in the huge bed. The orange neon light outside shimmered against the gauze curtains like waves at crepuscule. I was liking this place before I had even seen much of it. I enjoyed being alone, as the down pillows invited me into a world of comfort and thoughts of Sarah's raven hair, the lavender scent, the palpitations of her heart, and when we would meet again.

We walked along Gulf Shores, Alabama. No, she said, she had never been there before. The cornmeal-colored sand caressed her feet, swallowing her ankles and mine as well. See the fish? she asked. The green as tea water and their translucence made them hard to discern. One school after another made it difficult.

When I did see them, the attraction she saw in them was apparent. Sarah held my hand and we caught sight of some jets moving swiftly toward us. They were high, but so high as not to frighten us. The piercing sound of the planes engulfed the atmosphere. As they whisked by I held her to me and kissed her as much out of fear as love. Until that time I was reluctant to display that much emotion. The fear of losing her overcame me as though I would never see her again. Who has never felt that emotion, cannot say he has loved. Who said "man is who he is in the dark"? This was daylight and I am not afraid to say I was scared. And those pelicans drifting above us, in the wake of those jets; white-gray winged bird, so majestically sailing, then moving away into the distance over the water. And suddenly one by one descending into the depths of the Gulf of Mexico. At each touchdown, I kissed Sarah's cheek. She looked up at me; the rose in her complexion was so radiant that the sun hid momentarily behind a cloud. No one was more proud than I. Maybe she was allowing the memory of a failed marriage to wash itself away as the immensity of the Gulf could do. It had certainly helped me forget agonies of the past. She broke away and I watched her allow the waves to rush in, as she stood sideways. She jumped with glee and I saw a new side of Sarah, a woman unintimidated by the present, happy in her own space. I found my camera. My lens caught her, splashing and jumping as the waves embraced her. They held her the way I longed to: lifting, then releasing, only to do the same again. If I had been near a guitar, I could have composed a song in her name. No matter, I would do it right there:

If the sun were to grant me a wish
To stand next to you in the afternoon light
And if it be enough for sand and starfish
For coral and amber and all things in motion
And all things still, for me it would be and forever will

*That you were, and are and will be as close as the mole
on my hand
As the sand where I walk and the shore where I stand*

*She swan back to me, buoyed by my attraction and her own
skillful strokes. Her hair now shimmered in the sun, which had
returned. A sun so brilliant could not have hidden for long. It
ruled the day, but I enjoyed playing its game of hide-and-seek.
We were as children in sun, dancing our paso doble to tunes we
improvised. Sarah swam away again. Her strokes found favor
with the helices of waves, blue then green. She became a swirl of
butterscotch on the surface white foam. Sarah was at one with
the sea as any young dolphin. Her blue and white bathing suit
might have made her invisible, were it not for her black mane.
Was Gustave-Garpard Coriolis so inspired to study Newton's
Laws of Motion by a body as lovely as Sarah's? If so, who could
blame him? Angular and instantaneous velocities with her body
in motion made science pure joy.*

*I could not see Sarah now, given the sun's glare. I put on
sunglasses and saw a speck, but was not certain. I squinted to no
avail. Where was my nymph? Had Neptune reclaimed her?*

I awoke to the startling sound of the telephone. It was
a relic: One of those dumbbell receivers that we had back
in Panama, *que pesaba mas que un matrimonio*—that
weighed more than a marriage, as my Father would say.

I got dressed in a gray suit and white shirt and sky blue
tie and black shoes. I took the stairs just for the exercise. I
found the dining room empty. The waiter escorted me to
a table and told me to feel free. I ordered two poached
eggs, toast and yogurt. I did not want to eat much,
because I was afraid jet lag was sure to hit me sometime
that day. I had spent a wonderful night with Sarah, or
was it a day? I could settle on wonderful, in any case.

I went back to my room for my attaché case, and went
down to the lobby to wait for Ismael to arrive. He came at
seven fifty-five. By eight we were on our way. It was a

beautiful morning. The sun shone on the glass high-rises full of reflections of the country's history. None of it was familiar to me, other than the people's faces, whose skewed reference was from Genghis Khan action films. That was hardly enough to give me anything other than a Hollywood view: cardboard stage props.

We arrived at another glass tower and took the elevator to the eighteenth floor. A smiling woman received me and took me to a reception room. She gave me a name tag, and I clipped it on. I walked over to where coffee was being served. I took a bowl of it, as it was served that way. It was my first time drinking it that way so I was careful, having only seen cups with handles in my life. It was black and strong. I found some clumps of sugar and dropped one in mine. I took a few sips, and I felt revived enough to tackle the meeting.

"Excuse me," said a gentleman who had walked up to me from behind. "I am Yousef Jameer. I saw you come in with our driver, Ismael. I am from Borgi Solutions. We have been waiting to meet a representative from Rougetec."

"I am that person." I smiled and shook his hand.

We exchanged the usual banter about the flight over—that he hoped it had not been too tiring—and said he had arranged a dinner engagement, and to not get too busy that day.

We walked into the meeting room, where we introduced ourselves.

"I would like to welcome everyone here today and to introduce you to some very aggressive thoughts on how to make yourselves some capital in the near and distant future."

That is how the meeting began. It was Dr. Yousef Jameer's introduction. A series of slides followed: First, the mines where both shale and lithium were found in different mountain ranges in the country. There seemed to be no end to the 12,000-square-kilometer area. The satellite overviews were done in excellent resolution. Someone had taken care to explain where we were in the world in relation to the ranges. Then profiles of how the mining was conducted that gave the depths to which the excavations occurred and geotechnical findings. Pie graphs and numerical analyses had been worked up, so I took particular interest. This took four hours with an hour break for lunch. Then individual investors presented their prospects, which included copious details of financial gains in the mineral market in general, and with lithium, in particular. Jameer must have been joking when he said earlier that I not get busy that day. It was seven o'clock when we adjourned the meeting. Fortunately, I'd had no appetite that day. It was everything I could do to concentrate on the details, even though the meeting had been recorded, and CDs provided at the end of the meeting.

I gathered my thoughts and wondered when my mind would completely fail me. The coffee was quite the stimulant, so I was happy for that.

"You will come with us now, Dr. Davila," Jameer said, looping his arm through mine. "This is our Khazh hospitality."

I could not say no. I wanted to experience their hospitality. Every hour was an adventure with piqued interest.

The restaurant was a completely catered affair. A very elaborate display of vegetables. There was lamb in various presentations. There was chicken glazed and roasted. A beef loaf. There was no fish, however, which I wanted. I stuck to the vegetables and tea. I waved off the meats of every variety. I wasn't in the mood to say yes to something I did not want. The meeting had been too long, so my indulgence limit had already been reached. My lack of appetite did not stop the others. The one fellow from Colorado, the only other American, helped himself to an assortment of desserts, and seemed corpulently happy.

We spent an hour there, and I was ready to retire. No such luck, but we were off to a private club. There were four of us in our group, counting the driver. Wherever we went, the driver sat apart with one of the workers in the establishment. The division of labor, and therefore privilege, was apparent.

We arrived at a low-lit bar, where women were entertaining men. They sat having drinks, and talking as the singer belted out his words. I did not need this. I had to find something to do. I could not go back out in the street. Maybe they had foosbal, or something. I walked around to where I saw a singer on television. Why was it even on? The guy was still singing his song. Then the next singer started, a little lower in volume; at least pleasant. "Do you like her?" asked a woman I could not see well in the darkness, just the red sleeveless dress, thigh-high. "She is our best vocalist."

"She's good. What is she singing?"

" 'The trees in spring are lovely, with a heart as lovely as the day, with a spirit as fresh as the morning. Like your heart.' I don't know if that makes sense in English."

"Oh, it makes sense."

"Yousef asked me to come over and talk to you. Do you like our country?"

"Love as the trees."

"Let's dance," she said, taking my hand before I could answer. There was the floor with lights in it: their version of a disco. There were more women in that place than men. The night was early, so by two o'clock, the ratio would be closer to two to one. It was at the time five to one.

"I never been to America."

"You speak like a native."

"I was in New Zealand once."

"One would never know you had not spent your life there." We continued dancing. *This was easy. Just relax and let her do the talking.*

She was pretty, as the light from somewhere allowed me to take in her Asian ancestry. She was about five foot three in heels, maybe one hundred and twenty-five pounds. I would know better if we danced close together. She wore her long hair in a ponytail. It was black the length of her back.

"So how many languages do you speak?"

"Four. You have to know a few if Kazakh is your first language. Chinese, Russian, and English. These days, everyone knows some English."

"You hear it everywhere; well, I haven't heard much here, maybe soon."

The music slowed, so she moved in close. It was automatic. I didn't intend to do anything. Hadn't I had the most amazing dream with Sarah, and here I was in the arms of someone else? *It's just a dance. Don't get carried away!*

"So do you work here?" I asked.

"No, I'm with Borgi, too. I'm Anna Amarova."

"Dr. Amarova, the geologist?"

"Yes, Anna. I feel silly. I should have introduced myself."

"I am the silly one. I didn't picture a geologist in here. Well, I mean, I'm here, but I would not have picked this place, or, rather, I would have picked a quieter one. Gee, it's not coming out right."

"Oh, it happens to me sometimes. Maybe it's the jet gag, or I mean, jet lag. See, it's happening to me!"

"You are one clever geologist!"

"No, you're the clever one. I have read you work on the best companies to invest in based on a five-year record."

"I had to put something together on short notice. Such a study is better with more data." The song ended so we found a table. "What will you have?"

"Oh, I don't drink. There are so many calories in alcohol, but don't let me stop you."

"If I have anything to drink, I'll drop right here."

"Better not to do it then. How was the meeting today?"

"Too many presentations, but I suppose we had no choice. Everyone is on a schedule. I have two weeks to see all I can."

"In a few days we will go to one of the sites where lithium is being mined."

"I am looking forward to that."

"Tomorrow you have the day off, as there are no meetings. Can you have lunch? I would like to show you around."

"If that's the case, I had better turn in soon. Otherwise I will oversleep. I can take you now, if you like."

"Oh, you're taking me?"

"If you want to leave now, I will."

We walked over to Yousef and said good night. He was talking to some women. They didn't look like geologists, but I had been wrong earlier. No, I am sure they were not.

Anna took me right back to the hotel.

"How did you find your first night?"

"I was so tired, I didn't even turn on the TV."

"I chose that one because it is my favorite."

"It was a great choice, thanks."

"Our only hope is that you will like our country."

"It is attractive."

"Until tomorrow," she said, extending a hand.

I checked in at the desk and asked for an eleven thirty wake-up call. I would have said four thirty, had I not wanted to see some of the city. I took my jacket shoes and tie, and dropped diagonally across the bed. There was no need to count sheep, because none were in the pasture.

42

I woke up and glanced at the luminous dial on my Rolex, the graduation gift my parents had given me. It read twenty minutes to three. I stumbled like someone stuporous. A pant leg was tangled. I had to pull it off, inside out, and left it on the carpet. The maid would get it.

There was a knock at the door.

"Hello," I called from the bed. I got up, found the robe, and walked to the door. I opened it.

"Sorry to disturb you, but we called, and no one answered. It is now eleven forty-five."

"Would you bring up some coffee and a croissant?"

"Coffee, Sir?"

"Please. Just leave it outside the door."

I closed the door, and dashed to the shower. The hot water ricocheted off the shower walls, and felt really good. The fresh towels were nice, too. I got dressed as if I were going to the mountains. It wouldn't be that day, but soon enough. I went to the door for the coffee. I poured a cup. There was some black bread; croissant was lost in the translation. It was going to be an easy day.

I went downstairs. The cleaning crews, women for the most part, were working assiduously to maintain the four-star rating. The mirrored walls and gleaming floors would no doubt be shown in the next photo-journal the hotel produced. I passed one woman in uniform whose smile revealed a gold tooth. In the States I only saw that in the

South, where some women were in the fashion of displaying gold, star-shaped caps around their teeth. And there were the rap stars who displayed their wealth with a mouthful of capped platinum: Their way of smiling back at the ghettos they owed so much to, for giving them the wealth of colorful stories that form their anthems and drug-lore.

Anna was at the reception desk, perhaps waiting to request a call to my room.

We left the hotel. It was snowing lightly as we went outside.

"It snows even in April?"

"It is just another form of precipitation," she said.

"A geologist sees the beauty in everything," I said, climbing into the car. "Good morning, Ismael." I had not thought I would see him. "So, where are we going?"

"The Botanical Garden. I hope you don't have allergies."

"I was born in Colon, Panama. I'm at home with plants and animals."

"What kinds of plants grow there?"

"It would be easier to tell the ones that don't grow! We have so many kinds of bananas, at least ten that I know of. And lemons and oranges of several types. I am looking forward to what grows here."

"I haven't been here in a few years so let's see."

Ismael kept his eyes on the road, while Anna and I watched the snow accumulate. Workers busied themselves clearing the sidewalks and streets. Crews swept and salted the streets in what seemed an efficient way. Schools were open, as I saw buses roll by and stop at various intervals to pick up students. We arrived at the Botanical Garden, where Ismael dropped us off.

Entering the garden, I was struck by the humidity. I loved it though: Panama Revisited. We went right into the tropical garden, where it was easily 90 degrees. Anna and I were already out of our coats. I took off my sweaters as well. Anna wore a green silk blouse and blue wool pants. I didn't know how long she would be able to stand the heat. We were both overdressed.

"Would you like to hang up your coat?" she asked.

"Yes," I said, so we both walked back to the coatroom. "So, how long have you been with Borgi?"

"Over one year. It is hard to find work as a geologist. It is not all fieldwork, as you might have guessed."

"Still, you are out of the cold. This climate must be severe."

"Oh, it is. But this is my country. I hope to make a contribution."

"In addition, you will make a nice income."

"That's another attraction: the stock options. Borgi has done quite well, and I am glad to be part of that."

"You are one of the leaders in the group of young companies I have looked at."

"So you have looked at the others, too."

"Yes, and Borgi is impressive!" I said, as we entered the Amazon, again. "Those bananas look ripe enough to eat."

"There are some ready to eat at the exit where there is a cafe. At least that is where they were last time."

We walked along and saw mango trees, lemon and miniature mandarin trees. Epiphytes grew everywhere, producing glorious orchids, white and pink. The air was fragrant with flowers and butterflies darted about. I closed my eyes to take in rich smells of citronella and guava, the peppermint and cantaloupe.

"Where are you?"

"Back at home again, with the red moth!"

"I have never seen a red moth before. Only the kind that eat your favorite sweater!"

"In Panama, there is plenty enough to eat, so your sweaters are safe. There are even plants that eat other plants, like the strangler fig: a tree that reaches for the sun, while it shocks the life out its host tree."

We sat on a bench, near the exit of the tropical garden. They served coffee there. It was appropriate, as the sign said Costa Rican Coffee. I motioned to the waiter with two fingers, and with my left hand to me and Anna.

He came back with two cups. And I looked up at the canopy.

"What are you looking at?"

"Not at. For. I am looking for sloths. They must be up there somewhere."

"What are they?"

"Slow-moving mammals. They are hard to see."

"Ah, *medved-goobach*!"

"What's that again?"

"*Medved-goobach*," she repeated in Russian. "I can't say I have ever seen one in real life. If they *are* here, they are well hidden."

"This is good coffee. I have never been to Costa Rican, but it is so close to us. This is as close as I can get to it for now," I added, taking another sip.

"We could use a few tropical days right now."

"So when you are on vacation, where do you go?"

"I visit my family in Astana. There is lots to do there. I like the cinema. Any kind of films, really."

"So you are not married?"

"No. And you?"

"No."

"That's all. Just no?"

"For now. That's all."

"Since my father died, I am satisfied to help my mother. I have a sister who is married, though. She and her husband live in Moscow. We see each other once a year."

"What do they do there?"

"He sells electronic devices: the latest gadgets people crave. What do you crave?"

"Oh, I crave a lasting relationship."

"So, are you working on it?"

"Yes."

"That's good. I'm working on it, too. I want another cup. How about you?"

She went over to the counter and ordered two cups. I didn't even have any Kazakh currency, although they probably would not have turned down dollars. We walked over to a table near a window and watched the snowflakes accumulate in the corners of the panes.

"If this keeps up we may have to postpone our visit to the mines. We won't be going down in any case," she said, toying with the rim of her cup. "I hope you can wait."

"I am on your timetable. I have enough to keep me busy."

"One thing is for sure: the snow will not stop anything here. We will get to the mines, eventually," she added.

I liked the certainty in her voice. The inevitability of the future trip. The snowfall would end and the sun would return.

"Did you ever see the film *Distant*? A Turkish film that takes place in Istanbul. No? It's a rather sad one. There is one snow scene after another. One younger brother comes to Istanbul in hopes of finding work and stays with his older brother there. The brother who has an apartment is very stingy with what he has, really not wanting the visitor around, completely alienating him. The older brother is a photographer, taking pictures of tiles in a mosque. The photographs are what these tiled walls remind me of."

"I will have to rent that film. Could I find it here?"

"I am sure you could. I'll look for it."

Once again I had found someone easy to talk to. There was no urgency in her voice, just the relaxed tone and the acceptance of the eventual.

"Would you like to see some more?"

I said yes, and we continued our tour. We entered an area that had bonsai trees. The miniature world transformed even the diminutive Anna into a giant. A boy held a kite some distance away that had gotten caught in the tree. The craftsmanship was so believable that the boy came to life, and at any moment he would spring up into the branches of the tree. The delicate branches leaned in one direction as if inclined due to a strong wind, one that we would soon feel ourselves in the mountains. I thought of how long ago that kite flying was a beautiful pastime. Our handmade kites, *cometas*, as we called them, graced the morning sky. Those carefree days were gone forever, only to be revisited that day in that way with my guide, Anna.

"We should be leaving. They will soon close."

She said that, but I felt she was in no hurry for our day to end.

"I have to call Ismael to pick us up."

We circumnavigated the Amazon basin, fraught with its strangler figs and Venus flytraps, walking where the temperatures were comfortable.

Ismael came and we climbed into the car.

"That was a nice introduction to Almaty. They really made walking through the garden like the real thing."

"There is much to see here. You just have to know where to look."

This was a woman who spent her youthful life looking at resultant climatic conditions, and as any geologist knew, she knew that the earth changed not in years, but in thousands of years.

"So do you have a particular period that interests you?"

"I like the Paleozoic period, when you see the emergence of anthropods and all sorts of reptiles. Plant life like the conifers appeared, too, so there is so much that I tend to go on about it."

"You will have to tell me more later on."

"We'll pick up where we left off next time."

Anna and I shook hands in the lobby, and she left. It was a pleasant day. I looked forward to a quiet dinner alone, and milling over some spreadsheets. As I walked up toward the elevator, the concierge called me.

"Dr. Davila!"

"Yes."

"I have a message for you."

43

I picked up the envelope, put it in my jacket pocket, and walked to the elevator. My coat still had snow on it and it was beginning to melt. The smell of garlic and baked apples saturated the air. Dinner would no doubt be an attraction.

I walked into my room and took off my wet coat. Then I remembered the envelope and dropped it onto the bed. I removed my shoes and sat down on the bed.

The envelope held a scent of lavender: of Sarah. I had not perceived it for the aromas of the food.

"I was in your hotel today. So I left you this. Give me a call."

Sarah

I was smiling like I had won the lottery, and in a sense I had. Yes, I wanted to see Sarah, and yes, she was a tremendous challenge to me with her knowledge of American history. What I saw was the opportunity to learn what more about African-American culture and its musical heritage I had glossed over. I remembered catching a ride home in graduate school with an African-American a few times, and because I didn't know any of the musicians on his cassettes, he had asked, "Are you black?!"

"Well, not like you," I answered, because I wasn't. I could have shared *cumbias, son montuno,* and *guaguanco* with him, which are just as African as his favorite Confuction romp—but he only knew one language, and I knew two! He knew the South, but he had never been to South America, where I could have shown him some of his cousins. I knew dances that he couldn't pronounce, but that did not change the fact that we would be taking the same final. The real killer, though, was when he asked me after the next class, "Who was that fine honey that came out of the townhouse when I dropped you off?" It gave me an incomparable exhilaration to say *Es mi amante,* without dignifying him with a translation. He did get to see her again at the graduation ceremony for our master's degrees, when we strolled hand in hand on LSU's campus. No one was prouder than I. Euridice had earned her MS in mechanical engineering. She had studied the braking system on maglev trains, while I had written mine on additives to asphalt used in paving. I had already been accepted into a PhD program at Cornell. Euridice was headed to Venezuela for what was supposed to be a short break before returning to the States. The festive time after graduation with nightly parties gave no hint to anyone but my mother—she was such a clairvoyant—that Euridice would not be back and that I should throw myself headlong into my studies.

I had to laugh that here I was again, this time on another continent, but still chasing the dark-haired beauties. I *was* consistent if nothing else, but what outcome was I after? Did I even think that far? I wasn't into keeping score: filling some quota. If nothing else, I had learned what my father told me was true: If a woman is interested in you, she'll find a way to let you know. I looked outside. The snow continued to fall, but the streets were passable. *How had Sarah gotten to my hotel?* She had found a way. I was certainly company for her in this hidden-away country. I wouldn't mind having her head on my chest—again. No, it was beyond not minding. It was something I wanted!

"Hello, Sarah?"

"Yes, Roberto? How are you?"

"I'm fine, thanks. How are things on your end?"

"Things are going well. I met with a group of students at a college today. They nearly all wanted to go to Istanbul. That was good news. They were so enthusiastic."

Sarah was glad I had called, given the energy in her voice. She had not shown that emotion on the plane.

"I was hoping to see you before it got too late," she said.

"It is easier for you to come here. I will pay for the taxi."

"I can be there in an hour. Is that okay?"

"I will be downstairs in the lobby."

I hung up. And took a shower. We would go out somewhere. Since I saw taxis earlier during the day, I knew we would find one to take us downtown. I wondered what the restaurant scene held for us.

I was nearly dressed when the telephone rang. *She can't be here already!* I decided to let it ring, and get the message when I went downstairs.

I went to the lobby and did not see Sarah. Had Anna returned? That might be awkward but easily explained away.

"You received a call from your sister. She said she would call back tomorrow."

That was odd to receive a call from her. If it were urgent she would have said to call Panama right away. I sat down and read The New York Times Sunday edition. It was only a week old. I put down the newspaper. I was not able to read the Russian journals, though I found the advertisements attractive: There was one of a woman draped in red satin pouring a bottle of sherry into a tall glass. A man in a tuxedo sat playing a guitar. It was a Spanish airline and travel promotion to the Balearic Islands. *Looks inviting!* I had never been to Spain. My teacher talked of it with reverence. I was certainly beyond the hero-worship of Cristóbal Colón. My own explorations of his intentions led me to an individual who wanted to set up his own kingdom in the New World. The monarchy in Spain had a special chamber waiting for him when he returned from his last voyage: a prison cell. That was a cruel thank you for his daring, but he had left plenty death in his wake. One of the most advanced civilizations the Western Hemisphere will ever know, the Mayan, was left decimated after Colón.

The photographs of the blue water splashed against my face, making me think differently as I watched the snow swirling outside. It had at least stopped snowing, and traffic was nevertheless snarled. *Where was Sarah?* I suddenly did not want to go anywhere, expect upstairs—and not alone. I looked around. There were people entering and leaving the lounge, some quite inebriated. *Wasn't this a Muslim country?* Sarah would have to explain that to me. I liked the idea that Sarah did not drink. I had dated my share of lushes. Cathy was a lush and in the love-for-sale business, though she made a veiled attempt to deny it. Was that the kind of thing a woman broadcasted? She was a lady, when it was convenient: a real chameleon with her reptilian eyes and slithering to the ground body! And I was not beneath crawling, either! The circumstances at the time drew me to her lair. I was so far from that now. Even the thought of seeing Sarah did not have me lusting. She was so much more than a physical stimulant. Had I not said earlier that I was not out to make conquests? It was true. I hoped she did not want to take me *directamente a la cuna!* Or, directly to the cradle, as we say in Panama. It just doesn't sound right in English. Well, maybe it does to native English speakers. I looked up and more hotel patrons poured into the lounge as the music volume increased and died with the opening and closing of the double-doors. A woman's red face told the story of what she had been doing that day. The man who held her at the waist gave balance to her light gait, less she stumble. Oh, too late. They both fell, and too soon for the hotel attendant to save either one. Their bed would be their only friend, if not sodium bicarbonate.

I studied another magazine photograph. The woman was promoting a washing machine. The opening was in the front: The glass circle in a square. I liked this geometry, but a friend in the States advised me never to buy one because they leak. I was more interested in the smartly dressed woman: a slender blond in a white blouse, gray skirt and black heels. She was on her way out, probably to work in an office. The scene was entirely white with no sign of clothing or water.

44

"Hi!" It was a surprising greeting. I was pulled away from the laundry room to the lobby, again. "Have you been waiting long?"

However long, it had escaped me. Sarah was standing there, but I hardly recognized her. Her hair was up and she was wearing a long red coat. A white and black silk scarf graced her face.

"You're really dressed up! And in this weather?"

"You look great, too! Are you ready?"

"I am ready to go. What do you have in mind?"

"There is a club I want you to see. It's not far. I think you will like. I asked the taxi driver to wait."

I was no longer interested in staying put. The idea of getting to see more of Almaty was what I wanted. My guide was familiar with the city. I followed the lilt of lavender into the taxi. Even the cold could do nothing to untangle the intrigue of the night air. We sat in the back seat as we had been only days earlier on Turkish Airlines. This time though, we were both awakened by the crispness of the air, and I by the mystery I thought might unfold.

"I hope you like dancing," she said with the enthusiasm of youth, her eyes brightening even in the dark light of the taxi.

I took advantage of the moment and grasped her gloved-hand without saying a word, and looking down at it, I studied the texture of the red leather that covered the soft hand my fingers hoped to know.

She spoke to the driver in Russian. I know because she ended the statement with *Porjalsta*, a word which meant "please" and which was the most frequently used, in my short experience.

"We are going to a place that may remind you of home in some respect or another. You will have to tell me. It is an international spot, so being a foreigner will only make you feel at home."

The pressing of Sarah's hand in mine communicated all I wanted to know. I was ready for whatever the night might hold. As we trudged through the streets, the tires churned the buttery snow, and pedestrians did the same without as much success. The traffic lights were the common denominator. They regulated the flow with the precision of a music conductor. Ahead of us we could see the snow-removal trucks pushing clear the mush that the day had left behind.

I felt the soft coat sleeve and remarked, "Cashmere," to which she looked at me with tilted head. She could do so much without a word spoken. I guessed that was how women were able to go so far in life. Their hair up, with some strands falling, earring loops in the evening light, the double crescent, crimson lips, the angle of her nose, all shadows of empires past and in a flash: Visigoths, Iberians, Seljuq, Ottomans, and yes, if our ancestors ever met, it might well have been on my Mother's side: Iberia. As for my Father, he had stronger ties to West Africa. There was *un tumbao, a* drum, in the corner of the living room—perhaps the quietest member of the family, but a member, nonetheless.

"You went out today?" she asked.

"Yes, to the botanical garden. I went to the tropical forest. I hoped to see a sloth, but didn't see one. There were lots of great plants, though."

"Like Venus fly traps?"

"Yes."

Sarah spoke to the driver quickly, and he made a right turn at the next corner. We were on Gogol Street, very close to the club. The cars were parked bumper to bumper. It was Thursday, and people were getting an early start on the weekend. There some nice vehicles, smaller than I was used to seeing: Russian models and almost all black. The driver stopped, Sarah paid the fare and I registered another charge that I owed someone.

We walked into the place Sarah had described. The band was playing a smooth bossa nova. There was a female vocalist standing out in front. She sounded like Elis Regina. Sarah looked at me as if to say *I told you, you would like it here!* We discarded our coats and worked our way to the dance floor. Lights swirled overhead and I was in a new world, devoid of the cold snowland we had left only moments earlier. We were in the tropics: a mixture of Panama and Brazil. Sarah was a fine dancer. She told me during the evening that she and friends would go to Harlem and clubs in Manhattan to see El Gran Combo and Tito Puente, and had even caught Ruben Blades! "Have you ever heard of him?" she asked. Was she kidding? That was my brother! This woman was abound with surprises. And could she dance! If I closed my eyes, I was in Colon, again. But why close my eyes and miss the spectacle! Couples moved like they were from New York, totally familiar with the rhythms. The percussionist played his instrument with the familiarity that convinced me of the universality of the drum. Had he come from a family of drummers? He was certainly adept. The saxophonist and pianist made the floor rock. The syncopation they produced put us in the Caribbean landscape. The swaying palmettos, the suspended mangos, the breadfruit clusters over our heads all bore witness that they were among us. The tropics were part of our fiber. The band moved from Panama to Colombia with their *salsa* to *cumbia;* from Colombia to Puerto Rico; From Puerto Rico to Venezuela, and ended with a bolero: *Dos Gardenias.* But I was holding one of the gardenias. And the gardenia held me, transfixed. With the lights low, my mind was free to wander. The Caribbean and Pacific splashed against with waves of sound. The saxophonist now played his flute, as the vocalist sang a wordless duet with him.

"So, what do you think?" she spoke between the bass quarter notes.

"About this place, or you?" I asked.

My own silence seemed sufficient for then. The dim blue lights, the quiet brushes of the drummer, the consorting of other couples showed that Sarah had done her research like a true historian. Like the writers long before us, James Baldwin and Orhan Pamuk, who had written about Istanbul, Sarah was showing me yet another world a little farther east, where I was getting a new orientation. Even though the music was familiar, the faces were not. I did feel comfortable. How fortunate I felt! I had no idea how frequently someone meets someone on a flight to a foreign country and is in her arms less than seventy-two hours after landing. I wanted to say that it is infrequent.

"You would have probably found this place on your own," she said, just after the music stopped.

"You give me too much credit. I am lost once I leave the hotel."

"You found the Botanical Garden."

"How about something wet?" I asked, not wanted to revisit the rainforest. "Maybe orange juice?"

"See if they have grenadine," she said.

I walked her to a table and went to the bar. After a few minutes, the bartender got to me. The band began to play a second slow song. A woman in line spoke to me. I said

Hola, and smiled. She seemed satisfied, though I am sure she didn't speak Spanish. It seemed the most natural thing to say, given the atmosphere. I didn't hear any Spanish being spoken around me. I told the bartender what I wanted and returned to the table.

"So what is your friend's name?"

"Sarah," I said looking away as I sipped my orange juice. "What?"

"So you know a Sarah from Turkey, and Kazakhstan?"

"Oh, I meant you!" I didn't catch the meaning of her statement until then and laughed. "You know, red becomes you," I said, complimenting her red dress. "I like the detail around the collar."

"Thank you. I made this."

"You are one body of work!"

"Why, thanks, I guess."

"No, I mean it!"

"Ooh, a samba!" she said, motioning that she wanted to dance.

We walked onto the floor. I didn't know what they were doing back in Baton Rouge, but they couldn't have been having this much fun. This song had emptied the chairs. The floor was at capacity. Sarah's skin was aglow, the richness of an olive when it is ripe. The crescent mouth had become full. My heart raced to catch up with my feet. The *pandeira* and *cuica* contributed to the carnival. No one was dancing on the tables, but the women were shaking for all they were worth! There were fewer men than women, and some took liberties to dance with us as well. Sarah did not say anything but I kept things in perspective. The other Sarah found her way to me, and not until then did I give the blond a second thought. I was only interested in Sarah. Anything else was merely exercise.

It was eleven thirty when we decided to leave. It took another half hour to catch a taxi. By twelve thirty we had arrived at her hotel.

"I had a great time," she said.

I walked her into a shadow and kissed her.

"Call me tomorrow," she said.

I climbed back into the taxi, with every intention of calling her. I rode home watching the swirling snow from the day looking for new places to rest. The tires made tracks until we arrived at my hotel. I entered and walked to the lobby desk. There was a message. It was from Yolanda. *"Olvidate de los tacos. Regresé a Milano. Hablamos! Tu Hermana."*

She had taken this sister stuff too far! Why was she going back to Italy? Was she going back to school? I was so abrupt. She would no doubt send another message before I left Almaty. In any case, I would not contact her. I was really trying to overcome my attraction to brainy woman with amber frames, but I was such an easy mark. Sarah did not wear glasses, but I had fallen for her. If a woman didn't wear glasses, if she were from the Mediterranean that was good enough. I guess I had my Mother to blame. I always had a penchant for the Iberian type: She sang those beautiful song in Catalan. She played those flamenco records of Carlos Montoya. What was left for me to do? And when I came to the United States did not my own Tio Carlos have a record by The Impressions, *Gypsy Woman*? There was nowhere for me to end up but shipwrecked in the Mediterranean! Better that than to be one of those from John Donne's *A Burnt Ship:*

> *Out of a fired ship, which by no way*
> *But drowning could be rescued from the flame,*
> *Some men leap'd forth, and ever as they came*
> *Near the foes' ships, did by their shot decay;*
> *So all were lost, which in the ship were found,*

They in the sea being burnt,
they in the burntship drown'd.

I had in the past either leaped from (the case of Cathy) or been shoved from (in the case of Euridice) a ship I had manned, but somehow found no way of saving my crew. True, they did not die; just the relations: another life lost at sea, like my paternal grandfather, Jorge Davila de Llorens, somewhere in the Gulf of Mexico.

With my head on a fresh pillow, I wondered what I would do to send this new ship against the shoals of some shore. I needed my sextant calibrated. And why did I all of a sudden feel lonely? Had I not just had the most exhilarating evening in recent history? No, that was an exaggeration. But there was no denying the isolation. I got up and walked to the terrace. The snow continued swirling, and was quite high on the ledge. The wind whispered through the seam it found in the window. The blue and green blinking neon lights skipped across the crystalline glass that now formed circular webs.

I threw on my pants and a sweater and bounded down the hallway to the elevator. I was hungry. No, I just didn't want to be alone. I went to the restaurant. That place was like New York. There were people laughing. They were Americans, No, they were speakers of English as a second language. I ordered soup. The waiter said he had stew, so I said okay. It would take my mind off of being alone. I had had a full day, was into the next. No, I didn't want to watch the sun come up. The stew would weigh me down enough to sleep. I pulled apart the black bread and dropped it into the bowl. I looked up and there was a football match. A game played earlier in Italy. There was no snow wherever they were. What? Milano! I suddenly had less interest in the outcome that when I first looked at it. I buried my head into the bowl and finished it. By the time I reached the elevator, sleep had hit me. That was all I needed for a good night's rest.

45

I walked back into my hotel room, feeling differently about Yolanda. Why should I be morose about her leading her own life? Wasn't I leading mine? It was silly to think otherwise. There was nothing, no indication that we would have anything more than good times together. Two free spirits! There was no permanency in life anyway, was there? So why this stapled-together attitude? I would call her back to wish her the best; she had worked hard and had only a few of the successes that were in store for her. She had been so much more mature than I. The radio had been on all day: Shostakovich, Rimsky-Korsakov and Rachmaninoff. I went to sleep, shortly after hitting the pillow.

I went downstairs right after getting dressed. The driver would not be there until 10 in the morning. It was a little after seven. In the hallway was a poster announcing a live performance of a string quartet. It was Ravel, that evening, and all I had to do was to find the location, and to see if Sarah were available. I seemed to want my nights filled in order to escape the desolation the snow engendered. The sky was light but there was no sun. The cloud cover took care of that.

I sat down and decided on poached eggs, salad, yogurt and coffee. By the time I returned to the front desk, I had decided to send Yolanda a telegram:

Congratulations on your determination to
return to Italy. It seemed sudden, but you
know better than I. Best always, Roberto

As I wrote those words, I realized how cool they were: as though we had only ever been friends. That is how relationships end. They begin with such fire. Steel turns white at 2200 degrees Fahrenheit. Whatever temperature we did attain, our steel still cooled and left me as brittle as pig iron, and Yolanda needed to follow a different star. I thought of my last weekend in that Baton Rouge restaurant on my own in Beauregard Town. I had continued to make conjectures with both Euridice and Yolanda women in mind, and how the distance away from all of us continued to change, irrespective of each other. It was beautiful when you could calculate the distance, if were able to follow the trajectory, but what happened when you could not? And what happens when the atmosphere is such that the flight changes or the projectile is re-energized in flight. Those variables were the ones that powered relationship: *Incalculable ones.*

I sent off the telegram, and never looked back.

* * *

The agenda of the day would cover a mapping of the terrain where the mines were located. One of the presenters gave a slide presentation of survey maps, circular elevation and depression which reminded me of the thousands of years past, when all was covered with vegetation, then flooding, now all that was left on the surface were ridges on gray and blue, red and orange, pink and purple. You could follow the course of the watermarks as the presenter did with a pointer.

"You see all these colors represent what lies beneath the surface, but only by mining can we be sure of the mineral content beneath."

He moved his pointer to alphanumeric locations where various elements had been excavated. Kazakhstan had some many important deposits; it was just a matter of getting the machinery to the location. First, the topography, then making a way from a town to the mining sites. A Turkish company which manufactured heavy equipment was present to meet the challenge. It had the most extensive resume for the daunting feat ahead. The company, Toprak Yıldız, laid out a preliminary plan of five years for the construction of two sites. They only needed the companies attending the meeting to come forth with the capital. Some were reluctant to lay out millions. Others were ready to leap into the venture, as was Borgi Solutions. They had been in several joint ventures, and wanted to remain the vanguard of mineral exploration. Rougetec had the financial wherewithal to come on board, especially when they would not bear the brunt of the financial burden. I was there to persuade them to continue their exploration of lithium, because that was my specific interest. The United States was going to need a reliable source for the next burgeoning industry: lithium battery-powered vehicles, when the exorbitance of buying petroleum from OPEC had priced them right out of the market. Rougetec saw itself as the point-guard in the first quarter of this game.

By three o'clock the meeting had ended. I had more than enough information on which direction Rougetec should take. I wanted to get back to the hotel and research a few things. On the way back I asked the driver to stop off at a money exchange location. I exchanged dollars for *tenges*. It was not a difficult monetary unit to handle. Afterward, I felt more in control of what I could do and where I could go. As odd as it may sound, I did not want to go anywhere. The weather had something to do with that. Once that changed, I would want to see more of the city. My guides had been the best company, and the time spent with Sarah was most appealing. She would be returning to Istanbul, a destination Yolanda had mentioned as a meeting place, but I had no idea if I would ever see that city. Sarah gave me a reason to want to, though.

I asked the driver to drop me off at a cafe four blocks from the hotel. I assured him that I would be fine, and that he did not have to return for me. He found it unusual that I would want to go to a cafe, when there was a nice one in the hotel. I had learned to dismiss his curiosity, and left him as he watched me enter the establishment. I was escorted to a table. The tables were oak; a lacquered finish that shone like glass. The floors had a parquet design, which made me think the place was one hundred years old. The walls were dressed with paintings of masters such as Fragonard, Utrillo, and Miro. While I had not been that close to Europe before my trip to that country, the surroundings put me in a French film complete with the aroma of espresso and some sort of sweet bread. I spotted some fruit pastries and decided I would try one.

I told the waiter I wanted espresso and a pear cake. I continued to gaze at the wainscoting which was simple but in keeping with the cafe. I opened my notebook and poured over the data I had begun to collect. I would have enough material to submit to a periodical when I returned to the States. With the proper presentation, Rougetec would have a place in the lithium center industry of battery-making materials.

The cake was a delight, and the espresso strong, to the extent that I ordered a second. I would be up late. I looked outside and liked what I saw: a few couples walking slowly, and I thought how I might be like them, if I saw Sarah when she was off. I liked the anonymity I felt there in Almaty. Why couldn't I feel anything but that? I knew no one, and my time was spent unfettered.

"How was everything?" asked a man whom I had seen behind the counter.

"Great, thank you." He may have noticed that I had a journal in English at the table, so he asked in English. More than likely, because I looked very different from anyone else, he could not go wrong, asking in English. *I will have to learn a few phrases in Russian.*

I packed up my affairs, paid, and left.

I took the cold walk home to the hotel, my hand stuffed into the corners of my wool coat. What they say about dark colors absorbing heat should have an asterisk next to it *except in Kazakhstan. I was dressed for the weather, but all I could do was lose heat! It was nearly five in the afternoon and the sun was obscured by the tall and sometimes ornate buildings. The sidewalks were clear of snow, but banks were along the sidewalks. My boots gave me the added assurance I would stay on my feet, as I took it easy going home. I passed something I had not stopped to look at in years: a toy shop display. My interest was drawn to the toys and gadgets I loved from childhood. I walked in and immediately found something I always wanted, but never had: a gyroscope. They sold a heavyweight paper in different colors, so I bought a pair of scissors because I had in mind that I would draw and cut out a series of edifices, the likes of which I had never seen, but I had dreamed I walked through: Translucent structures that the world would marvel over and that I was sure I could construct. In my youth the only thing that fascinated me was playing the guitar, which was all I wanted to do. But after I left Panama, the universe held together by six strings gave way to a broader range of sounds and ideas. Acoustics lead to a study of mathematics. Mathematics of vibrations and how buildings absorb sounds and are built to withstand some tremors. Countries like Chile and Turkey are always in the path of earthquakes. One of my undergraduate friends, Fahad from Yemen, said that the Qur'an has a chapter named *The Earthquake*, which he recited. I remembered only a part of it:

> *When the Earth is shaken to her utmost convulsion,*
> *And the Earth throws up Her burdens*
> *And man cries; "What is the matter with her?"*
> *On that day will she declare her tidings . . .*
> *Then shall anyone who has done an atom's weight of*
>   *good, see it.*
> *And anyone who has done an atom's weight of evil,*
>   *shall see it.*

Fahad recited so eloquently. Just the thought of that day generated in me enough heat to forget the weather. I wondered if Sarah knew that chapter. I could have played my guitar to it, but someone might find fault in it, as I was not Muslim, and even if I were it might not be allowed in their faith. It was not like Christians. Music was part of the religious ceremony. The fact that I had not gone to a religious ceremony made me pause. I had managed well, in spite of not being affiliated with any chapel. I was not given to harm anyone, which was good in any practice of faith, of which I was aware.

It was a leap from the nascent tremolos of the guitar, but there was a relationship that an engineer could appreciate and the beauty the equations could engage any probing mind. I left the store as happy as a child. These were things to get me thinking, and enjoy my stay, certainly after Sarah had returned to Istanbul.

My room was an unexpected sanctuary. The heat was the sweetest of comforts. I would have thought after those coffees, I would have been up for hours. The cold had sapped the edginess I anticipated out of me. I would eat in tonight. That lamb stew I saw on the menu posted on the wall sounded good. I made a call downstairs for room service in two hours. I set up the gyroscope and played with it, then put it aside. I would come back to it later. I was happy to watch the smooth turns.

I took out my paper, scissors and a ruler I had brought with me. I measured and cut the translucent paper. The sheets were tan, blue and yellow. I folded each sheet vertically, and drew lines on them, two centimeters apart. I folded the papers such that they stood as intersecting vertical towers. I had two small flashlights that I propped inside two of the towers. I turned out all of the lights. The doorbell rang. It was room service. My dinner lacked only one thing: a visit from Sarah. It was already eight o'clock.

Not tonight. I called her.

"I was just thinking about you," she said. The bubbles had not left her. "How was the meeting?"

"You know, I am getting the hang of things. I am ready for my visit to the mines."

"I had a good day, too. I think the students just want leave this place. But some, yes, they only want to go to Turkey."

"I was thinking about going out again tomorrow night."

"Tomorrow is fine with me. Should I come to your place again?"

"Why not? How is nine o'clock?"

"Nine o'clock it is. See you then."

I said good-night and went back to my buildings. I was really pleased. I wanted to add something else, but couldn't think of what. I would construct two more buildings, gray and white, respectively. I was running out of room on the table. Still, the room looked better, now that it had my signature. I turned out the lights, allowing only the ambient street illumination. That was the realism it lacked. *And what about suspending them from the ceiling?* I would take them down before I left. Sarah might want one. I would certainly give them to her if she liked. I had seen a building by Calatrava in the shape of the human spine. I would attempt one of those. Just twist the rectangular cube into a rhombus cube, I said. I might have something new. I was not Calatrava, just Calatravaesque! Man, this modeling was fun! I needed some glue. Perhaps they had some at the front desk. I went down stairs. I passed the some rosy-cheeked couple from days earlier, stumbling from the bar. *Very spirited.*

They had glue, but what I needed was a glue stick, or rubber cement would have been even better. The man at the desk told me where I could find what I needed, but it was too late. I told I needed a taxi for tomorrow. I had the day free. They opened at 10 in the morning. I liked it when he said *"Korashow,"* as I left. I took it to mean thank you. I would have to get my hands on a Russian book, I reminded myself. I turned around and asked if I could have one of the magazines. He said "Whatever you like."

Then I surprised myself by saying *"Korashow,"* and he answered, *"Spaciba!"* Now I was armed with three Russian words. I could not remember how to say sloth.

I returned to my room, with the magazine that contained the woman selling the washing machine. She would be the backbone of the twisted spine edifice. She would be locked inside the structure. A permanent exhibit that only I would have seen.

I measured and cut, then layered the woman inside the opaque white sheet. I formed my rhomboid, which when you looked down into it, appeared like a series of offset parallelograms. It had potential in an architect's hands. I had the entire next day to explore the possibilities. I lay the pieces on the table and took a shower.

I dressed for bed and put on the radio. I had grown accustomed to the Russian pop singers. They sang as I counted sheep.

I woke up at six in the morning. The morning light was dim, but the streetlights were still on, perhaps because of the fog. My own cityscape was active. My chambermaid was busy doing laundry under the prevailing light. I would make a park. One of the buildings would serve as a parking lot. This was going to be Almaty Plaza.

I walked to the window. Sweepers were pushing the slush down the street. The streets were very clean, though a barrier of gray snow and black speckled the surface of the snow which at the same time separated the street from the sidewalk. I looked out into the morning and watched the dancing fog that was already dissipating. I got dressed to go out and find the art supply store.

I found the breakfast tables all but empty. Some men dressed in suits occupied tables, full of fruits and jams, eggs and sausages. I was in the mood for nothing heavy. I found a table some distance away from the conversation in Russian and intermittent laughter.

When the waiter came by we exchanged good mornings and I asked for coffee, yogurt, and toast with halves of quince, the most wonderful fruit of which I could not get enough.

After eating, I bundled up in a scarf and hat. I had on the sole wool sweater and my wool jacket. I would be looking for a pair of gloves which I had neglected to buy before leaving Baton Rouge. I would have had difficulty finding any there, since they start to sell summer clothes in February.

The fog had lifted completely, though the sky was still overcast. I had walked two blocks in a new direction. Children walked by, their schoolbags loaded down; their faces without much expression until they noticed me.

Eyes full of curiosity, but lips not moving, I wondered if they found my blue and white Peruvian wool cap and scarf, as intriguing as my face and height. In any case, I was different and new it seemed. I passed two teenage girls who nudged one another and smiled. I engendered chuckles from them. I came upon a store that sold hand-knitted woolens, which was what I was after.

"*Dubre ultra.*"

"Good morning. Sorry, But I don't speak Russian."

"Thank you is what I just said!" said the woman, showing a smile that displayed a silver tooth.

"Well, there is hope for me yet. If I am going to survive here, I will need more than just gloves."

"Where are you from? America?"

"You are the first to guess that right. I'm from Panama."

"We have more snow than Panama?"

"We have none! But if you want sun, we have enough to share."

"My daughter did a report on Costa Rica last year," she said, taking the opportunity to extend a hand of friendship. "You need gloves, yes!"

"That's why I am here."

We shared a light moment and walked around the store, passing hand-knitted sweaters and scarves, muffs, and hats. If Yolanda had still been in Montreal, I would have gotten her a sweater, but we were a thing of the past. Maybe Sarah?

"I have just made some tea. Please," she said, asking me to have a seat. Another woman appeared from behind some shutters. She did not say anything, just walked to wherever she was going. The first woman said something to her. The second, younger, perhaps half the age of the first, greeted me in Russian: the good-morning greeting I had only just heard.

"This is Fatma, my oldest daughter."

"Lovely morning," I said and, to myself, *Sauvecito, mi hijo!* I was going to have to take it easy.

"Fatma knows only a little English."

I succumbed to the urge after only four seconds. "Please forgive me, but she is lovely in any language."

A quick translation elicited a smile of uncommon beauty and teeth of orthodontist perfection.

I finished my tea, thanking them, and refused a second cup. I wanted to look at the gloves. Why was I in Almaty?

I was Kazakhstan to visit the mines.

"Geologist," ventured Fatma.

"Very close, civil engineer." That was closer than mathematician. She had already gotten her one hundred. There was no room for anything less. "You have some many nice things here," I said, finding a brown pair that matched my coat. "Do you have any sweaters my size?"

"We knit to order, Mr.—?"

"Davila."

This time Fatma shook my hand. I wanted to put it in my pocket.

"How long will you be in Kazakhstan?"

"Three weeks. Could you knit a sweater in that amount of time?"

"One week is all we need," the mother said.

"May I take your measurements?" Fatma asked.

"Of course," I said, removing my coat and then my sweater.

Fatma was about five-three and stood on a stool to meet me almost eye to eye. Her green eyes met mine and I wanted this temptation that the mother had orchestrated to be over. Well, maybe not right away.

"This is a nice shirt. Handmade, yes?"

Fatma was pulling out all the phrases from English 101 and 102. "Yes, I hands that make."

Fatma held the tape around my chest momentarily. "These hands make sweaters."

"And scarves?"

"And everything you like," she said.

"And everything likes you." I noticed that Mother had disappeared.

"Are you here alone?"

"Yes. Maybe we can see each other again, after the sweater is finished."

"I would like to do that. Where are you staying?"

"The Grand Almaty."

"Very expensive, yes?"

"Yes," I answered as she draped the tape around my waist. She slid the tape around my hips, her slender fingers flattened the tape and smoothed it around my derriere without apology. She wrote down the last measurements.

"Do you have a style in mind?"

"Yes. I will need paper to draw it." I watched for her walk away in her long green wool skirt, her own rear end held firmly in place by the fabric, her exquisite frame of size seven or eight. She was as graceful as Nadia Comaneci.

She returned as quietly as she had disappeared. A vapor is no less inconspicuous.

"You draw well. But you are an engineer."

"Do you have a brown with a rust in it?"

"Come back later today, and we will have it."

"May I make the pay arrangements now?"

"Make the deposit and the rest when you return, okay?"

I made the deposit, paid for the wool gloves, and promised to return in four hours. I would have to find that art supply store, and purchase that rubber cement, but I had fallen in love again. Fatma was an unexpected discovery. I had never seen a woman with such a combination of Asian looks. *Well, welcome to Kazakhstan!*

I left the knitting shop, with every intention of returning later. I walked, feeling better than when I entered for a couple of reasons. The gloves were especially nice, and Fatma was nicer. I did not see anything developing, though. She was making a sale, and I knew less about her than I did Sarah. I had made enough bad choices in life based on looks. But I was running out of choices, I told myself. There was no perfect woman, as there was no perfect man. Women made the choices anyway! We just went along with them. At least, that was how it seemed to me. I took an inventory. Yolanda was on my mind. She had it all, but she had pursued her dreams in Milano. *There had to be a guy in the picture.* She wasn't exactly the ugliest woman in the world, and she was possibly the brightest. I had always had a weakness for a woman in glasses, however silly that sounds. Those amber frames of hers made my knees weak. And being what women found handsome made me wonder how helpful that was. You had to keep finding excuses to stay focused on your goals. I walked past the art supply store before I realized it, and had to turn around.

I entered into another empty establishment. It was still early. It was small, but that did not matter, as long as they had rubber cement. I looked around, found some different paper, with a gloss. I found the cement, tacks and string, and walked to the counter and paid the female cashier. She was doing inventory, so there was no idle chatter.

I retraced the same path I had taken to get to the supply store. As I passed the knitting shop I glanced in the window to look at Fatma again. Her mother was at the window, smiling. I returned the gesture, waving my newly gloved hand, and walked on.

I arrived at the hotel with the zest of continuing my little project. I scurried up the stairs, not waiting for the elevator. The cleaners had just finished making the bed, as I passed one of the women in the corridor.

I laid out the new colors, dark against light, translucent against opaque. This would look better on the inside. This was really fun. With my stylus I cut rectangles where I had drawn on both inner and outer sheets. I offset the sheets and it gave a three-dimensional effect. This was turning into a fine endeavor.

I cut out models half the size of the original ones. I became enamored of the rhomboid shape and found myself with more models of that than any other. I cut some ellipses to use as ties to stabilize the buildings and add a feature of curiosity and color. They would articulate a signature of my own. When I reached for the rubber cement, I noticed the time. It was after four, so I decided to stop and go back to the knitting shop. I did not really want to break my rhythm, but knew that I would continue the following evening. The day would be occupied with meeting a mining company representative.

Fatma was still in the shop. She had a large set of wooden needles, and wore glasses as she worked.

"Hello again, Mr. Davila. I have what I think you will like." I followed her to where the new yarns were. They were in a woven basket on the floor.

"This is going to be hard, with so many beautiful colors."

"Maybe one sweater will not be enough."

"What about these two colors?" I said, holding up a brown with rust yarn, and a gray one.

"It will be ready in three days."

"You are fast!"

"You are a special customer." She took the yarns and made some notes.

"Here is my card." I handed one with the number of the hotel printed on it.

"Dr. Roberto Davila. I did not know."

"Roberto. It's fine. I would talk, but I want to wear the sweater in three days."

"Should I call you when it is ready?"

"Yes. I'll wait to hear from you."

I left very pleased to know the sweater would be completed so soon. I thought it would take five days, given my experience with dates falling through. In this culture the importance of keeping one's word might be paramount. I only hoped so.

The sun had set and the temperature had dropped. It was not at the freezing point, so it was bearable. The thick layer on my hands made a tremendous difference. The wool socks on my feet were another plus. I thought to have Fatma make me some socks. I was liking this cold place. Too bad I would not be there when spring really came around. I had noticed some buds on the walnut trees I passed. Spring was inevitable, and I would ask Fatma to send me some photographs of the trees. I would give her one of my buildings; or one of the suspended bridges I was considering constructing, if I could find a model shop.

I was using every ruse of avoidance not to face the evening with Sarah. Why did I think it was going to be a disaster? Didn't she agree to meet me? We had nothing to lose. She was going back to Istanbul, and I to Baton Rouge. Just take her out, kiss her good-night. I got back to those numerical analyses. *I had better get into the shower, if I were going to be ready when Sarah came.* My hands were full of cement, which fortunately came off easier than white paste. I was feeling like an Italian meal, so my goal was to find a restaurant that served pasta dishes.

I called the front desk and asked about Italian restaurants. The concierge suggested several, so I chose one of the closest to the hotel. I arranged my models, and cleared my workstation. I was proud of what I had put together. It was going to be back to work. I was scheduled to meet the mining representative at noon, so I was not pressed for an early morning. I didn't know how early Sarah had to be wherever she had to go, if anywhere. I left my room and went downstairs to meet Sarah.

She had already arrived! She was as beautiful as the dream of I had of her at the beach. Her coat was open, and she wore a sea-green dress. Where did she get that figure? Did she eat at all?! The stocking really contrasted perfectly with the dress, or was it that I could find no wrong with her because I wanted to be with her so? In those shoes she reached my eyes. If we did not get out of the hotel, I would be looking for room service menus!

"You just outdo yourself!"

"You set a high standard, but I am glad you like this old dress."

Sarah had to be kidding! How old could it be? Just a figure of speech, I thought. She wore her hair in a ponytail, with some that fell unmanageably into her face. As we walked outside, the breeze blew her fragrance of sandalwood into my nostrils and I grasped her hand for dear life.

"Are you all right?"

"It's the night air."

"It is brisk!" she said, pulling me to the taxi I had hailed.

This city abounded with taxis and vans, so to find one was not like other places I had been.

"Z----- Street and Trotsky!"

"You know your way around! Impressive!"

"I've been watching you," she said, leaning in close, so no heat would be lost between us.

"I didn't even ask, but I hope you like Italian!"

"I love it!"

"It's a new place, they told me."

In twenty minutes we were there. A small group of people left the restaurant and brought with them the lilt of garlic and parmesan so familiar to my olfactory glands. I was in Venice without having to leave this winterland. We walked into the dining area, where we heard the music of two violinists. They played so beautifully I was transformed. Sarah looked at me with approval, and happy with the recommendation the concierge had made. The decor put us in Venice to be sure: Paintings of striped-shirted gondola drivers navigating the canal, waves cascading against the walls of the city, created a setting for poets and *chianti*.

We sat down a table adorned with a white tablecloth and pink carnations in a vase.

"I hear this place in new," I told Sarah.

"I can still smell the wood. Maybe cedar. Look at that fireplace."

"And that mantle, my! It really adds a touch."

The waiter walked over to give us our menus. I asked if he would bring a bottle of sparkling water.

"I am famished. What about you?"

"I am looking forward to some kind of fish."

"They must have some pasta in tomato sauce. That would really please me."

"I see what I'd like. Pasta with fish in white cream sauce. And how was your day?"

"Fine. I picked up some art supplies. I started a little project I'm happy with."

"Really. What?"

"I'm constructing models of buildings."

"I hope to see them. I'd like to see something you've made with your hands."

"Look at the callouses," I said extending my left hand.

"Mmmm, the hand of a hard worker," she said, running her fingernails across it, while holding it. She seized the opportunity I had given her to hold it. We were exchanging heat, and I liked it.

We made our orders and resumed holding hands. "I have to make these minutes count. Time is passing too quickly," I said.

"And you'll soon have to rush back to your loved ones."

"I don't have any."

"No, that's my line."

"It's a parallel line," I said.

The violinists had found their way to our table. We were characters in a film, *The Venetians*. The Latin American meets the Turk, watching the embers that evening in Kazakhstan. Is she as free as he hopes she is? Is he as free as he thinks he is? Will they keep the fire burning? The song was unfamiliar, but the emotions were not. The musicians moved on to another table, and our dinner arrived.

We exchanged nothing but glances as we ate, as if words were unnecessary.

I was half-finished when I finally asked, "Do you want to take this somewhere?"

"Do you? I'm already there."

She was devouring me with her eyes. I was the willing sacrifice, but my poison stinger was still intact. Would she devour that, too? If she did, we would be one. One hands danced and she scrawled with her nail on my palm: I AM U.

I motioned for the waiter to bring the check. We did not finish our meal. The stray dogs would be happy when they rummaged through the trash. They would not die of hunger that night.

We got back to my hotel. The female at the desk smiled approvingly at us, as we passed her to the elevator. We kissed each other quickly on the elevator, paying no attention to the single woman in there with us. We all got off on the same floor. I held Sarah's hand as we walked to my room. I passed the key across the magnetic lock, and we were in.

The flashlight in the first building I made was on.

"Look at that! You're something else!"

"Do you like it?"

"It's so clever. I love it," she said burying her nose in my neck. I don't know if she looked at the others I had made: if she noticed the ellipses, the rhomboids, the German woman standing at the washing machine in the tallest building, or the parallel lines on the parking lot. I do know that I helped her with the bottoms on her green dress, the hook on her satin brassiere, myself to the lavender scent which my nostrils remembered all too well from the plane ride. This time, when we touched down, we were far from the baggage that keeps us apart: continents, passports, visas, language, culture and every other divisive concertina-wired wall that keeps two people apart.

I held her, tasting every curve on her body, every soft shadow on her neck. If she quivered, I caressed it again. From moment to moment, like a series of snapshots, like a string of pearls that told a story where one could not distinguish the end from the beginning. Sarah walked me backward to the window. The light from the sign across the street was what she was after.

"I wish you could see what I see," she said.

It meant so much to me. No one had given me that much attention since Cathy, when she ran her finger through my hair. I was a novelty to her. Euridice was the one I fell for. Yolanda filled a void that I had not cared if it were filled or not. If Sarah were like the others, she had yet to show it. Where she touched me made me tremble. I stood behind her so that the light, first blue, then purple, then yellow, then red, flashed against her olive skin. I held her breasts as best I could. Their wealth exceeded my capacity. Her hair now hung to her shoulders as it had when we first met. In the ambient light we were the same: nude adventurers. What Colón had not discovered in the New World, I would discover in Anatolia.

We walked over to the cityscape I had begun. She explored the miniature city, which she said reminded her of a model city someone had built in Istanbul. I was more interested in the mountain range and valleys surrounding the city. These mountains were soft to touch and I wanted to climb them. My guide was prepared to take me on an expedition. I would not need a backpack; just a willingness to follow. And Sarah took me deep into Cappadocia.

Can you see those white caps in the distance, through the clouds? They're immense! I know they're The Alps. From Turkey you can see them? Of course! Aren't they gorgeous? Not as gorgeous as you! Stay focused. Could I have some more of that pistachio ice cream? If you promise not to eat it all. I promise. That's all right. You can have all you want. I'm going to make some more just for you, because you like it so much. You're the best guide ever! And you're such a cooperative student. See that green water over there? Yes. That's the Euphrates. You mean where they say Adam and Eve . . . ? That's right. Can I have some more ice cream? You're going to get fat. I can work it off. Can I help? You took the words out of my mouth!

"What ice cream?" Sarah asked.

I had drifted off. Sarah had tied a tourniquet around my waist. The expedition had gotten dangerous, but I did not want to stop. Sarah and I snuggled to the light in the window as if we were watching a movie, or better yet, the screenplay we started several hours earlier at the restaurant. There was no need for seconds. We did our own stunts.

"I could stay like this," she said.

"Forever?"

"And a day."

I saw every reason to make that a reality. Things were so easy when you were in bed: equilibrium, where the sum of all forces are at rest.

"How many more days for you?" she asked, running her fingers through my chest hair.

"Fourteen."

"Why don't you cut it short and come to Istanbul?"

"I'll see if I can. If there are no snags with the mining company. I'll start working on it."

"It would be great. As it is, I only have four more days here." Her voice fell into the blanket, along with the weight those words carried.

"I'll work it out that I can pick up some books from a contractor. I just have to find an engineer who has written on lithium mining, and see if it is available in translation. If I can talk to him, even better."

"You're so resourceful."

"Maybe you can look too, since I don't speak Turkish."

Sarah seemed relieved. Her sporadic grips subsided. Her kisses on my chest continued.

"What are you going to do with those models?"

"I was hoping you would take one."

"I'd like that; having a piece of you. A building I may one day walk into. Yes, I like that. Have you ever done a building?"

"No, just models in school. I have done steel drawings, though. Without steel the building won't stand."

"So you have done them then. I would have said yes."

"A qualified yes."

"Do you know any architects?"

"Sure."

"Your heart began to race!"

"It did, didn't it?!"

"Architecture is another love of yours?"

"Absolutely."

"You're a marvel!"

"That's a lot to live up to."

"Well, it's true."

After saying that, Sarah couldn't get close enough to me. She slid over me to the other side of the bed, but concentrated on my back. Her hands went to work. No, not work—play! Where she found the stamina, I couldn't say. All I know is I was the luckiest man the world. I was ready to shout it, but I didn't want to get ejected from the hotel. The down-filled pillow kept my screams muffled. I pulled Sarah up to me again.

"I'm not through with you, by any means."

Was it Round Three or Four? I couldn't be sure. I was still standing and I hoped to still be, after Round Twelve. I was no Roberto Duran. *No más* was not in my vocabulary.

Sarah played my chest hairs like harp strings. I was the most well-tuned instrument in the orchestra. I took another sniff of lavender to revive me. My tongue and her neck were one. My tongue found an earlobe, then the ear, where it explored the cavern. I am not ashamed to say she moaned, and shed a tear upon my lips, at which point I stopped, as much out of gratitude as surprise. I took her breasts and kissed them alternately. We were one once more.

* * *

I came out of the shower to find her caressing two large pillows between her arms and legs. I started dressing, then decided to wake her.

"It's ten after eight. I don't want you to miss any appointments. I have a new toothbrush in the bathroom beside the bowl."

"You think of everything."

"The breakfast here is good. Nice variety. I saw salmon on the menu."

"Are you rushing me away?"

"You can stay as long as you like. I have my meeting at twelve," I said. "I wish I had a camera."

"Wait until I get dressed."

"There would be no point. I just want to capture your feet and legs in the morning light."

"In that case, there is one in my pocketbook," she said, motioning to where she thought she left it. "Oh, over there."

I reached it to her. She took out a flat red Nikon and passed it to me. I adjusted the curtains where we had stood in the neon light. Now the glorious sun shone on what she allowed exposure.

I took nine shots, hoping for the best. She wore pink toenail polish. It was spring, so I was interested to see her body in the summer: in a bathing suit, the color of that dress she wore.

"I'll get them developed before I leave. We'll have to take some more downstairs," she added.

Sarah walked to the bathroom as if used to being nude. She closed the door, and I continued getting dressed. I then walked over to the window. The snow had completely disappeared from the street. The sidewalks held on tenaciously, bonded to the ice.

I wore a white shirt, the green tie I had last worn in the downpour in Baton Rouge and a blue wool suit. In that unpredictable weather, I was not inclined to dress formally. The dress for Kazakhs, as I had noticed, were turtlenecks, shirts without ties. Since I represented my firm, I kept with American protocol.

I put the suit that I wanted cleaned and several shirts that I wanted washed in the laundry bag the hotel provided, and hung the bag on the back of the chair next to the desk. Sarah and I took the elevator down to the lobby. The attendant who had suggested the Italian restaurant was on duty. He smiled as we walked by. I escorted Sarah to a table, then returned to the front desk. "Good morning."

"Good morning. Are there any messages for me?"

He went to my mailbox. "You have three."

Each was in an envelope. Rougetec wanted an update. Reasonable. I had not called them, so I would as soon as I returned from the mines. Yolanda. She was working with a friend who had found her a job in Milano—a woman. A surprise. The third was from Lillian. What was going on with me and Yolanda?

Nothing! That was an easy question to answer, though surely not the one she would have anticipated. Lillian had invested some time into bringing us together around Rebecca's funeral. I wasn't pushing anything, though. Yolanda would be all right without me. The world was hers. She had the Midas touch.

The news from Lillian was the strangest, because she had to go through the secretary at Rougetec just to find me. I hadn't told her I was leaving the country. I had told almost no one. Not even my family in Panama. I should have informed them, but I just did whatever I wanted, without their knowledge. A postcard would be thoughtful, though. *I would mail them a letter, better yet. There was stationery in the room. Time to use it.*

"You were gone a long time. Anything wrong?"

"Just the job wanting to hear from me. Have you ordered?"

"I was waiting for you. You look preoccupied."

"I have to come up with something for the job, that's all. I just decided what to send them."

"I am sure it will be what they want. Too bad you don't work for an architectural design firm."

"Next life."

"Good morning. What will you be having?" the waiter asked.

"Two poached eggs and toast."

"And you, sir?"

"Orange juice and yogurt."

"I'll have something for lunch, maybe."

"Coffee also?"

"Yes, please," I told the waiter.

I reached across the table and held Sarah's hand.

"You mean a lot to me, Roberto."

"I want to say you mean more to me, but that would not be fair."

"Why not? I could stand to hear it."

I kissed her hand to confirm my feelings. "You forgot to take a model with you."

"So this is our last meeting? You might have told me!"

"I hope not! That isn't what I meant."

"I want to be sure," she said, this time kissing my hand. "Because I am coming back tonight. That is, if I'm invited."

"You're invited. Can you meet me here at eight thirty?"

"Yes."

"Then I will see you then."

We ate our breakfast. I went back to the room. I gave her a model. She chose one of the smaller models, just as colorful.

I saw her to a taxi and returned to my room to get my notes.

Why did I leave her thinking I would be able to change my plans? Maybe because I wanted to make our time together last. That's all. There was no other reason. Tourniquets had a way of making you say things that defied logic. And what was logical about love? Oh, I hadn't said the word, to her or anyone since Euridice. What was it anyway? A fleeting feeling divisible by zero?

There has always been something about me. When I was with someone, it was all about them. But no sooner were they gone than I felt the claws of death pulling me into what was the inevitable gloom of solitude, making me into, as Ruben Dario says, as a rock, something with no feeing. But I was not a rock. Was I a virus that can only live in the presence of a host? Yes, I was closer to that. I was like any other living thing which adapted to the seasons but was most alive in spring. And was this not spring in some faraway place; surrounded as any tree in spring by stranger's animals, taking what they could as in the case of bees, or bats, depositing pollen from other flowers, and keeping cycle going, until my time her was over. Maybe Sarah and I could find the happiness we had tasted up in my room. Would she be willing to return to the States?

And how to let Yolanda know that now was not the time for us? I should tell her soon, because we were not together. We had only gotten to know each other physically. I just could see us together on a permanent basis. I could hardly see myself with anyone like that, though Sarah pushed me in a new direction: her vortex. No! Why say that! There was no death lurking in our atmosphere. Only a feeling that we could not be apart. If death was anywhere around, I could not sense it. It was all in my head, clouds of doubt and the future commitment.

I walked outside in the direction of the taxi stand. Sitting on the sidewalk was a girl about the age of eight. She was selling tissues from a box. Her hair was matted and face dirty. Why wasn't she in school? Where was her mother? I pulled a few coins from by pocket, and dropped them into the box, not bothering to take any tissues. It was the most moving portrait I was likely to see. Her face raw from the cold. Were there no agencies there to protect orphans? I walked back and gave her a 10-Tyin note. I hoped it would be enough for her to leave the cold sidewalk where she sat on a box. She hardly budged. I had to move on because I had somewhere to be. I saw my own country in the fate of little girl like that is written on their face. It was no wonder the oldest profession in the world continued.

I found a taxi. I was twenty minutes from the building on Prokorfiev Street. I was eager to get to the mines. I hoped that weather was not prohibitive. Spring had declared itself, and I was its cheerleader.

I arrived at the meeting in fifteen minutes and introduced myself during the round table get-acquainted portion of the meeting. Fortunately, I had already examined the mining locations, specific to lithium finds. More recently the company had been stymied by a thick seam of granite. To undermine the granite, detonation devices had to be placed where they would be most effective, and do the least amount of damage to existing mine shafts. One of the senior vice presidents tried to humor me, perhaps, asking what I would do.

"Sir, I'm not a geologist."

"No, but as a mathematician what would you do?"

"Have you gotten all the lithium out of the existing excavated areas?"

"No, we haven't."

"Then until you have done that, I would not explore any new areas."

"Thank you," he said after a brief pause.

I was sure it was a strategy he had already considered, even if he was not going to pursue it. I had come that distance, so he would at try to make an ally, presumably a financial one, for a later date when exploration broadened to other locations, for different mineral deposits. I watched the slide presentation of the history of mining in Kazakhstan; some of which I was aware of, most of which I was not. The names of the players were completely new, and I recorded the meeting, even though the chief said I would be provided with a CD of the meeting. I told him that I was instructed early in my career to take copious notes. They found no problem with that. I did not want to discover a blank CD when I returned to the United States. Also, I was aware that the mining company executives spoke to each other in Russian in my presence, even though everyone was fluent in English. That went into my notes as well. They curry no favor with me on that score. Dr. Amarova shared the dialogue with me on what she thought were the salient point during our coffee break, but I told her I did not appreciate the foreign discourse; that before I returned, I would take an intense course in Russian.

"I would suggest the same," she smiled. "Nothing will get past you then."

"Unless they go to Kazakh!"

"Then I can help you," she laughed. "You noticed that we'll leaving tomorrow morning for a field visit. It is a two-hour flight and desolate."

"I am having a sweater knitted. I don't think it will be ready by then."

"You'll have a chance to wear it to another site, although I wouldn't wear anything nice."

"I will need something to keep me from freezing to death."

"We can pick up something after we leave the meeting."

"I will need to."

We walked over to the buffet lunch the miners had out for everyone. We prepared our own sandwiches and salads, then sat down together. As we satisfied our appetites, I remembered that Sarah was looking to come to the hotel that night. That would not work, since I would have to leave very early, and could not afford to rush. That was the first of the changes in plans that had to surface with a trans-hemispheric relationship.

I excused myself to call Sarah's hotel. There was a chance she would be in. She was not. I left the message that I wanted to meet her for dinner at 8; that I would meet her in the lobby of her hotel. I went back to the table and finished what was left of the sandwich. I didn't even touch my salad.

"They are ready to wrap things up. If you don't have any questions, we can leave now."

"I would like to get Mr. Stanko's card."

"Okay."

I got his card and told him I hoped to see him the next day. From there, I followed Anna, and we found the driver.

"It's good you have boots. Maybe a nice pullover and thick socks."

"You lead the way!"

At an outdoors equipment shop we found something for both of us. Had I not already commissioned Fatma to do my sweater, I would have bought two pullovers. One was going to be enough, with the Lycra top and bottom undergarments. I found some more socks. We would be spending two days in the mountains, so by the time I returned to Almaty, Sarah would be packing up. We had only just met, but were parting already. I enjoyed her company so. If fact I'd had nothing but a great time with all of the women I had met on that trip. I didn't know what the male to female ratio was in Kazakhstan, but I was doing great. Maybe it just seemed that way because I was passing through. I remembered how I balked at going there in the first place; that someone else should go. But I was the most available, because the other guys had families. In addition, I had to realize that I had the interest in this research of lithium mines, so I was suitable one.

Well, at least being in the mountains, I would stay out of trouble. I looked forward to seeing the sunrise on the mountain range. Maybe I would see a hawk or some vultures; maybe mountain goats and sheep. I was ready for whatever came my way—except mountain cats! I had seen a program about Siberian tigers, but maybe I was taking things too far. I remember as a boy walking across a bridge in the rainforest in Panama, smelling the distinctly pungent odor of an ocelot. They were not big cats, but neither were we: Gerardo, Ze, and I. We found our way out of the forest before our own fearful scent lead the ocelot to us. Of course, I was letting my imagination run away with me. I hadn't thought of them in years. I wondered where they were. Gerardo's sister, Corazon, loved snakes, even after she had gotten bitten by one. She said was going to be a snake doctor. We did not know the word veterinarian then. That's why we named her *Corazón de leon*—Lion-hearted. I became nostalgic then, in a way I hadn't been since childhood, when I was shipped off to *Los Estados Unidos*, where I had been educated and spent all of my adult life. My parents did me a favor, but the plan was most certainly my Mother's, as she had a brother who had already left the isthmus in search of the dollar that eluded most of us, unless we played baseball, or finished medical school. Had Corazon done the latter?

I thought again of a different leaving: Sarah would leave me; Yolanda had left me; Euridice had left me. I was indeed a man left behind. The only thing that hadn't left me was mathematics, and what was the probability that mathematics would not leave me? I prayed that I would not lose my mind like Sir Isaac Newton. Not that I was comparing myself to him, but you didn't have to be a genius for that to happen to you.

"How long are you going to look at those socks?" said Anna, pulling me from my reverie.

"Oh, you don't know what it's like to be far from your homeland."

"No, I don't. It can't be easy. Why don't I get you back to the hotel?"

We got out of the store, and were on our way to the hotel.

"I'll be there at seven thirty in the morning."

"Thanks for everything. Until then."

I walked to the telegram office inside the hotel.

> *Sir,*
>
> *Things are moving along nicely. I have recorded all of the meetings and look forward to conferring with you as soon as I return. Tomorrow we are scheduled to view one of the mines, so I am full of anticipation.*
>
> *Sincerely,*
> *Roberto Davila*

Next I sent one to Yolanda.

> *Que tal, Yolandita? By now you might be building an edifice to match Calatrava, or maybe my hero, Oscar Niemeyer. In any case, I am glad to hear you are following your muse.*
>
> *Roberto*

Finally, to my parents.

> *Padres queridos, estoy lo más bien, y por ahora no congelándome.*
> *Espero verlos este verano. Besitos a todos. Robi*

I'd told my parents that I was well and not freezing, and that I hoped to see them that summer. Somehow I felt better after those mailings. Now I had to get ready to see Sarah, for perhaps the last time for some time to come. My heart raced like it did when Sarah asked me about architecture, but my mind ran straight to Yolanda. She picked up the emotion, but not the correct attachment. *Take it easy!* I was going to see her, have dinner, take her, perhaps in her hotel, and go back to my hotel and turn in. An uneventful night, but this was a business trip. I did not have much time. I had to pack for two nights. The only pieces of equipment I needed were a handheld mobile, from which I could save and send messages, and a camera. I would be returning to the hotel, but I would pack everything, in the event I would need to relinquish my room. I packed everything away and was ready in a short time. I placed my models in an existing box. After another shower, I was on my way to Sarah's.

Sarah's hotel was nice, but a notch lower than where I was staying. The university did not have the inclination to go too far for its employees. Maybe they spent their money on administrative costs. I called and she said she was nearly dressed, to come up. I went up and rang the bell. Sarah answered it. She was not nearly dressed—not nearly undressed. She had on a magenta brassiere, and bikini panties to match. Now where could we have been going with her dressed like that?

"It's cold outside, but it's comfortable in here." She was getting lots of mileage out of those black shoes. When she wore them we were nearly the same height. "Come help me find a dress."

I followed the rise and fall of her cheeks, still tanned from perhaps a sunlamp, perhaps her phenotype. Was there any cure against lust? Did I even care? "How about this one?" It was what she wore when we first met, and her black hair and mine met. She held it up to her breast and back-peddled to me.

"Do you really like this?"

"All of it." My hands held her, and she, the dress. She tossed the dress onto the chair and backed me on to the bed. I heard her shoes fall, alternately to the floor. I found her waist almost too small but there was no letting go. Her legs were scissors once again, but with the circulation cutting clinch of before. I could live with this pressure, and I hoped that she could take mine. I was uncharacteristically aggressive and she could not tame me. How her panties found their way around my neck and one leg in my pants, I could not say. We managed to get undressed and found the rhythm that we had come to know and liked. The wooden bed creaked as if it were a metronome. And we composed so much music that night! The Turkish Suite, I had the mind to call it. All the lyricism of we could muster, all the thunderous palpitations of the timpani, the fluttering of flutes that Sarah evoked, the bass clarinet solos that I took and made for incredible evening. We never even mentioned dinner or dessert.

"Do you want some more ice cream?"

All I could do was laugh, remembering my dream, and what she was doing that gave me that thought. "Just do that again, and I won't need any."

She went to work with the alacrity of a cat. "*Powerful and sweet.*" Baudelaire had said. He couldn't have been more correct. And could they scratch! That suite was extending into a symphony. More instruments had joined in the strings where giving it all they had, and we had found the floor. It was not cold, given to the carpeting. She held onto the blankets and I held onto her. That room has become topsy-turvy. We followed the wan of an invisible and frenetic conductor. We were wet, through and through, and didn't care. She lead me into the shower

275

with her. It was small, but that was of no consequence either. My arms reached every spot she wanted me to.

"Look at this room!" she said. She walked over everything to find more undergarments. I started getting dressed. When I finished, I started picking things up. It was the mess seemed to be at first. In less than ten minutes, it was as it had been an hour earlier.

We put our instruments back in their cases.

"Why don't we have room service?"

"But I want to take you out."

"We'll have time for that another time. I really don't want to go anywhere."

"You win the first difference of opinion," I said.

"Besides, I want to stare at you building. I can't do that if I go out."

"And I stare at you, while you do that."

"All this staring, I am going to need new glasses," she said.

"What would you like?"

"Whatever you order, get two."

"How about some white fish chowder?" I said, "But you'll have to call it up."

Sarah made the call, and thirty minutes later there was a knock at the door. Sarah answered, and brought in the tray. She arranged the table so that we faced each other. The bowls were large and the black bread came with butter. There was a bottle of sparkling water and white cloth napkins.

"What time are you leaving tomorrow?"

"At seven thirty."

"That's so early."

"We are flying almost to Mongolia. I am eager to see whatever we can, but I only want to stay as long as necessary."

"Will you be going into the mine?"

"I was instructed not to, so I won't be. I have been in tunnels, but never a mine."

"It is so dangerous. I'm glad you are not."

Sarah had a way of holding my hand when she spoke. There was no way I was going into the ground, even if it had belonged to Ali Baba. And if it turned out to be a wondrous cave, my research was what I was after, the miners were only too eager to get the minerals out, so our company could do something with them.

My journal readings had gotten me curious about the financial potential for selling the byproducts of lithium chloride and potassium chloride: white potash as the latter was called. Anna could be resourceful in that regard. After taking only a few courses in geology and material science, I lacked the background in rock chemistry to answer those questions. I knew what questions to ask, though. Let the experts tell me what I needed to know.

"I had better head back, although I don't want to."

"Well, plan a break in late spring in Istanbul."

"And take it from there." I stood up and we embraced, tenderly. We had spent a wealth of time together, when it wasn't even a vacation. It was a business trip, the likes of which I would never see again.

"You know I never asked you if you were involved with anyone else. If you didn't want to tell me, I didn't want to know . . . and I still don't." We kissed and then she went for my coat. She put an envelope in my pocket. "All of my vital information is written on it."

"Here is another card with all of mine as well."

"I am pushing you out."

It was a reluctant push, maybe hoping I would stay, but I knew it would be too much work to get out in the morning. I wrapped myself up and I was down the hall. Outside I was disoriented. I found a taxi and gave him directions.

A half hour later I was back in my hotel but feeling a certain loss since Sarah had been so much fun, filling the anticipation that came with being so far away from everything familiar.

In my room my bag I planned to carry was already at the door. I called the front desk to keep an eye out for my room; that I would be gone for two days. I put on some music on the radio, and slipped off to sleep.

My alarm clock woke me up at six. News in Russian was enough to stir me further. In twenty minutes I was showered, dressed, and out the door. Downstairs, I had some oatmeal and tea. I had taken a seat in the lounge until Anna came bounding in. She was prepared for the weather: hooded coat, gloves and boots. Her coat bore the Borgi Solutions logo and she held two hardhats.

"This is for you," she said, reaching out to give me a hardhat and a set of earplugs.

We went outside, where the van driver waited for us. A short drive to the airport to the helicopter hanger was all we had to do. We sat down and had breakfast. I had no appetite.

"You should eat something. It's a long flight. Have you ridden in a helicopter before?"

"My first time."

"You get to see everything. That's what I like. It seats five people. Though we are the only passengers this time. The miners will be there when we arrive."

Anna was excited. Maybe for me, because she would have the chance to show me what she did for a living. Maybe because she liked to fly. I wanted to experience flight in a helicopter, too. It was more intimate than taking a plane. You were right there with the pilot, and you were certainly aware of the weather in a way I could not have otherwise been. We feel every gust, are affected by rain. The day was clear, almost completely cloudless, so we were going to have no foreseeable obstacles.

We approached the helicopter in a file, bending at the waist, as was typical. We sat down, found our seat belts, and buckled up. We had picked up more crewmen at the airport. They were mechanics, so with the copilot, there were six of us. Anna and I sat side by side, facing outward. The mechanics did as we did, only our backs faced theirs. She tapped my hands for reassurance. After the pilots made their checks, we hovered slowly and were in the sky. I was seeing more of Almaty than before. So many skyscrapers. This was a country of exotic edifices. Spires stabbing any clouds daring enough to come within reach were impaled without mercy. Other buildings let the clouds escape and float by unscathed.

In twenty minutes we were beyond the city. Spring had painted the pastures with a light beard of greenery. The trees stood in columns, marking country roads that wound in serpentine paths until they reached another farm.

"I love this part of the country," said Anna, finally speaking after a half hour of silence. She had to raise her voice, because of the engines.

I returned her statement with a gentle tap on her hand and a thumbs-up. That was sufficient. I just continued to take in the scenery. The colors changed from light green to brown to gray. Everything went gray to blue gray. This was a rockscape. Bleak and unforgiving is how I will always remember that first helicopter flight. I did not know what prehistoric period formed the mountain ranges of present-day Kazakhstan, but I closed my eyes and saw fluvial waters, wearing away for months on end; volcanic eruptions, putting crevices in the earth, establishing faults without flaw; dividing until land masses that only pterodactyls could cross, if such existed then. So that was what we saw then: miles of mountains that were not going anywhere until charges were set, and the rock eventually brought out of the mines, or some cataclysmic event made its appearance. As we flew over the ranges, the sun played in the shadows, creating ribbons of blues and oranges that brought life to land, so I said to myself that that sleeping giant would awaken, once the mines produced what lay under the surface.

Anna touched my sleeve and pointed to a clearing. There was no point in her trying to shout over the din of the engine. The plane tilted and descended, gradually gliding to the tarmac. It was just as desolate as any mine could be. There was a canteen: an oasis for the weary and dust-covered, and a series of trailers or steel boxes, end-to-end. Not a tree or any vegetation. This was a Martian landscape, as inorganic and rocky as if a volcano had deposited its spewed bowels centuries ago and left its *necroscape*. I could discern sulfur in the air. I had my gas mask at my hip, should there be the presence of chlorine, or the absence of sufficient oxygen. Anna carried a monitor to detect any aberrant readings, and I was going to stay close to her. She looked very comfortable in that fetid environment. I had not been enough places in the world to display the ease she assumed. As we walked the length of the road leading to the mine, I observed the rail cars lined up with rock, waiting to be unloaded.

"Are these cars full of lithium?"

"Yes, along with other elements and compounds. We extract kilotons of salts which are valuable. You will notice that no one smokes on this sight. Lithium is very flammable"

"Like sodium chloride?"

"Some, but we find more potassium chloride and lithium chloride."

"Apart from batteries, what are some uses for lithium?"

"It is used in ceramics, and aircraft. You also find it in thermonuclear weapons and heat-resistant glass."

"Is Kazakhstan among the world leaders in the production of lithium?"

"No. Chile leads the world with nearly 9,000 tons. We are nowhere near the top. Argentina and Australia are leaders as well."

"So what do you do with say, potassium chloride?"

"We sell it to companies who produce fertilizers and medicines. It is used for lethal injections, as well. You don't need much of it for lethal injections. Two grams would kill a man your size."

"And less for you?"

"Much less!"

Anna did have a sense of humor, but it was cloaked in serious subjects. She continued to fill me with talk of KCl and NaCl and LiCl.

"These compounds are used as gas welding flux of aluminum."

We climbed into a jeep that was parked nearby. I was glad to have her escort me along the temporary asphalt road that was parallel to the train of railway cars, filled to the top with rocks that glistened in the now weak afternoon sunlight. Anna drove by one cavern after another. After two miles the landscape changed little save for the unmelted snow. There were declivities and turns that spiraled downward into places where no light could find its way into the narrow road. Anna had the headlights on now, and honked her horn at every turn, to avoid any misadventures.

"Since you were instructed not to enter the mines, we will head back. We will leave in another hour, if that's okay."

"Yes, that's great."

Anna made a U-turn, and retraced the ground she had covered through the narrow mountain range. We were winding our way back when we heard an explosion.

"That can't be good!"

"I have not heard one of those in a long time. They aren't scheduled to do dynamiting. It may be a problem. I hope not."

Anna drove quickly to get back to where we started. When the jeep skidded, she slowed down, but her small hands held the steering wheel, and when necessary, her right hand grasped the clutch. We arrived to find the firemen spraying the area with some powder—I found out later as a precaution. Water would have done nothing but exacerbate the matter. It would not extinguish a lithium fire.

Anna conversed with the site engineer. "He said the miners had only recently exited the mine when the explosion occurred. Three of the miners were burned and flown to the nearest hospital. Unfortunately, this occurs too often. They take every precaution, but nature can change the rules whenever it likes."

I had nothing to say. I was indeed glad I had not ventured into the mines. I had no interest in entering confined space, anyway.

We boarded the helicopter that had brought us there.

46

Back at the hotel I said good-bye to Anna and thanked her for the tour. She did not say much on the flight back. When I asked her to let me know about the miners that had been rushed to the hospital, she only nodded. Somehow I didn't think she would.

After I showered I got dressed and walked down to the knitting shop. I was supposed to have returned to see the progress Fatma had made. Her mother came to the door, smiling.

"So good to see you again. Fatma will be glad to see you, too. Just have a seat."

I had only come for the sweater: to try it on, pay and leave. Fatma's mother served me some tea, for which I thanked her. I was looking out the window, enjoying the peppermint tea, when behind me I heard the clicking of heels.

"Dr. Davila! Where have been?"

I turned to face a radiant Fatma, wearing about a yard of rose-colored raw silk; her body exposed from her thighs to her ankles. She wore strapped sandals that gave her three-inches of added height. I tried to contain my looks but her outfit screamed at me.

"Very nice," I said.

"You do like it? It doesn't make me look fat, does it?"

"Not at all." *It makes you look hot!*

"Sometimes you just want to get dressed, even if you have nowhere to go."

"Well, let go somewhere!" I had said it before I had a chance to smile away the light-hearted remark.

"It won't take me long to get ready," she said, then spoke to her mother in Russian.

"Where would you like to go?" I asked.

"What about the cinema?"

"I will be my first in Russian."

"Maybe they will have English subtitles."

"It's okay. I'll follow the body language."

"Try on your sweater, while I change to boots."

I slipped on the sweater in front of Fatma's mother.

"She will love it! Do you?"

"I do!"

Fatma returned. "You look so handsome! Doesn't he, mama?"

"Yes. You should wear it tonight," said her mother.

"I won't take it off."

"Let me take a picture," said her mother, again leaving, apparently going after a camera. Fatma took advantage of the moment to smooth the uneven line in the back of the sweater. A line that couldn't have been there, as the sweater was perfect in every way. Her mother came back with a Rolleiflex 2x2 lens camera. Fatma took advantage of the pre-date photograph by looping her arm in mine. Her mother took several pictures: some with my arms around her waist. Little Fatma wasted no time.

"Have a good time!" were her mother's last words. It was as though I had a free pass to *let freedom ring.* And the way Fatma held my hand, I was going full-tilt to the penthouse! We were outside, both of us draped in wool, head to toe, and rightfully so in that weather. *Was it going to snow again?* I didn't care. I certainly felt freer than I could ever remember. Why I had to go to another country to feel that way, I couldn't say. All of the women I had met in the shortest span on time: Gül, Sarah, and now

Fatma, had been every bit as fulfilling in her own way. They all had something to say, and each held my attention. And Yolanda had every superlative a woman could have, I had only recently gotten to know. But she was gone. Yet the chain of lovelies had not been broken. What was most remarkable was that I had done nothing but be in the right place, continue to work, and return to my endeavors in my hotel room to emerge into the streets of Almaty, for new companionship. This turn of events would end at some point, but who knew when? We found a taxi, Fatma told the driver where to go, and we were on our way.

The theater was very small. There was a cafe where I purchased a coffee for Fatma only. It was a Turkish film. The film was story of a Kurdish couple, struggling to keep their marriage alive in occupied Kurdistan. The men were fighting for independence, while the women were looking for ways to leave the country, for good. Fatma was all but wearing the sweater she had knitted me: her head on my chest where Sarah's had been. A new scent filled my nostrils. It was hard for me to be as touched as I might have been by the narrative of the film, but for the euphoria of the intoxicants: *Was it jasmine?* All I know is that when I was aroused by the female protagonist's diaphanous pink gown, I found Fatma's soft lips. It was a series of short kisses. But they were so memorable, filling the void of a film that was brief on intimacy, and long on anguish. The couple found freedom in France, remained hopeful of returning to Kurdistan, *if that great day would come*, to quote a line from Archie Shepp.

The plaintive theme of the flute and string instrument, and rich panorama of the mountain ranges of Kurdistan were much like Kazakhstan of earlier that day. Only when I looked at the mountains of the latter, there was no vegetation. Their richness was in ores and granite; schist and lithium; the miners who worked in eminent danger.

Kurdistan was green as far as your periphery would allow. It was lush like the Panama of my youth. I could hear the owls and see the tanagers in flight. Did *they* have flying squirrels, too? I kissed Fatma again just to drink up the jasmine wine.

"What time do you have to be in?" I asked as we left the theater.

"I would like to get in by one," she said.

"Let me take you for something to eat. I noticed some nice-looking restaurants on the way here."

Fatma didn't say anything right away. I really had no intention of taking her back to the hotel, although she might not have said no to the invitation. Why push a perfect evening off a cliff?

It had begun to snow. We found a taxi and traced our way back to a well-lit street of restaurant. She had the driver stop and we exited the car, and walked the length of the boulevard. Fatma began humming the theme of the film. When I looked into her eyes it was clear that she liked the evening, and I had the feeling I had something to do with that.

We entered a bar. It was noisy but it didn't matter to us. We sat down and ordered sandwiches and sparkling water.

"So what did you think of the film?" she asked.

"The mountains. They reminded me of Panama." I had to speak up because of the din. A group of young women were laughing and were the loudest ones near us. She let what I said go without a response. She touched my hand instead. We were holding hands when the sandwiches came.

"The woman was very impatient. Is that the correct word?"

"She was frustrated. She wanted to scream—and did! Life there was at a standstill. Not going anywhere."

"Yes. That is why she was impatient."

"Right. And as a man, he had to fight for a cause he did not believe in. It happens all the time."

"It does?"

"When you join military as an obligation, you will be trained to kill for a reason you have had no determination in making. It is an obligation. It nothing else, the film showed the senselessness of war."

"Can you show me your hotel?"

"Why don't we do it tomorrow?"

"Are you afraid of something?" she asked.

"I don't want to rush this."

"You saw the film; how the friends in the war died, one by one. I do not want us to die like that."

"Death. You are so young to talk of death." I said that but could not forget what had happened earlier that day. The mines were coffins in waiting. "Let's go."

In the taxi Fatma and I watched the snow collect on the backs of cars, and sidewalks. I thought of taking her home, but she could have made that suggestion. I had been in enough taxis to know not to stand in the way of one. I was perfectly capable of causing my own wreck. Fatma's hands was keeping my body alert, and I liked it. Why did Sarah have to go? Why was I being massaged by this woman and feeling so good when I had no intentions of staying in Kazakhstan? *Just enjoy the moment. You don't know if you will even see tomorrow!* I told myself that it was as inevitable as Euridice leaving me. Who knew that Fatma would say she wanted to come to my hotel, but Fatma? I accepted the eventuality of things unseen: the glazed over pavements; a snowstorm in early spring; the inability of us to leave the hotel? Well, I was going a little too far with that one.

We were in my room. Fatma discovered my little city.

"Did you make all of these?"

"Yes. What do you think?"

"I think I want to see one of these buildings. Maybe here!"

"You know, I am thinking the same thing. I just have to find someone willing to go the next step with my ideas. Ultimately, I may have to do it myself."

"I believe you can! You just have to find the right place."

"I need to see what I am lacking and go from there."

"Lacking?"

"Missing. I never studied architecture, formally. I think these buildings will stand. I just need to enter a competition."

"Whatever you need to do, do it!"

Fatma had closed in on me. The *double entendre* of her words set my hands in motion. Fatma held my shoulder for support, as she removed her boots. She lost three inches of height, but I didn't care. We were headed for the equalizer. Fatma began to tremble.

"I am cold."

I pulled her in and massaged her all over. She had next to nothing on, so I wasn't surprised. Her cheeks were red, so I walked her to the bed, and pulled back the covers. She continued to shudder, so I ordered some tea.

"Put these on."

"They are so big," she said, at the sight of my blue flannel pajamas. The top draped past her thighs. The bottoms, well, would require major alterations. "I feel better."

She continued to shiver, so she went under the covers, with only her head exposed. "Are you going to bed, too?"

"I am waiting for the tea."

"What's that inside the town? It looks like a woman's body."

"You're able to see it?"

"Yes. What is she doing in there?"

"I liked her so much, I said she had to stay. She's part of the foundation."

"Like a captive."

"I'll see that no harm comes to her."

"Strange. Are you possessive?"

"Just in this case. It's something I could do, so I did. Besides, it's not a real person. Kind of like a doll in a house."

"Okay, then I see."

Next there was a knock at the door.

"Thank you," I said, giving the waiter a tip.

I poured Fatma some tea. "I bet you do take sugar."

"That's right."

I fought a pair of pajama bottoms and joined her.

"I like this," she said. She used my chest as a cat would a scratching post. "I can see you like it, too."

"You should have called your mother, when we got in, I mean."

"Don't you want me to stay?"

"I don't want you to leave."

"Then I'll stay. She knows I will call if I get into trouble."

What kind of trouble had she gotten into before? She seemed such a good young woman.

"Besides, she likes you a lot."

Was this some trap that I was engaged in? No. I liked where I was, and had already acted out my role. But I was not going to take her away with me. Things needed some direction, and I was the one to direct them.

"So what kind of trouble would she need to intercede in?"

"Girl trouble. You know."

Fatma continue to pull her nails through the dark grass beneath her fingers. She kissed it. But Fatma was so young.

"So you've been pregnant before?"

"Don't sound so surprised. You're American!"

"But you're not!"

"This has nothing to do with nationality. It is about where two people take things. And where we are taking them can produce a baby." Fatma was quiet, but continued to mine my body and mind, then stopped. "Because I made one mistake, I am not going to do it again."

"We don't have to talk about it," I said.

"I was very young and got pregnant. The boy was almost as young as I was. My mother made a difficult choice, that at the time I was against."

"So you wanted a baby at what—"

"Fourteen. That is right!"

"It happens all the time in Panama. In America, too."

"But what I did not want to face was how I was going to knit sweaters for my doll, and my baby, too. I was very basic. I did not have much time for a choice, so my mother made it for me. I'm glad she did." Fatma was holding me now, and not letting go. "And what about that sixteen-year-old boy? He was not finished. He made two more girls pregnant. But justice had its way with him: a nice little bullet in his head. A drug gang took care of him. No loss of humanity there, and I was glad that the other two girls had abortions. Girls are in this alone. The boys *don't have a heart*, do you say that?"

"Oh, we say that!"

I had no idea that on that snowy night, I would have Fatma's past opened to me. It must have been a tremendous floodgate to open. Fatma was not shy telling me about her life, which had all the realism of the autobiography it was.

"You met my sister. We were close, until she went to university. It was then that I looked for company, but the wrong kind. Drugs came with this new friendship, so did pregnancy. I really got lost in that counterculture. It was so easy to do. I got tired of it, but only after I was pregnant. I got so sick. I was going to lose the baby anyway, doing all those drugs. Birth defects, to be sure. My mother showed me pictures, and that was enough. I vomited, and was ready to go to the clinic. I was sick for a time after that, I got better. And I haven't looked back."

By then Fatma had climbed on top of me.

"Since then I have not been without my contraceptives."

Fatma was boundless, and cavalier. I was always cautious, for no other reason than watching cousin Carlito self-destruct. Fatma liked to take charge. She had this scissor move. I was not a wrestler, and while I had no interest in Greco-Roman, or professional wrestling, I was totally caught off-guard by her leg-locks. She was small and that was part of the charm. The pixie had me so sore. I would never forget her. I told her she could stay as long as she liked.

"Do you mean that? You're lucky I have work to do, or I would hold you to that."

"Don't you have elves to help us get the orders out?"

"Elves?" She looked at me, quizzically.

I just let it go. She had to do the work herself. Her strong hands told that story.

Fatma plied my body with the deftness of a Turkish bath master. She wanted to see me in pain, I felt. She had that bed rocking, and I needed the workout. I tried to replicate her scissor move and my muscles froze up on me! She laughed at me. She then massaged and kissed my legs back to life, with only a few spasms. I was totally hers. She pulled a bottle of sweet-smelling cream, and bathed my limbs.

"You are so strong, and big!" she said, pulling me. I was completely immobilized at some points. She liked riding me. I watched her shudder. I lost count of how often. My hands held onto her firmness. With the lights on, my fingers played with the blue birthmark on her right breast.

"You like that, don't you? It's yours for as long as I stay."

There she was reminding me that this time would eventually come to an end. It was that time together I would remember long after I had returned to the United States.

Fatma lowered herself to me, so I could caress her beauty mark. I tried to liken it to some form I knew. Paramecium! That was its shape. It really meant less than the color.

Fatma had sent me to heaven. A place I never thought I would see. Maybe it was the exhaustion of the day at the mines; the whirlwind of stories Fatma had shared.

"What about you? You're not married, are you? Don't you even want to be?"

"I do. I do."

"And?"

"I am going to."

"Well, let me know if you could live with a woman like me."

"I think I could."

"I wish I wanted to get married. I would marry you!"

"You won't have a problem, if that's what you want!"

"It's not so easy. A woman who has had an abortion in Kazakhstan is not the same as in America, I think."

"It wasn't your choice. In a country like the United States, some women have several abortions. I knew one who had three, which really makes no sense. Contraception is free there. I have a conscience, and like some singer said, don't have a baby, if you don't want one!"

"Or don't have a partner who agrees with you. That thing tore up my body. Inside I mean." She paused, as if looking for the words. "I cannot have children now."

I pulled her close again. There was nowhere we were going with that conversation. Not then anyway. She had let me off easily. She wanted to marry a Kazakh. I looked at her through the mirror, and she looked at my image.

"Did you ever think about shaving?"

"You don't like beards?"

"No, I do. I think I like you more without one."

She was scratching my chest again. "I really like this. Do you mind it?"

"No, it's a discovery. As for the beard, I've had it for ten years."

"Then don't shave."

"I may do it anyway. I need a new image. No one will recognize me."

"I will."

"Only you."

There we were. Two souls looking for a reason to extend our time alone together. I was looking at her derriere for perhaps the last time. She was perfect in every way. The fine black hairs that graced her body made me want her again. I began with her arms. She sat on me again, and there we were, as the blond stared at us though the parallel window panels. But what would become of Fatma? Did anyone else see what I saw? She was natural. But who did I want anyway? That was the biggest question. Did I even know who I wanted? I was one confused guy. I wasn't going to keep three women in limbo. I was likely to find myself alone very soon. Yolanda had already pulled up stakes. Sarah had a university post, and was no doubt looking at tenure. Now Fatma had thrown in her hat, however reluctantly. I was not sure, but I liked Fatma, because she was not really after me, and she had been hurt the most of the three. I was drawn to that: her openness, her pain. She was not the prototypical virgin of her country. She was tainted, but she was a strong woman, and unless I was wrong, again, she was genuine. She was going to make some man very happy. But it had to be a man who did not want children, from her loins, anyway.

I was no matchmaker, though as mathematician I could figure out her odds of finding a husband, but I wasn't interested in that kind of research.

"If I sent a ticket for you to visit me, would you come?"

"To America?" she answered with a racing heart. "I would love to!" Fatma began caressing me everywhere.

My suggestion had unleashed unbridled passion in her. The dawn was brushing itself against the window, as we had been up all night. We got up and went into the shower together. There we abounded each other with lather and the hot water washed us new again.

But after saying all that, doubts consumed me. Was she just too good to be true? Fatma had such exquisite form. A woman of five-three with the gait of a ballerina (I saw Elis Regina, again). Yes, it was true, I could find no fault in her. There had to be something that my glazed-over eyes had overlooked. Maybe her body housed some dreadful disease: the leukemia that carted Aunt Rebecca away; or maybe she was on some bipolar medication that made her appear perfect. Surely there were scars left from her teenage experience. Those queries alone made me want to back off. When had she last had a physical? Was I being too clinical? But wasn't I always? If I was thinking of spending the rest of my life with her, I had better be clinical! And why did I conjure up Elis Regina? Hadn't that great singer which I idolized died of a drug overdose? There I was convinced that the perfection I thought I saw was veiled. But at night, would I be awakened by the panther in my lair?

"Do you know I cook?"

"Ah, no. Like what?" I asked, pulled away from my inquisition.

"I can do all kinds of things with lamb. Why don't you come over tonight for dinner?"

"I'd really like that. Thanks." I walked over to the window. The snow was melting; water streaked down the window, people were walking in the streets. Fatma eased behind, holding me like I belonged to her. She pressed her lips against my back.

"Let me get you back home."

"You are lucky I live close by."

"So you won't be late for dinner."

"No. Never late for dinner!"

We were then face to face, standing nude. We found our clothes and began dressing. I helped her with her dress; she with my pants. It wasn't awkward. We were in no rush. I helped with her boots. And we left.

We walked the short distance to her shop. She opened the door. There was no sign of anyone.

"Can you come back at seven?"

"Yes. See you then," I said with an embrace.

Why did I feel the beginning of a distance between us? Was it something that began by my reluctance to go out in the first place? I was not feeling a particular need for company. I was being cordial, but couldn't I have said not tonight? No, I wanted her, too. My allegiance to Sarah would have to take a hiatus. No, I was the one taking the hiatus. Sarah was in Istanbul. Still, I was beginning to feel the distance between Fatma and me growing as my steps in the snow lengthened from her door.

Instead of going straight to the hotel, I walked to the place where the little girl sat, selling tissues and toys. I gave her some money, this time taking some tissues. She didn't look up. Her cheeks were scarred red.

47

When I returned to the hotel I had two messages. Two of the miners rushed to the hospital had died of oxygen deprivation. Perhaps Anna felt I would want to know. I did not know them, but my fears of the perils of that work were confirmed: Mines were coffins. *But how could they get the gold, if they didn't venture into the cavern after it?*

Sarah had said hello too and that she missed me. I missed her, as well. But I felt bad for what I had done with Fatma. I couldn't really dismiss it as just a movie date. It was over, but I had gone too far. I was in the end being selfish. What about Fatma's feelings? I was being as heartless as I had accused Euridice of being. I was taking on the characteristics of the world around me: self-aggrandizement. It was ugly, but I didn't create the design. As my Mother once said about sleeping with someone, if you aren't married, then what was the harm? I could live with that. I had to. But it wasn't something I felt good about afterward. That was the nature of a long-distance relationship. Didn't Euridice walk away like she didn't even know me? I was *une ombre de la rue*, as Edith Piaf sang. She was doing quite well. The more I tried to hold onto this ephemeral world I was building, the less I would be able to endure its painful surprises. I wasn't in Kazakhstan to find love, but to find lithium, and I had done that. It was time to return home, alone.

I arrived at Fatma's on time. I had picked up some flowers from a store across the street from the hotel:

yellow tulips. The flowers matched the silk tie I wore. I wore my favorite navy blue suit. I wanted to wear my best; something I learned from my Father: *Sea caballero, siempre.* And as I had done my best *to be a gentleman, always.* I let the aberrations occur behind closed doors. He had taught me that, too.

"Hello," said Fatma's mother, her silver tooth gleaming.

"These are for you."

"Beautiful!" she said.

I took off my boots and placed them next to the other boots by the door on a straw mat.

Fatma came from the kitchen, dressed in a black sleeveless blouse, and a long, red and black form-fitting skirt. When she took my coat to the closet, the split revealed itself. The outfit was not as harmless as it first appeared. I avowed to be good, but I could see she had not.

"What smells so good?"

"That is the lamb I promised you! Do you like turnips and eggplant?"

"I have never had them together. I am looking forward to everything."

"Hello, Roberto," said Fatma's sister.

"Hello, I am sorry I don't remember your name."

"Zayneb," she said, extending her hand.

She was another delicate flower. I felt very comfortable and was looking forward to dinner. As I walked into the dining room, I noticed a chessboard set up; a game had been underway.

"So who are the chess players?"

"Zayneb is," answered Fatma.

"She is probably good, too."

"She likes the game. And you?"

"I never learned more that the basic moves."

"Oh, you are being modest."

"Oh, that's not a game of modesty. Either you're good or you're not. And I'm not!"

"Well, the only thing you need tonight is your appetite," added Fatma's mother, taking my arm and escorting me to the table.

The table was set with white linen and napkins rolled next to fine chinaware. Stemmed glassware and cups which looked to be a century old, or older. Perhaps it was from the Ottoman Empire, fired by someone in their family. The designs on the plate indicated that. The Arabic calligraphy adorning the walls gave that indication.

"What does that say?" I asked.

"He who is best, is kind to women," said Fatma.

"And that would be—," chimed in her mother.

Man, did I feel like the lamb soon to be slaughtered.

"Now, you are making him self-conscious, right?" asked Zayneb.

"Is it so obvious?" I asked.

"It is a good thing to think about," said Fatma.

"But few men do!" said Zayneb.

"All men think about food," their mother said, bring out a steaming, casserole dish of vegetables.

Fatma followed her with lamb chops. They were adorned with every sort of fruit: plums, cranberries, blueberries, and apricots. When she set down the dish, she immediately started serving.

"Bismillah," intoned the women, alternately.

"Bismillah?" I added with inquiry.

"In the name of Allah," said Fatma. It is a prayer of thanks that Muslims say before they eat.

Fatma was dishing out the lamb, when I noticed pistachios and walnuts. Fatma had gone to some trouble to prepare this meal.

I shook my head in disbelief.

"I want you to remember us every time you go to a restaurant," said Fatma.

"I will, and sadly."

"Then you will want to return to Kazakhstan!" said Zayneb. "When are you leaving?"

"In four days," I said with reluctance in my voice.

"So soon," said Fatma's mother, as if seeing the hopes for her daughter dashed, forever.

A silence fell on the dining room. I thought of the Arabic inscription Fatma had translated. An emergency siren whirred past the house. Men walked by the house; their loud voices sent shock waves through the house. *How fast would it take me to grab my coat and boots?*

"But Roberto is going to send me a ticket!"

"Is that so?" asked Zayneb.

"Of course, it is," said Fatma.

"That's nice," said Fatma's mother, sounding unconvinced.

"So what do you think of Fatma's cooking? Isn't it the best?" asked Zayneb.

"Without question! You make it hard to leave."

"So what do you think of Kazakhstan?"

"It's beyond description!"

"I hope you will have good things to say about our country."

"Loads of good things." I added. Zayneb was making it easy for me to make my exit. Their mother, however, was no longer effervescent. I expected her to say in her own way *I'm ready to turn in. Good-night, Roberto. And keep your grimy hands off my daughter's tits!*

"So we may be seeing the last of you," said the mother.

Gee, she *was* putting me out. Not the way I planned it. But I hadn't planned anything! Not the trip! Not meeting Fatma! Not anything! "By the time I come back, you will have your own restaurant!" *And you'll be out of my life—for good!*

We were having coffee, when their mother said, "I have to get up early. Thank you for the flowers."

They were no longer beautiful. Their color had turned pale: sallow like the color of her face. The sagging cheeks, her lips were sealed, her silver tooth no longer in sight. She could have passed for a wax museum statue, until she moved again.

"But do try to pass by before you leave."

She was as stoic as Socrates. And her figure *was* less that Greek. No reason to be mean, now. Just get your coat and go, I told myself.

No, not a chance. You are seeing the last of me. Take a good look!

"I'll do my best." That was a lie to end all lies.

Fatma started putting away the food. They would be eating lamb chops and turnips for a week. I thought of the little girl out in the cold. I would take something for her when I left.

"Did you really like it?" asked Fatma.

"I loved every morsel."

"Morsel?"

"Everything was divine—great!" I needed to convey my thoughts simply. "I'll be thinking of that dinner long after I have returned."

"Zayneb is going to take so pictures."

Fatma put away the food. Zayneb started doing the dishes. I offered, but they would have none of it. I did pass Zayneb the plates and cups. I did not trust myself with the glasses. The set of cup and dishes alone looked to cost airfare for two. I sat down and finished my coffee. I toyed with the sugar bowl, then caught myself. I entertained myself by looking at the walls of the dining room. A shelf of old books that were no longer read. How did I know? The dust was collecting on them. There was a teapot with gold-rimmed glasses. I'd had tea from those very glasses days earlier. The walls were a brick color; the ceiling sky gray. There was no male presence, except, perhaps, the calligrapher, who had died centuries ago. I did not what to ask the father's whereabouts. I already knew more than I had asked to know. Fatma had volunteered earlier her heartfelt story, while asking me nothing about my own life. Better that way. Fatma took advantage of my sitting alone to brush against my back, and whispered, "My sister likes you. Don't think I don't know." That was a revelation! I was not looking to act on anything that would keep me in that family. I waited just another minute to say. "I have to leave. Thank you for an excellent invitation."

I stood and walked to the door. Zayneb took the lead.

"I thought we might play a game of chess."

"No, thank you. I am leaving."

That, I was sure, struck her as rude, but I was a straightforward as a checkmate with two rooks and a bishop. I wanted no part of a farewell. Fatma held my coat and said, "I want to see you tomorrow."

"I will call you," I said.

I had my boots on and coat buttoned.

"Thank you for coming," said Zayneb.

I nodded a goodbye to both, and left.

The cold air in my face was a slap of freedom. I turned so that both cheeks felt it. As I left, it occurred that I had forgotten to get something for the little girl. She was at home by then. It was nine thirty.

I'd had a full evening. I had succeeded in burning another bridge to the ground. They had built it before hitting bedrock. It was doomed to collapse under the weight of Fatma's life, our span of difference in what we wanted from life, and an unwillingness of me to bend down and pull her away from her culture. Some divides were not worth the energy to cross. And it took a lot for me to acknowledge that. I was so used to saying yes to everyone. I must like stray dogs. I couldn't pass one without finding a bone for it. But I was downsizing now. I could not save the world. Tomorrow I would make my last stop at the little street girl and give her a farewell donation.

48

In my hotel room I got comfortable. That was not hard with the kilo I had just gained. I sat down and went to work on my building designs. I liked working with gray paper. I also used clear sheets for a window. I decided to put another woman inside a building that would face the one I had already built that was similar. They might have appeared to a stranger as captives. That was my intention, at any rate. But they were no more captive than I was. We were all in buildings, out of the snow, and following directions. The new woman was dark-haired with a smile. Facing each other, they gave the impression they liked what they were doing. Models convey that self-assurance. They are paid handsomely, is it any surprise? I had a real penchant for rhomboids. It was time to move onto another solid. I would do some sketches in the coming days. Tomorrow I would devote my time to tying together my report for Rougetec. They had been awfully good about giving me my space. They had never been a micromanaging corporation anyway. I only had one incident where I told a boss to "back off"; that he would get what he was after and some if he let me do my job. He said that no one had ever told him that; that he wanted to make sure I knew the importance of the project. I didn't believe those words. He just did not think that some upstart employee would dare tell him what I did. I delivered on my promise, as I had done before. I later asked to be transferred to International Accounts, which is how I ended up in Kazakhstan. That, in addition to the fact no one wanted to go so far away. When I got back I was going to put in for a vacation. I had not seen my family in a long time. The thought of seeing Colon again got me excited. No place on earth was more humid, but I knew how to dress: All white linen, handmade sandals, a Peruvian straw hat. And the beard was coming off! Ninety eight in the shade dictated a slow pace. A glass of tamarind on ice. Those were the comforts that awaited me.

49

I woke up at six thirty. I turned off the radio, as I had tired of the Russian rock music. I had just gotten out of the shower and thrown on my robe when there was a knock at the door. It was room service, asking if I wanted coffee. I told him no, thanks. I had not seen him for some days. And I supposed he was working on his tip before my departure. I went to my desk, now full of buildings. I began folding them. When I was done, I placed them in a portfolio, where they would survive the return flight. Next I lay out the documents for review. I would not look at them again until I returned to the States.

I culled over fifty pages of narrative and charts along with a chronicle of daily activities. I gave particular detail to the mine visit: the unfortunate incident of the deceased miners. I sent my report ahead, so that I could hear from the company while I was still in Kazakhstan, before I left, should they want any clarity. Three and a half hours were all I needed. There was also the DVD of an early meeting with all interested parties, and the contacts which that and subsequent days brought forth. I was pleased with what I had gathered. The intimacies were most unexpected. I was not completely sure my U.S. passport did not have something (everything?) to do with the status I held. I wasn't a rock star, but I could not have asked for more attention. I had completed an assignment I did not want, at first, and now I had seen it to the end, and was looking forward to returning home. I was also looking forward to seeing Sarah in Istanbul. With the bulk of the work behind me, I could take in the sights, unfettered by anything.

I packed away my clothes, only pausing when I folded my sweater and hat. I kept my scarf out, because I would wear that on the plane. I had thought of giving a building model to the little girl on the street, and one to Fatma. No, only to the girl on the street. Fatma might build a false hope about any gift from me. Wouldn't a ticket to America be more than enough? It would be too much, in fact! Better to leave without as much as a sound.

Fatma would forget me with time, but before she did her words would produce a maelstrom of invective that would swirl and pound against my heart: a stone of granite that had already started to show signs of wear. Water can do that. It tells a story words cannot. The footsteps of Roman soldiers who march the spans of Spain, the rugged Pyrenees, and hills of Carthage ceased, but the aqueducts remain. My little life story held much less history, but was still important, if only to me. The chambers of my heart beat, even if no one heard their echo.

It was Saturday. The little girl would be out peddling whatever she could: maybe one of those bracelets she fashioned from aluminum cans. I would buy one from her and give her a building, if she would accept it.

It was after four in the afternoon, a time I was sure to find her on a pleasant day. Maybe she would be having a chocolate on her box. But when I arrived, she was not there. I looked across the street, but she was not there either; just a woman sweeping the sidewalk. I asked her about the little girl making hand signs, but to no avail. I had been there enough time to know a little Russian, but I had not spent my time doing that. I was feeling silly by then: walking around with a building in my hand. I had begun to see people looking at me. There was nothing to do but look at someone who didn't look like them. I decided to go in the store in front of which she sat and leave the paper building.

"She dead yesterday," the shop clerk said. He must not have understood me. His bad grammar cut me a dagger: three words, three wounds. I described her again, because he could have thought I was talking about someone else. But his next act removed all doubt. He showed me a photograph. It was she, her hair falling from her wool cap, a dark blue coat, and a joyless face. My heart sank. It was the coldest day of my life. Why had life given me so much and given her so little? Was it better to have died on the street than to have perished that early spring, than to have been devoured by a society that would take her down dark streets and lost in the shadows?

I asked what the cause of death was; it was in desperation. He could not tell me because we did not understand one another. What did it matter? Pneumonia? A broken heart? Either one was fatal. Her look seemed to be one who had given up to death's awaiting embrace. Now she was gone, and I was leaving, too. I gave the shop clerk the building. He smiled, and I said nothing, going back into the sunny day.

I walked back to the hotel, straight to the bar. I ordered a glass of rum and a lemon. It was the first time I'd had that since I arrived. Sarah's not drinking had convinced me of the health benefits. I squeezed the two lemon quarters into the glass, and drank it down, feeling only the burn. That was for me. The next one was for her, and all the other hers I had been insensitive to. Another lemon half dripped into a glass, and that next glassful caught up to the first. I'd had enough. I was still sad, which meant I was still sober, a caring person, which an intoxicated person did not tend to be. I didn't have to worry about the sadness escaping me. It was one with me. I didn't want to be like the couple leaving the bar that leaned against each other for anchorage, laughing themselves into oblivion. I would return to my room. There would be no one there to share my feelings, no book of mathematical matrices to take my mind from the ever present face of a little forever gone; like the face of the girl on the cover of National Geographic. Was she Kazakh, too? Did it even matter? There were faces like that in every country. Eyes green, gray, brown and every complexion were in the little ones left to raise themselves. Where was the fairness the world spoke of? That girl brought me to a reality I chose to ignore: the bitter street, with no chocolate to eat.

50

It was after midnight. Though the manager thought it unusual, he granted me permission to take a swim, as long as it did not exceed one hour. That was more than enough time for me. I was no Olympian. I just need to wash away whatever memories would leave me. The water was very cold, so after twenty minutes, I'd had enough. I draped my robe around me, and returned to the lobby to the manager. Then I saw Fatma sitting on a couch. I was speechless. What was she doing there? And at that hour?

"I could not sleep," she said, her voice laced with the innocence of a child. But she was no child.

Did I think I could just walk away, and she would not come looking for me? I was a trip to America. I had promised her a ticket, perhaps in haste, but I wasn't willing to sponsor her. *Just give her some money, and let that be that!*

With the manager in earshot, I walked her away from his curious looks, to the elevator.

We were in my room where she sat, still her overcoat on.

"You are all packed."

I did not say anything except, "Some tea?"

She just sat there, then took off her coat. Why was she wearing that short dress she wore the night we went to the theater? To flood my head with memories; memories I had tried to drown? She looked so forlorn. I got a chill between how she looked and the cold water I had just exited.

"I just had to see you."

I didn't think I would see her like that. I mean, I thought it would be as I was departing, if at all. As I had convinced myself, leave things the way they were, albeit incomplete. Stories are only complete in the movies. In real life, stories are never complete, unless death enters. But where relationships are concerned, someone new always comes in. Fatma was back with me because she hadn't met the next one.

"You know, I am not sure I should have come, but when you leave, it will be too late. I will be alone again without you—without a friend. You think it's because how we were together. But it is more. I like your company. No, I love it. But I cannot say I would like to have your love more than your friendship. Do you understand?"

"Yes." I handed Fatma the cup of tea. Our fingers touched.

"Do you really? I hate to say it, but I am lonely here. My sister and I are friends, so I am happy for that. But soon she will marry, and I will be left with my mother, knitting and staring at the walls."

"You just have to get out more. Take some classes. Meet people."

"That is what I called myself doing that when you came into my life."

Why was she not going beyond me?

"You live in a big city with lots to do. Why, in the short while I have been here I gone to lots of places. There is no end to cultural venues. Soon the weather will be warm. People will be out every day, right?"

"I suppose," she said, looking into her cup.

I spoke to her as I looked out the window at the empty streets. I had never seen them so void of life. Not even a stray cat. Fatma had eased up behind me. She held me around the waist. Her nose found my back; her hands, my pockets.

"Help me with my boots?"

Why did I think we were just going to talk? Then I would take her back.

The boots came off, and so did the dress. She wore black undergarments.

"Are my breasts too small?"

"No, no!"

Where did that question come from? I thought. She was small, but her breasts were not. Her feet were small, but not her legs. It was too cold standing when the bed was right before us.

"I wish I had known you were coming. We could have swum together."

"Let us go now! That's something we haven't done."

The manager only smiled when we walked past him. Her towel wrapped around her seminude body might have drawn attention, but at one thirty in the morning, no one was there. As her heels clicked their way through the mezzanine, I turned to catch a glimpse of the manager looking her over. Yes, she could turn heads at any hour.

Fatma slipped into the water as smoothly as a seal, and like a seal, she wore nothing. That I had heard was a practice of Europeans. Fatma bore none of the trappings I had known in America. Why should she have? It was nice to be in a space where we were free to do whatever we liked. Fatma swam the length of the pool, got out, and dived in again. She was having her own fun, and I only on occasion swam beside her. We swam for perhaps thirty minutes, then dried off. She shivered, as I dabbed the water that dripped from her hair, hair that now shone like August tar.

"I am cold," she said, trembling.

I provided all the heat my body could muster, and we shuddered our way back to my room, to the syncopation of Fatma's footsteps.

I gave Fatma another towel, as the one we had shared was too wet. I fixed some cocoa, which she drank like someone who had been rescued from a lifeboat.

"You are a dear friend."

I paused in front of her and she kissed my thigh. I was not expecting that sort of gratitude, having left her without the intention of returning. Before leaving her home, I did not dare to look into her mother's eyes again in life. Her look would have turned me to stone. My limbs were as weak as I could have ever remembered them. I was fortunate that Fatma only wanted to snuggle. I rolled back the blanket and we both formed a cocoon, and slipped into a world of innocence.

We were in bed until two in the afternoon. Neither of us had anyplace to be. We just stayed in my room. I had enough energy to order room service. But we just shared a sandwich and orange juice. After letting our food digest, we left for another swim. In the gift shop, Fatma found a brown, one piece swimsuit, which I purchased for her.

Again, there was nobody in the pool. Maybe it was too early in the year, or swimming was not a favorite pastime. There were some men playing foosball in the game room we passed, but the hotel was absent of activity otherwise. At any rate, Fatma and I needed no one else. We swam the length of the pool several times, and it was most enjoyable. After an hour, we left the pool.

When we passed the front desk, the manager motioned to me.

"Dr. Davila, I have something for you."

"Thank you."

"Aren't you going to open it?" asked Fatma.

"Yes," I answered simply.

Fatma waited for me to do so, but I did not care for her to share my private world. She did not say anything, although her body language told me she did not like what she thought might be secrets. She was right. I had lots of secrets. She was perhaps ready to live with them, if a ticket to the United States was in the balance. There she could lose herself like so many foreigners did every day.

"You know, I want to give you and you sister something before I leave. I want to get that today. Are you up for a walk?"

She smiled at the thought, and held my hand. We returned to my room and got dressed. As she dressed, I looked at the message. It was from Paul Martin, the friend who had given me the lead for my present job. He was a senior mechanical engineer with Rougetec.

Roberto,

Are you ever coming back?
Everyone asks about you! Well, not
everyone. You have gotten a few calls
from an interested party. She just
leaves the name Milano. A last name, I
guess. Maybe it's another assignment!
Moonlighting as a secret agent?

Talk to you soon,
Paul

Paul would have loved this trip, as he loved to travel. Since he had gotten married, he remained Stateside. He had two children, too, so he was less inclined to venture too far. We had a lot in common. We had attended undergraduate school together. I missed his wedding, being in Panama at the time, but would have been there, otherwise. He was a funny guy, in a quiet way. He loved to dance, and even picked up salsa, Latin dancing. He would be in our townhouse a lot, as there were female students from Latin America there on the weekends. He even picked up Spanish, so he enjoyed the cultural exchange. Our convivial atmosphere was essential to the happiness I experienced in Louisiana, when I was mired in studies. The parties did get too loud for the *americanos.* *We were americanos,* too. We did not share their getting drunk until two in the morning, then turn out the lights, though. Someone must have called the police, and the macho men came right into the house and pulled the plug on the stereo, the bastards, *esos cabrones*! If we had been all white, like them, a respectful, "please turn of the stereo," would have sufficed. But we were one state away from the Texas Rangers. We never caused any trouble. We got our degrees and left the country. Many of the LSU students would ride through the neighborhood playing music loud and shouting racial epitaphs. Once some good old boys with water pistols squirted a Venezuelan with some liquid that got into his eyes, and it burned. I told my Uncle Carlos about it and he told me the story of Emmett Till. It is one of the most horrific episodes in North American history. I was not ready to hear it, but he said I needed to know how ugly white people could be; that while I was in the South, to be aware of the land that produced that and other heinous chapters in this land is your land, et cetera.

I don't know if Gilberto Rojas' spirit ever recovered from that incident. He left after a time, without finishing his degree in geology. He was the one who taught me how to derive Maxwell's Equations. He introduced me to Phil Collins, Boston, and Quarterflash.

51

I was so far away from all of that. I was in a land that had shown me nothing but love. Why did I have to go so far away to find these human qualities? This was where I needed to be to find some peace. I had done what the job required, produced some nice-looking buildings, made some friends and, unfortunately, had gotten entangled in a web of women where I had yet to determine who was going to be the black widow. The widower was easy to find.

Fatma's workload increased coincidentally with my arrangements to leave Kazakhstan. I made arrangements to stop in Istanbul for three days, and then return to the United States. There was no hurry to get back there. I had forwarded everything, and had gotten only good news from my seniors. One told me he was glad he did not have to brave the temperatures and snow. If he only knew how I spent most of my nights, he would have been envious. I knew how not to let the right hand know what the left hand was doing. That went for him and everybody else.

Fatma regretted not being able to see me to the airport. Yes, I would stay in touch. No, I would not forget to send her a ticket. Anything more than that was not in the deal. The best I could do would be to look for a suitable replacement—for me. She would have no trouble finding someone. The standard that she would have to meet in her country would not be the same in the States. If a woman were honest and had the domestic skills she had, guys would knock each other over to get to her. I had known only one woman to knit in my life before Fatma, and that was my grandmother, Paula Carolina. She was mute, but she spoke so beautifully with her hands. I had not thought about her in a long time. I wished I had learned to communicate with her. I left Panama so early and she died while I was away. She was my father's mother, smooth skin, the color of asphalt. There were so many stories I would never know about her. Now that I was so far away and she was gone, why did I long to know the distant? Just concentrate on what you know, or might be able to answer. Had I gotten to know Fatma? She certainly wanted to tell me her life story. I had gotten to know plenty about her. It was silly to do, but I tried to compare her to someone I knew, and could come up with no one; only a composite: Niki Karimi, the Iranian actress, Audrey Hepburn, and Ayanat Ksenbai, an actress from Kazakhstan. Fatma really did resemble Ayanat the most with those almond eyes and that disarming body.

I did not know that last actress, but saw her in the travel magazine on the flight to Istanbul. The afternoon light, dark and red, gave her hair a brown hue. Maybe it was brown anyway. I put the magazine back in the seat-pocket in front of me.

I closed my eyes and not even the occasional rocking of the plane disturbed my slumber. When the stewardess tapped me on the shoulder for my meal, I waved her away, as I was not hungry. An hour later we were starting our descent. My connecting with Sarah in the airport was going to make things easy. She had suggested Turkish Airlines, so I told her when the flight was scheduled to arrive: 16:35, Thursday afternoon.

I worked my way through the lines that looked like cattle chutes. I found the sign for foreigners. (I was always a foreigner. I remembered the time with Carlito at the Penn Relays when some boys jumped us. I felt the same awkward feeling. Then I was new to the States, and did not know the culture nor language well. In Turkey I knew neither the culture nor the language, either, but there were at least no looks of hostility; only a natural curiosity, which I had as well.)

The agent looked my passport over. My face matched the photograph. He just waved me on after he stamped it. I wondered how Sarah would greet me. I witnessed no open signs of affection. Couples did not smile. Kamal Ataturk Airport was not JFK Airport. It was quieter, and again, no smiles. People were serious and the women wore scarves, for the most part. Did they hold hands in this country? What an odd rumination! They must have, right? I had nothing but questions on my mind.

Downstairs, I waited at the serpentine luggage pick-up, where I looked for my suitcase. There was no sight of my bag. I hoped that that did not mean anything. But hadn't Emilio Restrepo lost his suitcase on a flight from Venezuela to Florida? Hadn't Maria Cartagena had her new panties snatched along with her cell phone from her luggage? When she found the bag, it had been sliced with a knife. *Who stole panties, anyway?*

"Roberto!"

It was Sarah. She called me from behind. When I turned she was standing at the exit gate. She was completely in white. She wore a white raincoat and green and white scarf. She fit right into the moving landscape. I waved, then continued, following the moving luggage. I spotted my bags, grabbed them, and moved to where she motioned me.

All of a sudden there were people coming from everywhere, converging into that narrow exit. I had two bags now. I would no doubt acquire another one in Turkey.

"Hi! What took you so long?"

"I don't know. I was just going through the motions. I didn't know what to expect."

Sarah was so animated. It was as though she didn't expect to see me there. She seemed nervous. *I* was nervous to be sure. Unlike my feelings in Kazakhstan, I really felt I had gone back in time. We were in a taxi now, and passed by areas of Istanbul which had to have taken centuries to build. It was a feeling of reverence I could not have anticipated. I pointed to a mosque. Its minarets challenged the clouds, as if to say "I will reach you yet!"

"We will have the chance to visit many. After three days, you'll want to come back."

Sarah had given the driver directions, so he did not say anything.

"This is the European side of Istanbul, where I live. Tomorrow we will take the ferry to the Asian side."

"Is there any difference?"

"Oh, yes. As an engineer, you will appreciate the differences."

The sky was growing dark, and we had come to her apartment building. The street was on a steep incline.

"Nice building," I remarked.

"It's two hundred years old."

"All this wood!"

The mirrored vestibule and chandeliers looked priceless. A large tapestry hung in the hallway entrance. I didn't know the Islamic period at the time, but came to know it was from the eighteenth century. We walked along the gray, marble floor and entered the elevator. It was the sort I had only seen in French films: a black steel cage that exposed the floors as we transcended through the building. I wondered if that type existed in other countries. I had never ridden on one before.

We entered Sarah's apartment and removed our shoes, a habit that by then I had gotten used to. It was a brilliant way to keep out the germs one collects on the street.

Sarah showed me to the room I would use. I put down my bags, and admired the space of the room: a table and chair, a bed and a blue carpet, perhaps also from the eighteenth century in a white-walled room. There was a sofa bed already opened for my comfort.

Sarah took me through the apartment that was equipped with two bathrooms, a living quarter, dining room and another bedroom. After the tour we embraced.

We were off to explore Istanbul in the twilight. We meandered down the street, and crossed a large boulevard. We worked our way through the throngs of people, passing shops and cafes. The window displays were so inviting that I knew we would eventually stop at one.

We arrived at the banks of the Bosphorus, the broad expanse of water that divides Istanbul and, at the same time, Europe and Asia. This was a fact I did not pay attention prior to my trip to Kazakhstan, but I was in Istanbul now, walking the length of the banks, listening to a foreign tongue, universal laughter and looking at Asia. The night was dazzling as if in celebration. People were taking advantage of the cool spring evening, swollen with life, young and old. As we traversed the wide path, I noticed some couples sitting on the huge boulders that separated us from the splashing water, the water that carried the freighters and ferries.

"So, you finished your work in Kazakhstan?"

Her question came from nowhere. Thoughts of Fatma immediately filled my pause. She was the only work left incomplete.

"Uh, yes. I forwarded that. They didn't have any questions. I inundated them with graphs and narrative. They'll get a summary when I return."

"I'm sure they are pleased with your diligence. Maybe your next assignment will be here!" she said.

"I'll have to find a reason."

"I certainly hope so."

The earlier nervousness had disappeared. She was on her own turf. I was following her. We made a turn toward the boulevard. We crossed it, at the semaphore. The word *semáforo* had never left my mind. Nor had Euridice, now a bittersweet memory.

A semaphore was what Euridice had been to me: the signal that had directed my life, that had given it meaning. It would take a long time for the signal to change, and I was willing to wait.

"What do you call that in Turkish?"

"Semafor," she said.

"You have traffic like I've never seen!"

"There are over thirteen million people, so yes, we've loads!"

"This the Hagia Sophia. It was once a cathedral, then converted into a mosque by one of our greatest engineers, Sinan."

"Those buttresses are tremendous supports."

"Let's go inside," she said.

The chandeliers held many light tubes. The stained-glass windows must have allowed for a great amount of light to enter, given the size and number.

Later we went to the Blue Mosque. Inside I noticed suspensions from the chandeliers.

"What are these?" I asked, then discerning they were eggs; huge black ones,

"Ostrich eggs. They keep spiders from spinning webs."

Although it was hard to believe, Sarah was my guide. I was at that point, taking notes. As we walked around the mosque/museum, some people prayed. I was the first time I had ever entered a mosque. It so was quiet, we could hear the ambient street noise. Sarah stopped to take some pictures of me. She asked a man to take one of us, and he took several. I smiled in courtesy.

"Teşekkür ederim," Sarah said to him, and we continued our tour.

We walked the steep ramp inside the mosque, and encountered tall mosaics of Mary and infant Jesus. I was surprised to see them in a mosque but they had not been removed because (as Sarah explained) Muslims believe that Maryam and Isah (Mary and Jesus) are Muslims, too.

We left the Hagia Sophia interior, and circumnavigated the edifice. I stopped whenever I wanted to take in the nuances of the structures: its flying buttresses, its four minarets and the fading rust color of the exterior. It had survived earthquakes, yet still stood as a majestic testimony to centuries of civilizations: Greek Orthodox, nascent Islam, Ottoman and secular Turkish.

We went to a small cafe where we had some green tea. It must have been made with very young leaves, as the color was so light.

"So what did you think of that?"

"Amazing!"

"I hoped you would like it. The engineer, Sinan is responsible for many of the alterations to the structure that made it stronger. It was so many centuries ago, yet continues to give us something to be proud of."

I was even more impressed with how quiet that city of some thirteen million was. Maybe I was just overwhelmed by going back so far in time. It was a lot to absorb. I wished I had brought my sketchbook. I would have to buy some postcards, though I did not think I would forget the essence of the day that tea helped remind me of.

"Have you taught his work history classes? You seem so knowledgeable."

"No. It's just stuff you learn in school, kind of like George Washington," she added.

"Georgie never built anything like that!"

"He was a military general, right? But what's that about the cherry tree? Didn't he like cherry pie?"

"For all I know, that is just a fable. Besides, I think everybody likes cherry pie."

"Exactly! Why would he chop that tree down?" she laughed.

We were back on the street. We found our way to a tram stop. We caught one and took a ride through that glorious city. There wasn't a thing that did not interest me. Something happened on the tram that I won't forget. A woman had gotten on the tram and sat down. A short interval of time later, the driver passed money back to her. But he did so person by person until she had the money! I was sure that would have never happened in The Americas!

We got off the tram, and walked a steep incline to a military museum. Inside there were paintings of the halcyon days of Islam: people making the trek to Mecca; the siege of Vienna by the Ottomans; swords with Quranic inscriptions; and wide-blade standards which gave me an appreciation of the size the men who wielded them must have been.

When we left the museum we paused for an enactment of soldiers performing a precise drill. The costumes were a replica of the ones worn during the Ottoman Empire. I didn't know any Turkish music, but I thought of "The Nutcracker Suite," because of the practiced way in which they moved. The drummer kept excellent time as the men marched to what in centuries past might have been their possible death.

We walked the *Cadasi*, as the streets are called, with the freedom of the spring breeze that blew by us. Istanbul was not a city of demonstrative people, I noticed, which is why when I noticed two lovers in the park exchanging words, I paused. Sarah looked at me and opened her mouth to speak then closed it. The young man raised his voice and spoke in a belittling manner. The woman held her head down as she sat, her hands in her lap. I wished he would have stopped. Did he notice that she had resigned? That he had won? Where was the referee in this street-pummeling of the female? In the States I had seen quarrels among couples, but invariably the women won: even after their wigs had been knocked askew, and eyes blackened. Their mouths still on automatic with a plethora of unmentionables, which in some cases spurred the unleashing of left hooks and upper cuts. How could a man do that to a woman? If words were meant to hurt, that is how they engendered the flurry. And I could see when the police arrived was how they rained nightsticks on the man with no mercy: justice was served and several nights in a cell for the prize fighter. Oh, he had fought with such bravery: he 180 pounds, his common-law wife 135 pounds of swollen eyes and what must have been a smarting rib-cage. There would be no words exchanged between them for a while. She would stay in the house he had bought. He would have to reconcile his disagreements before they would be like two crows again.

"You seem distracted," Sarah said.

"I was going back in time. I have seen that before," I said, cutting a glance at the couple putting on a show.

"It's a Turkish tale."

"It's a universal tale. No subtitles needed."

The sad smile Sarah gave me showed she understood that it was universal.

"How have you managed to avoid close relationships?" she asked.

"How could I avoid them? Don't I show the scars?"

"Maybe now you do! You have danced around them."

"You mean danced right into them."

"How is that?"

"I followed you to Istanbul."

"This isn't a trap. You are here by choice."

She was right. There were no shackles around my ankles. I could have waited to come to Istanbul with Yolanda. I had cleverly avoided meeting her there, only to be there anyway. But I wanted to be where I was. Sarah had made me a guest. We were walking as colleagues, because being together increased interest among the pedestrians. But we were more than colleagues. We were certainly aware of that. But the environment was so civilized that we dare not hold hands. It was not like anyplace I have ever been. Either people were pretending to be aloof, or waiting for the moment to break from the spell that held them captive. For fifteen million people, I felt that two million eyes were on me!

"So how do you feel about this place?"

"It's fascinating!"

"And you would return?"

"I'd go where there is good food and work."

"So all you need is work, then?"

"Exactly."

Sarah and I had managed to dance around the intimacy issue. If we were going to be close, it would not be in her apartment where, as the Iranians say, "The walls have mice, and the mice have ears."

I was comfortable about that. Again I felt myself creating distance. No expectation, no commitment.

"And speaking of going, where are we going?"

Sarah had finally broached the in entrapment issue. But why that term? Didn't I want to be there? If that was the case, I was not being coerced. Still the suddenness of it all gave me reason to know that she had an agenda, and I had better make mine known, or invent one.

"I think we have a chance to make something happen. Something beautiful."

"You know, I have been meaning to tell you something. It has been hanging over me, but I was not sure you would be around for long. You see, I was in a relationship after my divorce, and long before I met you. I have feelings for him, and he for me. But you have entered the picture and the distance between us (I'll say Mr. Y.) has grown. I need to know if you understand."

"I found it odd that you would be by yourself; a woman with so much going for herself."

She shook her head as if to say "No."

"Seriously," I said. And looked at her in the green and beige silk scarf and wondered if that was her protection against me, or onlookers. Or was it another device to keep me at bay? It had certainly done the latter. She had managed not to arouse me in the least since I had arrived there. It was not entirely due to Fatma's thigh-clinching, which left me with a sweet-soreness that would be hard to forget. "So I entered number two?"

"But a strong second," she interjected.

So everyone was playing the field. Euridice had played, Yolanda was pretending not to play it, Sarah was playing it, and I could not leave myself out: I was a major player with loves on two continents, since Yolanda was now in Italy.

"So where is Mr. Y?"

"He is in Buenos Aires."

"So you like Latin men! What is he doing so far away?"

"He's a medical researcher."

"And when did you see him last?"

"Three months ago."

"In South America?"

"Yes."

"It's no surprise that you knew all those Latin songs. And you dancing! You are quite a bag of tricks!"

There she was looking like a poster model for religious donations to some Bosnian cause, and all the while doing the samba every chance she got. Why, she was better than the character Rinehart in *Invisible Man*! I didn't really want to ask any more questions, because it was nothing more than a catharsis for Sister Sarah. And I was just about to send in my vote for her Mother Teresa award! Send it in any way! She deserved an Academy, though she had starred in no movie.

"You're incredible! I am glad you finally brought it up. I give you credit."

We were walking again. As we began, the couple we had seen earlier passed us, holding hands.

"I didn't know we would get this far, that you would actually come to Istanbul."

"Well, I'm here, in this city of minarets and surprises. Funny, you know I am not disappointed. I want to congratulate you."

"Like I said, I didn't know it would get this far."

"Well, that's why they call it life: It gives you the test, then teaches you the lesson. And I've never been a good test-taker."

"I wouldn't go that far, Dr. Davila. Two disciplines: mathematics and engineering."

"My Mother said I was brilliant, but she didn't mention a failure at love."

"The test isn't over yet."

"So the final is not over? You mean there is a bonus question? I can hardly wait! I better bone up! You might just come in my strong suit."

"Love is your strong suit."

"What will become of me?"

"Another day in Istanbul. I have really enjoyed it."

"Truly."

"It exceeded my expectations. The next time I come, I'll know what to expect."

"There is so much more than you have time to see."

She missed my sarcasm completely. If I did come again, it might well be with Yolanda, I thought. That is, if she was still single. I wondered what she was doing, with all that globe-trotting. Maybe she was just pursuing her studies. Her drawings sure were compelling. How did she find the time to produce so many? I would have to ask her what her focus was. If it were buildings, I had some entries for her.

"You are so mature," she said.

Is that what I was? Then why did I feel I was in a burning building, wrapped in a wet blanket, crawling to the fire escape?

"I am thirty four. I would hope I would have found maturity by now."

It was clear that Sarah had made her choice some time ago, and was waiting to have me on her turf to spring the news to me. She was no less clever than I had thought her to be.

"So when are you headed to Argentina again, in case I plan a trip? But I don't think we would be on the same flight anyway."

"I won't be going until December. It's summer there. But you knew that."

"But I have never been there. In Panama it's eternally summer."

Why did I suddenly wish I were there in the infernal heat and hundred percent humidity? I could not wait to see my isthmus again. But I had to return to Baton Rouge and deliver my report. Then I would request an emergency leave. They might wonder why I had never mentioned going to Panama before. I was so content and hidden away in my comfortable home in the Bayou State, of gator-tails and mud bugs, etouffee and shrimp po'boys, of rice and beans and catfish, pecan pie, which I had given up on because it was too sweet. I had fallen in love with Community Coffee. I was sure it came from Costa Rica. But where I was going there was a host of things I was going to rediscover.

52

In the airport I opened my laptop to find a letter from Yolanda. I hadn't told her I was going to Istanbul, for obvious reasons. Now that my plans had fallen through, I was free to hear what she had to say. I had all but ignored her telegrams, in search of *paisajes nuevos*—new landscapes, as my father would say.

When I thought of Yolanda, I asked myself, did she ever know a bad day? *Si tenia problema, nadie lo sabia.* She never let anyone knew if she had a problem.

> Roberto,
>
> I haven't heard from you in some time. What's this silence mean? I spend my days totally engrossed in drawing. I wish you were here to see what I have turned out. I would send you one of these charcoals, but I don't risk the voyage. They would be smudged to no end. Two days a week I spend my mornings in the Piazza in Milano, sketching structures that absorb my interests, in this place that is timeless, yet holds centuries of wealth. Today, I was forced to seek the shelter of one of the cafes because of a shower. People scurried out of the rain. I found an empty table and set up my tablet. The

waiter was so nice, bringing over a cup of coffee. I am a regular, and he likes my work. He mentioned that he has a daughter who is an art student, though I have never met her. Like his smile, the sun returned. But it is your smile that warms me most.

My studies are progressing well, though I spend nights awake to meet the deadlines. I am developing dark circles. I will look like a raccoon by the time my master's is complete. I am studying for my license as well. That way I can have my own firm. I will need a civil engineer with some buildings ready to lobby exhibitions. Do you know anyone with creativity and a good structural sense? Let me know if you think of anyone.

So have you returned to Baton Rouge? What did your coworkers have to ask you? They must be full of questions. I know I am. When you settle in, give me a call.

And what about my shoes? Did you see any you thought I would like, and could not resist getting me? No, just recover from the jet lag you must be suffering.

Love,
Yolanda

Her letter was more than I deserved, considering the heel I had been. She knew how to work me. She knew my weaknesses and my loves. Still, I had changed to the degree that whatever I was missing was inside. That was the void I had to fill to be happy. I could not bring happiness to Yolanda or anyone else, otherwise. Yolanda was whole with her art, and the success her architectural projects gave her. Therefore, she could then reach out and touch others. She had certainly touched me, so I needed to pull my life together and stand like the buildings I too wanted to see stand one day.

Yolanda. What she was not did not interest me. What she was could be summed in the short missives she had written me: a woman with the capacity to care—about me! I certainly had the ability, and more importantly the willingness to do likewise. I had longed to find what I saw in her: a woman who could balance her life as steadily as Yolanda in a new pair of stilettos.

I looked down at the shoeboxes at my feet. She had asked for one pair and I had gone one better. I knew her foot like my own.

I returned my attention to the laptop, knowing I had made the right choice. "Dear Yolanda," I wrote, "I have a surprise for you."

About the Author

Nadel Harvey was born in Philadelphia, Pennsylvania. He studied civil engineering and mathematics. He has worked most of his life as a civil engineer. He enjoys reading and playing piano when he is not writing. He is inspired by listening to music of Thelonious Monk, Elis Regina, and Göksel. He speaks six languages and lives in Izmir, Turkey.

www.ingramcontent.com/pod-product-compliance
Lightning Source LLC
Chambersburg PA
CBHW050920250626
47155CB00001B/312